Chapter 1

Robert Cafferty stares into the fogged cheval mirror, almost begging the worn-out frame to hold steady. The dark mahogany frame bears matching birthmarks on either side, collateral damage from decades of manipulating the frame's height. He briefly ponders its circuitous voyage from a French furniture shop, perhaps to a home in the 16eme Arrondissement in Paris, and yet, eventually to a haggard antique store in Youngstown, Ohio. He surmises that years of groping from teenage girls, who dreamt of proms and weddings, must have stressed the mounting brackets loose and caused its unsteady movements.

"Maybe someday I will fix this for you, Mom," he whispers as he kneels and centers his long, athletic frame within the mirror's oval. Cafferty observes his hardened presence, the result of years spent boxing under his father's steady gaze. His skin is thick, toughened like a hide yet drawn taut around his jaw like a drum. His focus on weight, on his opponent, and the gravity of his environment jettisoned anything resembling baggage.

Cafferty tugs the athletic-fit Oxford shirt and gives a final look to the dark herringbone suit and its endless, signature criss-crossing chevrons, goading an eye to find one stray fabric.

Satisfied, he springs forward, his burst causing his tie, slung over his shoulder, to limply fall into place. Cafferty smirks and tugs at the piece, a pointless attempt to straighten permanent creases born from years of storage and inferior materials. He snickers quietly while flipping the tie, revealing an off-center "RAC," and gently traces each of the letters while quietly whispering, "This is for you, Mom." He retrieves his fedora from the nightstand, leaves the cramped guest bedroom, and quietly walks into the living room.

Cafferty hesitates, the newness of the space immediate and perplexing, a stark contrast to the bedroom he just left. Sleek, modern light fixtures have replaced cumbersome chandeliers, enough so that Cafferty no longer feels the urge to duck. The old, ribbed, paneled walls are gone, and in their places a linen-white paint graces coarse, textured walls. The faux wood blinds have displaced frayed curtains, once resembling neglected car dealership flags. The kitchen cabinets are new too, their clean, thirty-six-inch boxes appearing even larger than the modest, 1930s-built home ever intended. An unsteady, almost fleeting aura hangs about the room, as if the shine can only last so long.

It looks flipped, he pans to himself. Pulled from the foreclosed heap and buffed up for a quick sale. Except for the floor. It would not meet anyone's current definition of "modern" or new." And Cafferty doesn't have the heart to change these, despite their outcast standing. Not yet, at least. These original oak slats are the ¾-inch variety, hewn from local wood. Cut from a single tree and installed by craftsmen, they bear every drop of sweat, nick, and grime the decades have served without complaint. He further reasons, they aren't pressed laminates from some offshore factory, likely produced alongside PVC pipes and sent by the shipload to a massive home improvement store. That flooring, he huffs, would peel like an onion, and its shallow, almost plastic sheen is contrived, gaudy even. *Not yet, though,* he thinks to himself again.

Cafferty navigates scattered newspapers, resembling dingy lily pads, as he approaches the wheelchair facing the wall. A grainy, black and white photo sags within a faded gesso frame, its oak leaves chipped and irregular. Two men, replete in drab military fatigues, stare back from within.

"Why is she facing away from the TV?" he asks testily to the caretaker. "Carrie, why is she…"

"Because the people are watching her. Freaks her out," she responds indifferently while cracking gum. Carrie Boddington sits facing the TV, desperately wearing twenty-something fashion despite a face wearing cigarette smoke nearly as old. With a career in single parenting since her early teens, she is too old to start a new pursuit yet too young to care for another.

"Do you think it might help perhaps not watching TV, then?" Cafferty offers.

"Bobby. She likes looking through those old newspaper clippings and talking about dancing with her friends," Carrie says, with a roll of her eyes.

3

"What friends?" asks Cafferty.

"Exactly," spits Carrie, holding her hands up, exasperated. "No one has come through those doors the entire time I have worked here, yet she carries on conversations with people named Christina and Mira. Er, herself. You know what I mean."

"Ah, okay," says Cafferty.

"She is happiest when she speaks about dancing. Even her fingers loosen up and bounce to whatever cadence is in her head at the time. So, the TV ain't bothering her," she reaffirms, again presenting a hardened shell to the man.

Cafferty plucks the scattered clippings and approaches the chair, mindful of the swollen feet dangling lifelessly. "Hello, Mom, what are you doing today?" asks Cafferty. The feet appear to prop up a figure draped in a pink nightgown. Surprisingly, her frame is rigid and thin. It lacks puffiness typically reflective of someone sentenced to confinement and certainly, one whose calves are like large loaves of bread. Rather, her frame hints at a conscious effort, a hidden pride that simply won't give in to fate.

His eyes latch onto the limp compression stockings clinging loosely around her ankles. "These things aren't doing a whole lot of good way down here," he whispers, stretching the material with a firm pull.

"Hi, do I—umm, I'm sorry. Do I know you?" Mildred Cafferty begs. She recoils stiffly against the wheelchair and dislodges long-forgotten papers wedged between the armrest and cushion. A craggy

4

pile of black and white sheets accumulates on the floor like a remote switchback, surrounding the anchored woman. Atop her lap lies a forgotten, cellophane-wrapped *Youngstown Press*, dated 2014. Her fingers clutch the plastic like a relic, something like the last of its kind.

"Yes, Mom. It's Bobby, your son, and we are here in our home. Do you remember where we live?" Cafferty asks. He delicately adjusts the compression stockings over fluid, choked calves and a labyrinth of vessels.

"Of course, we...oh, what is it?" She bangs the armrest. Two rusted screws peek through the material, evidence of an enduring struggle . "Goddamn it, yes, I—I know where we live. It begins with that sign. It looks like...the thing that you pull from the bird we cook. Fuck, ooooh, that thing...what is it?" She slams her hand into the chair.

The words hit Cafferty like a sniper's bullet, precise and mechanical, a thousand yards away from anyone suspecting. He swallows hard, and as if in shock, ignores the lethality of such a wound.

"Yes, Mom. We live in Youngstown and it begins with a *Y*, the same shape as a wishbone. Mom, did you find anything in the papers today?"

At her feet lies a reprint of the *New York World-Telegram* dated August 14, 1935. She grabs at the pile but is immediately restrained.

"Oh, Jesus." She winces as her joints grind like misshapen cogs. With each pang, Cafferty senses a prick within his chest. He plucks and refolds the paper before gently placing it on her lap. She fingers the faded letters as if nudging the ink for a cue. At once, she bubbles.

"I remember this. We sat in front of that old radio when he signed the Social Security Bill." Her hands mesh together in a fleeting moment of synchronicity.

Cafferty observes the woman and begins to smile. "That old walnut Zenith radio," he blurts.

She continues, her voice cracking with excitement. "A brand new America.... And soon they built the, ooooh, dammit, th-the annex for the Social Security Administration right there." Fingers, gnarled like a treble hook, poke beyond the front door of the home. "The steel mill kept us in our home during the big drop, but that New Deal gave hope after the mill.... Wait, *what was first?*" she huffs as her trembling hand slams into the armrest. Her eyes, fed by a depthless spring, begin to well again. The bout of frustration, like others, ticks by like another mile marker on a road to nothingness. Cafferty's smile evaporates as he organizes the events like a suit of cards.

"That's good, Mom, you remember the Youngstown Steel Mill, Stock Market Crash, the New Deal, and the Calder County Social Security Annex. Now can you tell me about this one—do you remember this day?" he asks, pointing to a faded *Life* magazine photo atop the "Cathedral of Learning." She marvels at the grandiosity of the image, causing her to warm inside. A smile beams across her face, piercing the sea of confusion like a beacon.

"Oh yes, yes I do. Pittsburgh beat the Yankees in 1960. What is that called, the bat with the ball?"

"That's baseball, Mom, and yes, Pittsburgh beat New York in the World Series," Cafferty states as the stockings concede to gravity again. "I remember we went to St. Stanislaus and had a social after that."

A smile coalesces on her face, softening the deep grooves etched into her skin. She draws a breath and hums a beautiful melody as her eyes slip shut. The subtle vibrato emanating from her lips guides her fingers through choreographed movements she has done a thousand times before. The movements soothe like an ether, loosening her joints and transport her to a world far away. She is as light as a prayer.

"She always loved music," Cafferty whispers through a soft smile of his own. "And she loved 'All I Have to Do Is Dream,'" he adds to no one. The final note of that song drifts from her throat and is buoyant, as if reaching for a belfry.

"People were so happy, and the city was alive with the mill. Everything was good." Her voice steeps in the moment.

She toes the pile beneath her, observing the pages slipping against another until they freeze. Her smile flees as she shifts painfully, glaring at the *Youngstown Press* dated September 19, 1977. Her eyes cinch as her hands clench together as if wringing the memory from a gigantic sponge.

"The people, they were crying. The whistle blew and then it just stopped one day. Thousands of people never, ever went back to that mill. Where did they all go?" she whispers. "Only a few stayed behind...and then, well..." She hushes with a final squeeze of her hands, choking a moment she'd rather have forgotten.

"It's okay, Mom. That was so long ago now." A sudden crack rips the moment as the caretaker fumbles the TV tray, startling the pair. Cafferty stares at the woman, who acknowledges the steady burn with a simple shrug.

"This thing is cheap, don't blame me," she fires.

"This isn't how it should be," Cafferty mutters, his jaw clenching and pursing his lips. His gaze finds his mom again, who has lost the moment and instead sifts through a grisaille world of nameless faces and foreign static. Her eyes, hollow and lusterless, resemble peepholes, observes Cafferty. Peepholes to a snared soul, just begging to be free.

"Umm, I'm sorry.... Who, um, who are you?" Mildred offers apologetically.

"It's me, Mom, Bobby. Tell me something. Do you remember this tie?" Cafferty carefully guides her hand to the slick fabric, helping her flip it, revealing a cursive "RAC." The letters appear to slant, affording a sleek look, as if running. "You *made* me this tie when..."

"Of course, I remember. You got hired by that company. I—uh—I'm not retarded, you know!" she blurts out.

"Of course. Yes, Mom. Bain & Bain is the company. And today, I am driving to my retirement party with the same tie in honor of you."

The words evade her as she withdraws her hand and instead retrieves the *Youngstown Press* dated December 24, 1995. "Parson's Juvenile House of Horrors Shuttered" looms in sturdy black font. Mildred glances at the message and sags, as if remorseful. "I remember that day. We all heard whistles for years over there. They never stopped, day or night, but winter.... Winter was always the worst because it was so cold and quiet. No birds, the grass-cutters, or w-w-wind in leaves. Just whistles. But I never heard the whistle again after Christmas. What is it now?" asks Mildred.

"They made it into a Veterans Administration building and hospital now, Mom. I would hope they are doing some good for the community from there."

Cafferty spots a final newspaper resting upright against the wheel and places it in front of Mildred. She beams. "He is the best, American as it gets," she says, thumbing the headline that reads, "Johnny Carson Has Died." "I see him every night on that...oooooh, goddamn it." She pounds her forehead, causing Cafferty to restrain her arm.

"See?" A sarcastic offering arrives from the caretaker.

He ignores the jab and gently fingers her rumpled hair, soothing her. As his fingers part a tuft, he notices purple splotches dotting her scalp. His fingers dab at the marks, but they are buried deep and remain. Cafferty glares at the attendant as if trying to suck truth from a stone. "Do you know how this happened?"

The caretaker, shifting toward Cafferty, fingers the medicine organizer. "Mr. Cafferty, your mom has a dozen medicines she must take. It's getting harder and harder for her to swallow. Sometimes, you have to work to get these pills down."

Cafferty recalls the doctor's words from months ago: "Dysphagia…weight loss…dehydration…and finally, aspiration pneumonia." His head bobs in silence as he leans to kiss her forehead. "I will be back, Mom. I love you."

"If you see Mira, can you ask if we will go to the dance tonight? It's over at St. Stanislaus." She smiles, tracing a finger to imaginary movements.

"Of course, Mom. If I see Mira, I will ask. It would be wonderful to see you dance again." Cafferty rises and strides toward the door. His eyes never stray from the worn oak rails beneath him, as if they're anchoring him while the world spins with uncertainty around him. Only upon reaching the door does he notice the old hardwood dipping beneath the new walls, as if swallowed.

Beyond the door, the September dawn sky casts a soft glow over various shapes. Powerlines span like tentacles in a murky sea, plucking at the wooden poles until they split the earth and concrete around them. Modest vehicles, like an anchor chain, cram bumper to bumper on either side of the street. Behind them, the small row houses huddle together in the early morning chill. But what strikes Cafferty most is the quiet. No whistle, no bustle, no movement of people. It's as if the city is still sleeping, content to stay in a dream world.

Cafferty tugs the car door and pokes the engine to life. Its voice is chunky, staging a silent protest to the changing seasons. Soon, however, it finds a steady cadence and stout timbre among its peers. Cafferty pinches the bridge of his nose and fills his lungs. He clings to the breath like his mom's hand moments ago, staring directly at the face in the rearview mirror. A steady whoosh escapes from his mouth until he is empty. "This is for you, Mom."

Chapter 2

"Hey, which way to Forbes Avenue?" prods Cafferty. A stout figure, resembling a dingy fire hydrant and clad in a Pittsburgh City Works reflective vest, ignores the request as he leans against a stop sign. His thumb flicks against a small glowing screen, as his eyes sink into a trance. "Excuse me, can you please—"

A arm rises, and mechanically waves the car through. "Follow the detour signs. This road is closed," he grumbles.

The car slaloms through a sea of cones, narrowly avoiding chasms and mammoth concrete tubes on either side. Soon, he is halted by another man in dingy yellow and confronted by a wall of city lights, brighter and newer than anything he has ever remembered. He squints hard into the colors as if trying to reach the end of a horizon. It occurs to him that the thousands of bright lights, a polychromatic tidal wave, resemble eyes peering throughout the city. Every foot of pavement yields a glare that is distinctive, yet not congruent with any single design. The eyes seem to jostle with one another, each vying for pavement from the other. Yet, with each frigid neon stare, and despite their genetic differences, they somehow appear bound by some living entity. *It's like puppies fighting for the nipple,* he thinks to himself.

Cafferty senses the bright eyes surveying him with skepticism, poking and demanding to know *why. Why are you here? What relevance do you have to the present, and more importantly, to the fu-*

ture? Do you still have a purpose? Things of your generation's de-sign—rotary phones, a department store...hell, the entire INDUSTRY this city was built upon—are all gone. Cannibalized by the future.

Cafferty grips his steering wheel, uncertain as to why these observations have come so easily and with such brutal candor. Almost immediately, the similarity hits him like a brick. *This is what my father's generation saw. Immigrants from Italy, Ireland, Russia, Poland, every corner of the Earth, came here for the mills. Each language, each hour of available work, housing—everything made these people scrap for every square inch in the hope they could buy the next generation hope. They too ogled every new arrival, sizing their very substance while beating back the fear of change. Or more specifically, how their purpose would also expire.*

Cafferty glances at the man in yellow again, this time his hands lifted above his head. "Traffic is bad enough—let's go!" the voice bellows through the windshield. Again, he navigates narrow paths, while his windshield is overrun by signs and steel dinosaurs baring craggy brown teeth. After nearly rear-ending a car, Cafferty pauses for a cement truck that's navigating an impossible turn.

He stares out the window and observes people, each tethered to a bluish white haze emanating from their hands. They slip past each other indifferently, only occasionally offering a cold glance. It's a clumsy, toothy smile, hanging from a boy that catches his eye. The boy is not focused on a screen or looking earthward, but instead gaz-

13

ing up at his father. A smile forms on Cafferty's face as he recalls his father.

Bobby Sr. once brought him to Pittsburgh decades ago to watch the Steelers play. While the game escapes him, he recalls the people and the sky. His mind and work ethic were shaped by that visit, and by the no-nonsense father who took such pride in a city built on steel. He stares hard into the windshield as the cement truck teeters precariously on the curb, nearly banging the crosswalk pole. He recalls, *Men were sturdily built, seemingly discharged from the same bucket and cast by the same mold. Faces and clothes were powdered black, proof of an honest day's work.* Cafferty squints his eyes as if he is once again walking among them, examining their very fiber.

The sky felt heavy with curtains of steam and smoke enveloped the entire valley, permeated by one flashing advertisement: A-L-C-O-A. He remembers his dad saying, "If you are ever lost, find the AL-COA sign. It is on the south side of the river and can be your lighthouse for guidance."

A loud horn and a firm tap to his hood snaps Cafferty back to reality. The thought races through his mind as he lifts the foot from the brake. *I can no longer see Mt. Washington, let alone the lighthouse I once knew.*

Soon, he encounters fifty-five stories of glass and steel stretching toward the heavens. The structure, designed to turn over itself every five floors, resembles the rifling in a barrel, he thinks. In

14

the middle, a bulging disc of glass encircles the spire. As he observes the bulge, he notices little flicks in the glass like ants, appearing to hang above the city. "Jesus, no way," he mutters.

Cafferty marvels at how different the building appears after twelve months, the time needed for him to work the Forca deal. "I have got to make this work," he whispers to himself.

Stepping off the elevator into the banquet room, Cafferty is overwhelmed by the grandeur. Waiters, crisply outfitted in black and white, slip between tables and offer thimble-sized hors d'oeuvres. Their lips ripple with unfamiliar offerings, sparking commentary among the attendees. Black truffle arancini and squash blossoms with pimento ricotta seem to pair with highbrow music, which is too much for Cafferty's brand. He hesitates momentarily, appreciative that he will likely never again encounter a food he cannot pronounce or wine he cannot appreciate. However, tonight, he recognizes that such pageantry is habitual, even urgent for those footing the bill.

His eyes scan the room, seeking those who find the pomp equally spurious. Immediately, he is drawn to a fiery glow from the corner of his eye, racing between tables with little control. It's his longtime mentee and colleague, Jonas Bloom. Jonas' effulgent strawberry orange hair swishes atop a rail-thin body with as much substance as a scarecrow. His waxen complexion yields a lifeless, almost mannequin appearance, which has earned him the nicknames "Mort" and "Snerd" from his shameless peers. Cafferty immediately smiles, always appreciating Jonas' tenacity and trademark insults as a honed self-defense mechanism.

"Sweet baby Jesus, you still have that fucking thing?" Jonas says, pointing dismissively to the tie. He quickly extends a hand in Cafferty's direction, yanking himself toward the roughcast figure. "Hey, go ugly or go home, right?" Jonas fires, chortling at his own joke. "How much did Goodwill pay you to take that—"

"All right, all right," Bobby states, pointing at the orange plume in front of him. "Do you know what the best thing is about me moving on?" Cafferty fires. "Not only do I not have to hear your amateur-hour bullshit anymore, but more comforting is knowing this building has more mirrors than a funhouse. Every floor, every elevator, and every bathroom, enough mirrors to make Narcissus blush. You'll be staring at *the* punchline for the next twenty years," he fires with a sly wink.

Jonas booms, sending a jolt through his wiry frame. "Nice, right on the money!" he exclaims. He hugs his longtime friend.

"All shitting aside, Bobby. You have had one helluva run and I couldn't be prouder to have learned from you." Jonas' smile drifts from his face and he stares at the ground, in deference to the man who has accomplished so much. "I wished to hell you weren't leaving. All of us thought you had another decade in you, at least," he finishes wistfully.

Cafferty takes the compliments in stride, offering a humble reply.

16

"It's time, ya know, Jonas? We had a good run and God knows I will be near. Does anyone from the Rust Belt ever really leave?" he asks rhetorically. "It's in our DNA, no matter what the pursuit might be." He slaps his friend's shoulder and clenches his tight jaw, feigning a stone-cold glare. "Besides, being around your shitty jokes always makes me appear funnier than I am."

"Touché, my friend, touché," smiles Jonas.

The ceremony marches forward, as the formality is tempered by a motley cast of characters delivering their breed of levity. One by one, speakers regale Cafferty, counting him among the best lawyers ever. Each speech elicits rapid clanks against the glass throughout. Jonas, atypically emotional, delivers a crisp but meaty summary of Cafferty's life and impact on Bain.

"Over three decades, Bobby has led the strategic approach and subsequent awards of multiple revenue streams within one single vertical. That vertical—the steel industry—of course was, and is, our bread and butter. Whether speaking of consolidations within the industry, bankruptcies, lobbying, or trade issues, Bobby was always one step ahead in strategy, and never left us—or, more importantly, our clients—without an effective counter."

Jonas, long an admirer of Cafferty's amateur boxing prowess, often sought ring references in honor of his friend. "I always told Bobby I thought years of boxing would have made him punch drunk, you know, caused him to misfire every now and then. And Bobby would tell me, 'Jonas, you have to be hit to be punch drunk. The object is to move away from where the fist is going, or even better, hit him first...and ALL of that can be seen in a man's stance, footwork, his eyes, that twitch in the left shoulder, their change in breathing....that one 'tell' that every single man has. All businesses, or more specifically, business situations, have 'tells.' That is, certain weaknesses in the positions they are arguing, the composition of the team arguing the positions, the timing constraints of a particular decision, the ability to assume a level of risk, etc. Each of those constraints narrows the ring in which they can maneuver. I simply learned to hide my tells better than most.'"

Jonas steps away from the microphone momentarily, admiring the simplicity yet enduring effectiveness of the advice. He continues, highlighting a few of the firm's most notable wins while cleverly noting the partnership of the clients in attendance, in particular Forca.

"It is quite appropriate that while Bobby worked some rather difficult situations so early in his career, as the domestic steel industry fell on exceptionally hard times, he has come full circle in nurturing the rebirth of that same industry. From the first moment he began lobbying on behalf of the domestic steel industry, from pursuing anti-subsidy cases to anti-trust cases, he has been front and center. I'd like to think Forca, and the partnership with Bain, is the pièce de résistance of that collective effort. I'd like to raise a toast to my colleague and dear friend...Mr.—" With applause cutting Jonas short, he cackles like a hyena, vibrating his orange plume.

The sea of twill and herringbone obliges Bobby to speak. While he is emotionally detached from the scene and occasion, he is committed to ending this phase of his life. He delivers a quintessential Cafferty speech, measured yet witty, but with a presence commanding respect.

"I will leave each of you with some final thoughts," he states, seeking eye contact with every person in the room. He grips the podium as if it were the shoulders of a friend, drawing a deep breath.

"There are three life lessons my father taught me. The first of those lessons was to find your purpose *in life* and work your ass off to *give life* something by which to remember you by." The words echo with a gravity and suggest a more noble product than the scattered shrimp tails strewn across white cloth tables. "I feel we have built a history in Bain for which no single person can—or, more importantly, should—be individually remembered. There's not a professional in this room who would state it any differently, or even contemplate their self-importance over another—we were uniquely close as a team, and the Bain accomplishments will be remembered by life as such." A thunderous roar rattles the delicate glass flutes resting atop tables. Cafferty courteously affords time for the team to bask in their own glory before latching onto the teak-trimmed shoulders again, hushing the crowd.

"Every so often, ask yourself the question, 'How will life remember me?' I have done that, and it is time for me to put my individual stamp and purpose on life." The applause rings genuine, but more reserved, as the message still marinates within the group.

"The second lesson my father taught me, which is equally important, is to always leave on top; never quit when at the bottom. 'Top' in this context is relative, but each of us deep down inside, if being one hundred percent true to ourselves, knows what the 'top' looks like." He pauses momentarily, allowing the words to settle. He draws nearer to the microphone, as if bracing his voice against an unseen current. "Don't quit when you've already started the obvious descent and leave a bum hand for others to play." Cafferty shies away from the microphone momentarily and clears an unexpected hard lump, one that has festered for decades. "To put it a little differently, everything—a career, a card game, hell, even Joe Louis—they all have an expiration date. Once you pass that expiration date, you begin undoing life's diary of you. Worse yet? You begin denying others the opportunity of crafting their life's diary. Find a new purpose while you are on top."

His message sizzles like a shooting star, racing past eyes and drawing mouths wide open. "Look around you—you are surrounded by the brightest team in the entire tri-state area. I leave this game proudly, knowing we did our best with our time together, and our collective diary in life will reflect such. Thank you all and enjoy your evening."

An ovation begins rippling throughout the hall as a bald, sweaty mass grabs the microphone, his eyes nearly shut. "Hang on,

Bobby, one sec." The crowd hushes, curious to see what could be so important as to break the moment. "You mentioned you had three life lessons, yet you only spoke of two. I, for one, would be very interested in hearing the third."

A clattering of forks and crystal begins echoing throughout. "Yeah, what's the third, Bobby?" a voice bellows above the din.

"Did I say three?" Bobby winks. The crowd hushes.

"On the drive into town today, I marveled at the construction all around me. Every turn I made, I saw traffic cones, signs, concrete, and glass. Gone were the streets I once knew traveling here, and even entire buildings have disappeared. The old ALCOA sign is no more. Hell, an entire industry—the very product this city was built upon—has evaporated and been replaced by newer industries, technology, brands of people. In any event, it occurred to me that change is universal and perpetual. Nothing remains the same."

He pauses, reaching for his water, the ice cubes deafening throughout the hall. "I am not a religious man—much to my mom's chagrin and despite countless days spent as an altar boy in Youngstown. I think my last confession, ironically, was in seventh grade after stealing wine from the cruet. Imagine two young boys decked out in their cassocks drinking poached wine before mass." The room erupts with laughter as Cafferty patiently awaits before carrying on. "But seriously, I'm still trying to figure out what the word 'spiritual' means, so even doctrines, core beliefs, and what comes after all this"—he motions to the sky beyond—"continue shifting on me like

21

castles, year to year. But I digress. I couldn't name one thing that remains constant.

"So, we must embrace the changes time shapes while maintaining the very purpose we individually seek. Adapt, but do not lose yourself in the mix." Cafferty settles on the last note, nodding. "Hell, that sounded better than I thought it would," he jokes, his impeccable delivery causing a rip of laughter. "But then I walked into this very room, and immediately my entire theory of universal change fell apart like a house of cards. Something was *exactly* the same," he warns.

The room steeps in silence. An audience peers around the room for any obvious sign. Hushed chatter flits about the room as to what might have been the cause. Cafferty plucks the microphone from the podium and emerges from behind the wooden barrier.

"What is the one thing that will *never* change? Jonas Bloom will always be the grandest jackass to ever pass the bar, and will eventually find his true purpose as a five-foot, eleven-inch traffic cone on Forbes Avenue." The place erupts as Jonas chortles at his friend's final shot. "Thank you all for the fantastic evening and enjoy the party."

As the mob descends upon Jonas, firing additional barbs, Cafferty slips between bustling staff to the back nook. Music fills the hall, but idles on an unfussy set, garnering hoots and frivolity from the group. It is an unlikely place for refection, yet Cafferty finds himself staring at the retirement plaque still encased in its prepackaged shell. "Purpose," he says quietly to himself, thumbing the crisp etched lettering nipping at his fingertips. The letters bite harder as he drifts into thought.

I want to give others, like you, Mom, a place that affords dignity and understanding. Dignity, of course, to those who suffer from dementia…. I don't know what you feel, see, think. It crushes me to think you do not know who I am and how much I love you. Language, faces, shapes, names—all of this is gone, and I imagine it is like being kidnapped and shot into space…no sound, no air, just moments passing in a swirl of uncertainty before the final fall. I want to surround people like this with appropriate help. But there is another piece of this puzzle—those families who watch their loved ones spiral into complete anonymity, both to themselves and to everyone they see. This is equally damaging and I hate even saying this…I don't know which side of the table is worse. If my pursuit helps one family reconnect—gain one minute of what life was before the fall—that is fulfilling a purpose.

Cafferty stiffens abruptly as if he has spoken aloud. His eyes examine the orchestrated movements of waitstaff ferrying dinnerware back and forth. No one seems to care or even notice that Cafferty has chosen this buried spot, distanced from the energy. But soon, a man sporting an unmistakable beard and impeccably tailored pinstripe suit slices through the ebb and flow. The thick black pelt covers the man's face like a wooly scarf, accentuating his jawline with the subtlety of an anvil. The growth extends beyond his chin, almost appearing as if his head is attached directly to his chest. As the figure approaches

Cafferty, however, a flash of white teeth peeks through the tuft and elicits warm laughter from both.

"*Ah, Tudo bem, Helio,*" says Cafferty. The stocky, dapper Brazilian embraces Cafferty, sending a firm slap to his shoulder.

"*Otimo. E voce?*"

"*Tudo,*" says Cafferty.

"Make me one promise, Mr. Cafferty: Please don't forget to keep practicing your Portuguese, even after this night is over. You've handled yourself quite nicely in such a short time—Paulistas might mistake you for one of their own," he breathes with sincerity. Cafferty nods to the surprisingly young CEO, his commitment bound by the respect fashioned during their collective pursuit: resurrecting the Youngstown Steel factory in its new form—Forca.

Cafferty recalls meeting the man, marveling at the naiveté or audacity, perhaps both, of the youngest son of the befallen Forca CEO. He would cite the inherent "trip wires," Cafferty-isms that were more ominous than "red flags," Helio would encounter in his new role—nepotism, corruption, canceled contracts, but most importantly, the failed confidence in the product itself. He recalls the bloated font blackening the man on the front page, suggesting Forca had become "as flimsy as tin." Helio would only smile at the comparison and press forward with a relentless pursuit, his call to action even testing Cafferty's appetite for risk.

"Of course I will work on my Portuguese, Helio. It's got to be easier than what we've been through."

"Do you mind if we have a seat for a moment? There's something I'd like to give you," he says, while motioning to a vacant table nearby. Helio retrieves a hefty, silver facón sheath adorned with an inscription of "RAC." "I don't want to pull it out here, but we have decorated the blade for you. I hope you enjoy it." Helio slides the satchel across the table, but Cafferty stops short of looking inside. "Oh, I also brought a nice Scotch for you, my friend, because I know how much you appreciate a fine single malt," Helio chides, a nod to Cafferty's naiveté for such pricey spirits.

Cafferty chuckles while admiring the leather satchel bearing the gifts. "Someday, I will find the right occasion—no, the right occasion will find me—to appreciate this drink, I promise you," he states convincingly.

For the first time all evening, the gift strikes a chord, presented modestly by a friend and not a client. Cafferty appraises the tucked-away setting, where the lighting is purposely dimmed, obscuring the gears and mechanics of such an event. *This* is *Helio*, he affirms quietly to himself.

"Thank you, Helio, from the bottom of my heart. This means a lot to me. I want to tell you something. For two years I have watched you handle difficult and at times absurd questions about your company, your father's role in the allegations, all the contrived bullshit to undermine you and the rebrand of Forca. You have grown into an amazing leader and I will always respect you."

The words surprise Helio, as he considers Cafferty's words and sudden transparency.

"Look around this room, Helio. I was part of this for thirty years. I am not fond of math, hence why I became a lawyer." Helio raps his knuckles on the table, affirming Cafferty's unfailing candor. "But if I had to guess, this party ran upwards of one hundred thousand dollars." Helio scans the room, and, after fingering the jazz band and magnum red bottles, nods in agreement. "We paid one hundred thousand dollars for this, and all but the waiters will forget the names of the hors d'oeuvres by lunch tomorrow. They will forget the band, and the ice sculpture will be poured down the same drain as the dishwater in the kitchen. All of this is gratuitous."

Helio presses his lips together, sensing something beyond frivolity. His eyes meet his friend's, as he dismisses the scene with a casual wave. "I have known you for some time now and this is out of left field, as you like to say. Is there something else you want to tell me?"

Cafferty offers a quick smile, while tapping his friend's wrist. His eyes cast down at the table in front of him while the last twenty-four hours race through his mind.

"Helio, I have a mom who cannot remember to eat. She does not know when to go to sleep or when to wake up." Cafferty scrapes stray black lint from the pristine tablecloth, dropping it to the floor. His jaw clenches, as if unwilling to part with a secret. "Helio, she cannot remember how to use the bathroom, and sometimes her care-

26

taker waits for a commercial to clean the woman." The words overcome Helio, causing him to sag. "Do you know what she is still so capable of doing, despite the loss of everything else? She can cry. And at times I think she does so because that is the only thing she can do that says, *I am still alive inside.*"

Helio leans closer, as if perhaps listening for a sound buried within his friend.

"Yesterday, she forgot my name. That is nothing new, and sadly a circumstance one must grow to accept with this disease. But it was when I asked her if she knew *her* name.... It was as if life walked up behind her and jerked the entire living room rug out from under her."

Helio extends his hand, resting it upon a still shoulder. "What can I do to help, Bobby?"

"My purpose came too late for my mother. I own that. But there are forty-seven million others like her afflicted with dementia—that's more than the entire population in Canada, or Australia. Can you imagine that context? Do you know there will be three times that number by 2050?"

The words press Helio into his chair, as he contemplates the sobering reality.

"What I ask is for Forca to assist in funding a memory care facility in the very geography in which they will soon capitalize. A facility that goes beyond an apartment complex that bathes, dresses, and feeds. This facility will be designed specifically for the needs of dementia care, a safe environment. One that focuses on less medication and more nutrition and wellness, social interaction. A facility that serves the family's needs, the outreach aspect of the programs." Cafferty pauses, considering his own words and what his mom will never know. "I will manage all aspects of the program and will push for as much support as I can get, including Bain as well." Cafferty pauses, observing a waiter scrape half-eaten shrimp plates into a garbage can. "This is an opportunity for Forca to not only cement their integrity locally, but also fight what will likely impact portions of your workforce, your family, or you." Cafferty slowly slides the facón knife across the table and looks his friend in the eye.

"Helio, I would ask that you consider what I have said for one evening. Tomorrow I will accept this beautiful gift of yours as a sign of my retirement or signifying your willingness to partner in the fight. You owe me nothing and I will forever respect you either way." Cafferty leans back and carefully watches his friend, quietly pondering whether he has marred his friendship, leveraging the heart for business. He recalls declining two tickets for a São Paolo premier soccer match two years prior, telling his new colleague, "Let's keep the business at hand over the heart."

Helio stares at his friend and gently swirls the ice in an empty glass. "You know, a wise man once told me to keep the business at hand over the heart."

The words prick Cafferty like a thorn. "Touché, my friend."

Helio chews on an ice cube while eyeing the transparent man in front of him. "Well, people might think I have lost my mind too, but I say fuck it. This sounds like a cause very much worth pursuing, Bobby. I will do whatever I can to support you."

The words stun Cafferty, causing him to imagine what might be possible. Before he can utter a word, he is beaten to the punch by the younger man.

"So, is there any time better time than the present? I don't believe so. Can you come with me, Bobby?"

Helio retrieves the churrasco knife and escorts Cafferty to the front of the room, splitting conversations in mid-sentence. He clanks a glass with authority, commanding the respect due the firm's largest client. The chipper music abruptly halts with a dissonant thud. Even the most notorious mouthpiece, J. C. "Bullhorn" Marshall, stifles his machine gun rattle for the moment, if for no other reason than that a man is wielding a churrasco knife. Helio motions for David Shilliday, the firm's senior partner and most rapacious fist, to join him up front. Shilliday obliges, instantly recognizing the cold, white glow of camera phones capturing yet another moment. Helio clears his throat and flicks the microphone to life.

"Today I came to present a retirement gift to a friend. This churrasco knife—one coincidentally carried by the gauchos for fighting—was meant to symbolize the end of Bobby's long journey. The many struggles and successes throughout his career, and certainly those which supported Forca's cause. However, this evening the knife represents a new journey, one which will require every bit of strength and collective fight we have as a community, as partners. As such, it will be a symbol of Forca's commitment to join the fight against Alzheimer's."

Whispers bubble through the silence. "Alzheimer's?" says one. "Like, forgetting things?" breathes another. All eyes are fixed on Helio.

"Forca has committed to a one-million-dollar pledge for the…" Helio clasps his hand over the microphone and whispers to Cafferty, "What's the name of your organization going to be?"

An astonished Cafferty rubs a square jaw, now sprinkled with the day's growth. "It will be called the St. Stanislaus Memory Care Facility."

"A one-million-dollar pledge for the St. Stanislaus Memory Care Facility."

The ballroom offers a cautious cheer, the very kind doled out for an extrinsic solution such as snake oil. Helio seizes an opportunity to leverage Bain—or more accurately, David—like a colossal vice. He recalls a vodka-propelled comment, like a Molotov cocktail, David Shilliday lobbed at him the first time they met. *"The apple does not fall far from the tree."* David misjudged Helio's English comprehension and the comment still smolders within.

He squares to David Shilliday, his frame rooted like an oak, while a slight crack reveals teeth from behind the beard. "Forca challenges Bain to a $500,000 contribution to this global epidemic and to help us fight this enemy in our own backyard." The room chatters and hisses, like a pressure cooker nipping at the seals. A grating whistle leaks from the PA system, almost needling someone to respond.

Shilliday, perpetually on the qui vive for parting with money, shudders at the thought of a negative public image. His decision to fight dementia, or worse yet, ignore the fight, will make the social community feed in minutes. He knows he has been licked. *Checkmate, you sonofabitch*, Shilliday thinks to himself. A smile presses across Shilliday's pouty mush as he surprises himself with what leaks forth. "Bain & Bain will commit to a dollar for dollar match with our strategic partner, Forca."

Helio presses his hand into Shilliday's, firing a wink and a smile. Shilliday scurries offstage, cornering the firm's accountant with questions concerning tax breaks. Cafferty reaches for his friend's arm.

"Muito obrigado, Helio. I cannot thank you enough."

Helio stands pokerfaced, examining his friend. "Nothing is free, Bobby. There is one promise I need from you as well."

Cafferty leans in. "Of course, if it is something I can do, I will—"

"That tie. You must promise to never wear the tie again—it's hideous!"

"I will see what I can do about that," winks Cafferty.

31

With one brief pass, Cafferty wishes his colleagues luck. He politely declines a drink with Jonas. "I've got to get back to Youngstown. My mom…," he says as he motions toward the exit.

"I understand, Bobby. We all do."

Cafferty pokes an oversized "lobby" button in the elevator and, without a sound, feels the new-age capsule begin to descend. Drawing a deep breath and closing his eyes, Cafferty feels an odd sense of déjà vu and begins removing the tie. He recalls the moment he removed his boxing gloves, as an undefeated amateur, and hung them on a rusty nail in the attic. He never touched the gloves again, and instead let life recount that chapter of his story as often or as infrequently as it wished. This was the last time he would engage as a lawyer, defending as he was taught and as he was compelled to do for others.

He tucks the tie neatly alongside the knife, briefly trying to smooth a permanent crease he knows will never lie flat. As the capsule reaches the lobby, it slips open, perfectly flush with the floor and seamless against the shaft. Moving briskly toward the exit, he never once looks behind him, only at the flickering neon eyes beyond the firm's entry.

Chapter 3

Mayor Donnelly stands facing the Youngstown Regional Veterans Administration, while nervously fidgeting with a jagged chunk of weathered shale. He observes the piece disintegrating into a damp red dust with relative ease. It's the same brick that almost eighty years ago was duly described as "suitable for any paving and building needs," which withstood the harshest of bitter winters. However, today it has no more resolution and character than damp chalk, only made worse by a surprisingly chilly September rain earlier in the day. He thumbs along the ragged edge of the facade and watches as another piece of the shale falls to the ashtray-colored sidewalk below.

The mayor is shiny and stiff against the shale backdrop, like a new flag that has been unfurled and has yet to face harsh conditions. His face, free of cracks, suggests an uncomplicated past and one that lacks any significant story to tell. He rubs his hands together vigorously, as if trying to remove paint, before plunging them into suit pockets. "Darn it, of all days," he mutters to himself as his hands find nothing within. Though he typically clicks a rhythm on a cheap plunger pen to stave a nervous stutter, he has forgotten his safety tether today. He plucks a jagged shale crumb again, rolling the piece delicately between each finger.

His first thirty days as the political visage of a no-nonsense city were noteworthy only due to a teen pelting him with a half-eaten sandwich, marring the misplaced trench coat he chose to wear at his introduction. The transplant councilman from rural Ada, Ohio, had surprisingly won the Youngstown mayoral election, graduating from the political confines of a little league game to the big leagues.

He spots a dull-gray, utilitarian F-150 slowing near the curb in front of him. Two lake-blue eyes pierce the windshield, cracking the drab, gray cloud surrounding the driver. Abruptly dropping the shale, Donnelly maneuvers around the hood to greet the man departing the vehicle. Cafferty moves with a purpose, emitting a command presence more akin to an officer than a retiree. Cafferty extends his hand and presses firmly.

"Good morning, Mr. Mayor." Cafferty's eyes size up the man before him. He notes a thin veneer of some sort, something slightly out of place, like his mom's refurbished house.

"Good m-morning, Mr. Cafferty. Thank you for coming," says Mayor Donnelly.

"Please, call me Bobby."

"Sorry, Bobby. I wanted to say that I am sorry for your current challenge, your mom's condition."

Cafferty, while listening, inspects the building in front of him, as if at a viewing, pursed lips and a sadness hidden somewhere in the lakes of blue. Instead of responding, his fingers trace along the orangish red streaks running across the fractured gray grooves. *It's like it's been mortally wounded*, he thinks to himself, recalling the various iterations of the building. *Like life has slowly leaked life from within, bleeding down the staggered blocks and pooling on the side-*

walk below. Its breathing is labored and with each draw of air, more life is pushed onto the sidewalk below until it lies motionless.

Ignoring the skittish babble from the mayor, Cafferty speaks. "This wasn't just a building. This was a life, more constant than the North Star. The Calder County Social Security Annex, the St. Stanislaus Church, and the Youngstown Steel Mill were the three patriarchs of this city. If you were ever lost as a child, you were told to walk to any of the three and you were guaranteed a familiar face, a hot meal, and a hand leading you back to your parents. There was communal pride and respect between the immigrants—some fresh off the boat—an unspoken bond that we were one and building a life together." Cafferty walks to the corner of the building, where a portion of the brick has given way to a rusted, tired girder.

"Whenever I want to see my father or grandfather, I don't go to St. Stanislaus' cemetery. I come to this spot, because they are still living right here."

Donnelly clasps his hands together gently, as if arriving to the wake a few moments late. He is respectful to the man eulogizing a friend.

Cafferty quietly responds, "Thank you, Mr. Mayor, for your concern about my mom. It is greatly appreciated."

Cafferty pats the building and turns his attention toward the Mayor. "Now then, please introduce me to the new director."

As the elevator doors shut, a cavernous groan echoes through the shaft, bucking the unit upwards. Slowly, the groan settles into a staccato squeak, as if giggling at the two men. "Ah—it's almost as if this elevator heard the punchline a thousand times," chimes Cafferty.

Donnelly chuckles. "The elevator's name is Otis, or so I am told by the folks upstairs. See, he's even got his name tag," Donnelly says, sarcastically pointing to the faded "Otis" manufacturer's tag. "Apparently he sounds like a different person all year. The colder it gets, the higher-pitched his giggle, like he enjoys it."

Otis chirps as the unit shimmies against the shaft. "See? It's crazy. But the hotter it gets, the more pissed off he becomes. 'Ornery Otis,' just groaning like some crotchety old man."

"He never laughs during the summer?" Cafferty shakes his head. "He would be the only unhappy person in Ohio during the summer." Otis heaves a deep breath and stifles a giggle, lurching to a stop. As the doors part, a giant of a man observes contractors debating a floor's load capacity. He reeks of disdain, his folded arms stretching across a red and cream Lacoste polo as if watching an incompetent court jester.

The man is Dawson Phillips, a former Division II football player from Georgia, and a recovering misogynist. Recently banished to the least desirable project within the VA, his career and image were castrated among his peers. But here, within these confines, he feeds his thirst for power with despotic control and perpetual scolding, as if slowly grinding weary bones to powder. He doesn't want them, but *needs* the vets and contractors assigned to his buildout.

"Bless your hearts, boys," he begins in a lofty manner. "Let's be a little smarter than the floor. That dog ain't gonna hunt." His southern euphemisms are as equally misplaced as his worn Sperrys. "Glue it and screw it. Just get this thing movin'," he finishes as he snaps in the mayor's direction, his fingers reorganizing his dishwater blond hair into a perfect part.

"Ah, I didn't even hear Otis fussin'," Dawson spits, as if ambushed. "Usually he's real good about announcin' company." The mayor offers a hand, but is cut off by Dawson, his voice deepening as if scolding a child. "You're late, Mayor, and I'm mindin' a tight schedule here."

"I understand, M-Mister Dawson, but if you don't m-mind, I would like to introduce you to Bobby Cafferty.... He's the—"

"Oh, hey, Bob...or Bobby.... Bobby sounds like I am speakin' to a little leaguer back in Ball Ground. Do you mind if we call each other by our grown-up names?" he lobs dismissively. "Look, I heard about your mama and it's a damn shame, her losin' her wits and all with that. What's the na—

"Dementia," Cafferty interrupts calmly.

"Yes, that. And I would do anything I could to help." Dawson leans in, his frame towering and shading the tiles between them. "Hell, I bet half the people in this place have got some kind of dementia. But I got one mission and one mission only: I am going to jam the three outlying VA clinics into this rust pail of bricks and bolts in nine months, and then head back down south where I belong."

37

Donnelly toes the ground in front of him, dipping his heading remorsefully. "I am sorry, Mr. Dawson, for wasting your t—"

"I understand, Mr. Dawson," Cafferty fires, his jaw firming into a blocky mold. "I respect and hope you meet your goal, sending you back to wherever you are from. For me? This *is* where I am from and this *is* where I will be long after you serve your punishment for that horseshit you pulled in…, Where is *it*?" Cafferty squints, his brow now furrowed.

Dawson peeks to his side as if looking for help, but only catches a contractor staring back helplessly. The shadow disappears between the men. "Ah, it's Ball Ground, Ball Ground, Georgia," a stunned Dawson states, his cheeks reddening as if slapped. Otis fires a giggle three floors below.

"Yes, that's it. Ball Ground," Bobby acknowledges. "I will send you back there on the same schedule you seek. Perhaps that might even fashion you into a more honorable man than you deserve. Or…I will simply send you back there." Cafferty's voice stings. Dawson, a bully woven into his DNA, wobbles on his feet. His stance looks as if it might crumble.

A sudden uncontrolled hack bursts from the corner of the room, startling the trio. The men spin toward the man, anchored uncomfortably in a wheelchair. He resembles a rotting bag of spuds, with knots and discoloration painting his body. "Fucking told *you*, didn't he," the voice crackles with jagged glass. Cafferty and Donnel-

38

ly stare at the man, his face spalled like an atlas, valleys carved from rivers. Donnelly gasps.

"Bad boys, bad boys, whatcha gonna do?" the voice taunts the dethroned bully, eliciting an undercurrent of giggles throughout the floor.

Dawson waves his hand, shooing the owner of the voice. "Jesus, Mary, and Joseph, that guy. No one will be sad to see him go, except maybe Seagram's...and the flies." Dawson turns his attention back to Cafferty, shielding him from the man in the corner.

"Mr. Cafferty—Bobby—if I can help, then I will do so." Dawson dangles a meaty paw toward Cafferty. "Just understand"—he motions to the fountain of barbs—"they put this goddamn place together in the dark."

Cafferty simply stares at the hand. He scans a room decidedly larger and more contemplative than the man in the corner, who spills bitterness. Cafferty feels eyes settling upon the trio, not as a distraction but perhaps something more. Cafferty's voice lowers.

"As you know, the Department of Labor will house three of their Disabled Veteran Outreach specialists here. I know you and Mayor Donnelly have already discussed the importance of this workforce in his broader outreach programs. Ohio has upwards of eight hundred thousand vets, and with this building serving as a regional hub for placement and medical services, I have no doubt there are skills here that can help. And it certainly doesn't hurt your résumé, placing veterans back into the workforce." Dawson nods, acknowledging points he has heard prior. "I am not asking for your help with anything. Just that we can do what we are trying to do. Do you understand?" he finishes.

"I do," states Dawson flatly.

"Then if you'll excuse me, I have another meeting to attend." He abruptly twists, leaving Donnelly and Dawson in a frozen stance.

As Otis' doors begin to narrow, Cafferty observes the now-silent lump in the wheelchair staring out the window at the bus station below. The man appears to understand the scene unfolding, souls descending the bus steps onto an unnamed street, in search of something. A trace smile hangs on the corner of the man's mouth. Then, as if the man scripts a different ending, the smile scurries off, causing Otis to giggle.

Chapter 4

Richard Cost stands alone beneath a U.S. flag that extends from the shamrock green walls of Pittsburgh's Franklin High School. The thin oak post supporting the flag appears to press down upon him with the weight of a forest, leaving the man with a permanent slouch. His trademark cranberry merino wool sweaters of the past now resemble faded crop tops. Their haphazard journey of washer to dryer has leveled enough shrinkage on the garment to expose his belly button through the undergarments and appear to constrict at his shoulders. His once thick brown hair would tousle about during his frenetic writing style. Now, his clammy hand rests upon his bald brow as if he is in a constant state of pained observation.

He gently rubs his fingertips across a vast and shiny blackboard, his eyes scanning the surface for perhaps a hint on what to do. Light dances around him before plunging into the starless pool, hypnotizing the man who has seen this somewhere before. *Where does the light go? It cannot just stop*, he thinks to himself. He strains his eyes, as if trying to bore a hole into the surface. But the chalkboard resists, with more vigor and more patience, revealing none of the secrets within. "Fucking thing," he whispers into the void.

His hands tense. The digits constrict the damp chalk, awaiting a prompt, any prompt, to simply start teaching. His back hunches and spine protrudes like a reptilian ancestor of some sort, a beast millions of years in the making and an obvious target for sneers and stares. He no longer educates of past eras, deciphering events as if the world were his lab animal, a tool for *his use at his whim*. He has become the animal, pinned to some dissecting board, exposed for all the world to examine.

"Hey, Dino!" growls a crooked-mouthed man-child from the back row. The figure who has spent years eviscerating fragile under-classmen has a favorite new target. "You know we get Principal Skynnar when you ain't here. He gives a shite-ton of homework. Quit slackin', old man. No one likes a *quitter*," he claws. "Hey, Gator!" he shouts as his eyes squint shut for the assault. Nervous laughter bub-bles throughout the room. Richard is unaware as his eyes continue chasing light, as it dives into the pool in front of him. "I'm talking to you!" A gnawed pencil crashes into the chalkboard, yanking Richard back to the present.

"You gonna teach up there or have another seizure?" This time he garners hoots from around the room. "Because if you ain't teaching, I don't have to be here," he spits. Richard slowly spins and shuffles toward the class, his loafers scraped wafer thin in the front. His toes bubble over the soles, the leather revealing a worn outline of toenails cutting through.

He stares at peculiar shapes in front of him, seeking a lifeline to something familiar and safe. However, he senses drowning in a sea of swirling colors and a wall of sound. The tidal surge crashes into him, marooning his body somewhere beyond the present.

A clatter of chairs and desks rumbles over the laughter as students form a large circle. An impromptu teenage convention begins with frivolous gossip and antics, again usurping History 207. "I am a te-teacher," he stutters, trying to convince himself of the parody. His eyes flit about the room, magnetized by sounds and laughs that he is late to pinpoint. "Crazy" fires from the corner, stinging the frozen target. "Looks stoned" follows. "Just old," "stu—," "cr—," "batsh—" The shots blend together, nipping at his fate like vultures picking over dust and bones.

His eyes settle at last on a girl in the front row, where the absence of noise is the oddity. Her eyes are mysteriously dark and somber, a stark contrast to the lust-filled mob gathering around a witch trial. The din fades into a quiet whoosh, ambient noise without a source. He gazes into her black peepholes, noticing the light pass *into* her. A space within her illuminates and he observes tiny figures, one larger than the other, through the peepholes. "They are…hugging?" he whispers to himself. "I know that," he confirms, smiling. "I can actually *feel* that hug."

After a few moments, the light no longer passes, as if the peepholes are slipped shut. The little girl leans closely and cocks her head, as if she needed to protect a secret from the bully behind her. She whispers, "I am so sorry, Mr. Richard, I wish I could help you remember now. But I promise you, very soon you will remember."

His mouth splits for a moment, and an innocent, apologetic smile appears on his face. "I'm sorry, honey. I've never seen you in my class. Do I know you?"

The next morning, Richard arrives again at Franklin High School. The parking lot is cloaked in darkness, with a single light sputtering atop a wooden post. Glass shards sparkle against the moon above, fossils of a recent spate of vandalism. He shifts the still-moving car into park, emitting a clang against the aluminum football bleachers. The engine gasps and lunges, dying from the misuse.

"Wh-What is—where are the kids?" he mutters into the wind-shield, pulling the door handle. He extricates himself, as if he is la-boring against the clench of a crumbled steel cave. The crisp autumn air pricks his bare arms as he shuffles in no particular direction. Minutes become hours as the man lingers behind a soft glow on the horizon, eventually assembling into an orange ball from the east. His journey halts on a highway ramp as a loud screech startles a lost man.

"Richie, what are you doing, buddy?" begs a balding man in a suit. "You will freeze out here. Where is your coat?

Richard smiles at the man, his face familiar but out of place.

"Where are the lights, do you—umm, have lights?"

"What do you mean, what lights? My car lights are on."

"No, not your car lights…the colors that blink." He points to a red light flickering in the distance.

"Sometimes they scream, you know, the…sirens. Have I done something wrong?"

"Richie, I am not the police. It's me, Principal Skynnar. Come on, buddy, please get in." Richard stiffens.

"Jesus, Skynnar—I kn-know who you are," huffs Richard. He shuffles around the car and arrives at the passenger side, staring at the handle. For a moment, the handle appears insignificant, merely silver matter against the shiny red door. However, a flicker from within Richard, perhaps curiosity, begs him to pull the oddity. The door releases and Richard climbs inside the car.

Skynnar leads Richard to his office, a congested space littered with class pictures, diplomas, and walls of textbooks. It smells like a dank closet, yet something about it titillates the lost man.

"Richie, have a seat." Richard observes the man pour dark powder into a machine and flick it to life with an electric pop. Immediately, an earthy scent clings to the air, wrapping around the room like a warm blanket. A black syrup oozes from the machine, pooling into the mottled pot beneath it. The scene comforts Richard and he smiles.

"It's almost like…an—what do you call those old-time cups that the feathers went into?" Richard inquires, his eyes fixed on the dark puddle.

"Do mean an inkwell and quill, like for writing?" Skynnar offers.

"Yes—I remember a quill and an old-time inkwell in my house. Th-this is many years ago, but…I can still see the inkwell and letters. Cards too." Richard shifts on the chair and rubs his hands, wringing the last bit of chill from his body.

"What letters and cards, buddy?" The coffee machine fires three beeps as a bright red light pulses from the machine, stealing the moment.

Richard points toward a brass-framed class photo dated 2013, angling skyward from the desk. "Geez, are those your kids? They look so old in here."

"Yeah, buddy—the twins graduated high school in 2013. Do you remember helping move them into their dorm with me the following fall? Remember IUP?" Another beep fires from the machine, like an insolent child demanding attention.

"You know what that thing looks like?" Richard says, staring at the sound's source. "It's like—"

"Like an inkwell," Skynnar states regretfully.

"Yes! Exactly, how did you know?"

Skynnar takes a deep breath as his shoulders sag. He pours a small amount into the cup and hands it to the man.

"Richard, it's time we focus on getting you well, seeing professionals who can help you." Richard stares into the black liquid, his hands trembling and pushing ripples back and forth. "You know I would do anything for you if I could—and I've tried. We have had substitutes teach some of your classes. We've had Mrs. Dixon even score your students' tests, and as you know, she's got the PSAT preparation classes."

Richard bypasses the voice, seeking out the wash of colors, faces, and trophies behind the man.

"The school board completed its annual assessment. As you know, they were in your classroom in October. Not just yours, of course, but all the teachers'." Skynnar shifts uncomfortably in his chair. Richard's eyes cling to one picture, its image magnified and placed into a cheap, four-piece, plastic frame hanging directly behind Skynnar.

"That assessment, coupled with your classes failing the state testing, means, well, I've got to do *something*. Do you understand what I am saying to you, Richard? If we do not improve the scores to an acceptable level by June, we will lose a third of the state funding. We can't—"

Richard rises and shuffles toward the large photo behind Skynnar, labeled "1983 St. Patrick's Senior Class." He studies the photo, tracing the silhouettes as if hoping to feel the life within. He settles his finger on the image of two kids laughing, their muscles flexed, in dark green jerseys. "Who is that?" mumbles Richard.

"Richard," Skynnar says, his voice breaking, "that's us, that's you and me. Do you see our football jerseys there? We had that senior photo taken right before our homecoming game. Me, you, and the guys all decided to wear our jerseys instead of the oxfords."

For a moment, Richard snares a fleeting memory from within, burning fast and bright like a tracer. "Geez, Skinny. We won the game pretty handily if I recall? Shut 'em out. I remember they crowned you king of the homecoming court."

For a moment, Skynnar forgets his career, state-funding scores, and the board he reports to, and witnesses a friend being consumed by quicksand, leaving him heartbroken.

"Yeah, Richard. We got after 'em pretty good that game. We were playing th—"

"Knights, the Kingston Knights. I remember." Richard swirls the coffee against the silence. "I think it's time for me to go home," Richard states flatly.

"Yeah, buddy, let's get you home."

Richard settles in his car and turns the ignition, watching the yellow and black streaks pass by. Soon, shapes and noises begin filling the parking lot and sidewalks, like the high tide rolling in across a deserted beach. As the masses pool near the front door, steam puffs from the students as they chatter and ham it up in the cold fall morning. Richard engages the drive, and the car dawdles toward the exit of the school. As he approaches the main road, he encounters the mascot, a large bison with lusterless black eyes.

He stares into the image, squinting and blinking as if trying to read the wooden animal's mind. However, the image stares harder, unflinching and dispassionate, refusing to give an inch. A sudden flicker within jolts a memory of the young student, her eyes so revealing and her words comforting. He smiles until the burst of a horn behind him chases the memory for good. He hears a voice from behind him, encouraging him to move. "Don't worry, my friend," booms Skynnar. "I will follow you until we get you home."

Chapter 5

Otis fires a volley of giggles as the brisk October morning tickles his elevator shaft with a gust. His mood has become increasingly jocular as of late, at times adding "thwacks" after a giggle, as if appreciating a joke with a slap of a knee. He shimmies as he approaches the third floor, momentarily stifling his laugh short. Within his grasp, he ferries a streetwalker who is woefully prepared for the elements. She stares into his faded elevator control panel, using him as a cheap mirror. With a final huff, he opens his doors with a hard gasp, depositing his load. His mouth hangs wide as he ogles her scrambling across the dingy white tile.

She, like others of her breed, seeks shelter during the biting freezes. Her luck had been good with the past VA administration, as they had turned a blind eye to policies. Despite the hard life of an alley dog, she bears strikingly soft, smooth-looking skin. She covers the random men and rare showers with a heavy scent of lavender, a calling card that remains long after her visit. While she fears nothing of the gypsy pit life, she is petrified of the cold. Now, the building frets under new management, as Dawson has no mercy for those stiffening beneath the bridges.

The third floor bustles like an ant colony as contractors outfitted in blue and white hard hats transport materials and tools, contributing to a greater cause. Their movements weave through onlookers donning faded military field jackets, who appreciate the distraction from endless days.

Suddenly, a bellow roars and the ants respond with an urgent pace. Otis whistles and giggles beneath them, needling the group.

"I told you to get some goddamn grease for this bucket. It feels like I'm in a blender!" The voice rips up through the elevator shaft, splitting above the third floor chattering. As the elevator door opens, Dawson fumbles and drops the blueprints, causing some derisive payback from the vets.

"That's why you were Division II football, right there," shoots a familiar voice. Dawson glares at the gathering, trying to identify the culprit. *I know that smell—where is she?* A brisk cloud of lavender hangs atop an undercurrent of pungent sweat and paint. His eyes trace the outline of the room, landing squarely on Trixie, hiding beneath a card table.

"I told you to stay the fuck out of here or I will have you arrested," he forbids. Dawson looks for any other target to make a point and fixes his stare upon the man plopped inside the grasp of a faded silver wheelchair. "I would do the same to you, but even county lockup wouldn't take a vagrant dead man."

Danny, the decaying vet and perpetual thorn, ignores the jab as he settles into a frozen pose. His eyes flit about, observing a fly buzz around his arm.

"How in the fuck is a fly living in the winter?" he quizzes no one. Soon, Danny spots another fly, skittering across the window overlooking the bus station. A smile casts across his mouth and he bubbles with excitement, imagining where to begin. "Hey, Dawsie—do you realize this place is infested with flies? They've got to be nesting in here, laying eggs and shitting all over the place," he fires. "Half the boys here are down in sick call, and I got a hunch why. I might make my way to the phone this afternoon and call the *real* Veteran Affairs, report this ate-up dump," he singsongs.

Danny cups his hand and creeps the makeshift net toward the creature, which now rests atop his pale blue vein. With a lightning-quick swipe, he catches the fly in his palm, almost capsizing in the process. "Haha, you little bastard," he spits, looking around for any validation but receiving none. He shakes his hand fast, banging the creature within and throwing the fly against the tile below. With a jab of a puffy foot, he strikes the floor awkwardly, trying to kill the creature.

Dawson, still simmering, reloads for a volley against Danny's irreverent tone. "By the way, the medical floor is downstairs, not here. I don't want you leaking whatever you're rotting from all over my floors!" Dawson snaps, waving a chubby finger like a wand.

"Don't forget what I did for you and all those other banjo-playing hillbillies in Georgia, Dawsie," Danny snaps. "Bet ya if I had a pair of tits and was a few decades younger, you would try to slap my ass too, maybe even fuck me—who knows? I mean, that's your thing, young girls and all."

Danny feigns cupping enormous breasts, embellishing curves of an unnatural proportion. "OOOOOOH, my Dawsie," he moans erotically in a screechy soprano timbre. "Ohh, Dawsie, bring that big, fat ass over here and make little Susie cry. Oh PAAAAAAA-pi, Pa-pi—" Danny is holding serve, much to the amusement of a smattering of vets.

Though Dawson started his reign with an iron fist, Cafferty's public square-off knocked a chink in that armor. Danny aims to ram a sword straight through and cripple the bully forever. The smattering of vets, previously occupied with board games, are now seizing a more interesting use of time.

Dawson fumes and pushes rolls of blueprints into a young contractor's hands, knocking him backwards. He squares toward the silver buggy and trudges toward Danny, his face reddening with each step. He halts within a foot of Danny, hovering above him. Danny's hand lurches for a moment toward his wheel, until he realizes his back is against the corner, with the bus stop three floors beyond the window and a mountain of a man directly in front of him. His arm hangs extended as his hand rests against the wheel.

"Look into my eyes, you old man, and hear what I got to say to you," Dawson gravels. "The situation back then, when you might have been able to wipe your own ass, was God-awful. They were so fucking desperate, they would have taken *anyone* into service. Christ, they *drafted* people!" he chortles.

"Before you pull the military card with me, let this sink in—you were a cook. You see these men around this room?" He points a meaty finger, like a blackjack, at bodies who have grown silent. "You weren't like them, do you understand me? Do you know why you were a cook?" Dawson asks, his blond eyebrows furrowed together, like a sandy isle in a sea of blood. Danny sinks in the chair, as if awaiting the wick to reach the charge.

"Let me tell you why. Because someone noticed you in basic training and said, 'Now *there's* a coward, there's someone that will run away from his own shadow.' You were stuck in the only place that wouldn't put someone else's life on the line. You boiled and fried while everyone else was sacrificing to earn their 'soldier' title.

"You know, down in Georgia, we had a word for that job, you know, where you made food *for* people." Hisses scatter about the room, but no one speaks. Danny deflates against his chair, like a marooned jellyfish on a searing beach.

"Bet none of these fine soldiers here knew either those things about you. Coward. Cook," he states firmly, pausing on both words for full effect. Silence envelopes the room. Even a brutish Otis, normally game, can only gasp somewhere beneath the scene. A couple of vets return to a game of checkers, mumbling incoherently. Eviscerated in front of the people he will ever know, Danny contemplates his life, summed up by a nomadic misogynist and a DD-214.

Dawson clucks his tongue, setting the hammer on an imaginary revolver, and fires a bullet directly at Danny's forehead. The recoil lifts his hand high into the air with a resulting concussion felt throughout the building. "That dog will hunt!" he mocks, pleased with himself. He winks at the saffron corpse and begins fingering the part back into his dishwater blond hair.

"Now, if y'all will excuse me, I've got deadlines to meet," he blurts as contractors begin to scurry.

Danny slowly spins his chair away from snooping eyes. The same eyes that slow for a grisly pileup, pining for the moment a body gives up the ghost. He locks his stare on the fly he crushed moments earlier. Its body is battered and adhered to the floor by its own vital fluid, yet it desperately flicks one wing, dying to live.

"Why?" Danny says. The bug fights a pointless fight, spinning slowly against the broken wing. With each movement, the fly paints the floor with irregular circles, using every molecule of self to continue moving. "Just...let...go," Danny whispers as he watches the spinning wane to a twitch and eventual stillness.

As chatter restores to the floor, a stout-built figure in white emerges from the more reserved cargo elevator. She plods like a freight train secured to rails, a labored movement, but one that would mash anything in its path.

Eschewing greater nurse's pay in larger cities, Nurse Abby arrived in 1997, a tenure only trumped by Otis. Her early calling as a Missionaries of Charity nun—the "brick terdhouse-tough order," she once quipped—endowed her with an extensive repertoire of Catholic hymns. But somewhere during the process of "molding a life for

Christ"—the docility, the subjugation of one's self-esteem, the acceptance of medieval-like hardship as a merit badge—she began to lose finesse, which would have benefitted an aspiring nurse. If there was any hope to develop that skill, it was doomed from a body resembling two hundred pounds of mashed potatoes stuffed in a fifty-gallon bag. However, no one dares to complain, particularly those receiving care from her.

Affectionately known as "The Princess of Prick," she is famous for inserting a catheter without missing a note as she hums "The Prayer of St. Francis." Her voice almost makes life bearable for the patients, who appreciate what equates to Heaven's jukebox.

"Let me hear it!" calls one of the men, setting his red checkers aside with a smile. As she moves toward the man in the wheelchair, Nurse Abby smiles at no one in particular and trills the air with the opening notes of "Amazing Grace." "You know I could listen to you all day," offers the man as he slinks back in his chair with a gratuitous smile.

Abby pushes a modified cart, which casts a striking resemblance to a gurney. Bland, revolting liquids lie atop the cart, including one large white aqueous solution that could pass for Elmer's Glue. She nudges Danny's back with a hard knuckle, her favorite method of communication. "Honey, if I tell you to show up for your feeding, I need you to show up," she says softy, belying her adequate frame.

He raises a scrawny, blotched arm and half-attempts to dismiss her. However, his weakened condition is intercepted by a meaty hand. "I have been working hard at dying since about 1979," he grumbles. "I am as close now as I have ever been, and if I want to skip a meal, or whatever the fuck it is you are putting in me, then it's my ch—"

Nurse Abby gives a firm slap to Danny's head, the least likely spot to spring a leak. "Albumin. And honey, there are other people of faith on this floor as well. I'd appreciate you minding your tongue," she states matter-of-factly.

"Besides, no one dies on my watch, Danny. Or at least no one dies on my watch hungry You know that pretty little young thing that shows up on the second shift? The one that you, the other heathens, and even Dawson goo-goo-gah-gah all over? You pull that Bobby Sands hunger strike drama with *her*," she fires. "Even when my mom was dying, God rest her soul, she still went to her grave with a full belly." Nurse Abby quietly walks through the sign of the cross before setting her eyes back on the tray.

Danny wags his head at the remarks and begins settling in for a restless midmorning feeding. Abby selects a shiny, silver needle and methodically wraps a dark yellow cord around a limb only slightly larger, pulling the cord until it vanishes against his skin. "Jesus wept" he whimpers. Danny cringes and fires a look of disdain at Abby. "That thing should be pumping up car tires or a basketball, not a human." He motions to the needle. "Why do you think I don't show up?" The question falls flat as he is jabbed twice and winces from the errant strike. "Christ, Abby, don't you make a living tapping veins?" Danny fires with a crackle and gurgle.

"There it is," says Abby, satisfied with the connection. A slow, steady flow of substances enters his body as Danny begins speaking quietly to the half-listening nurse.

"I ran away from life at that bus station." He motions across the street. "I stepped up on that platform, I pulled out whatever bills I had in my pocket, and I chose the very next city that was on the schedule. I didn't give a damn if it was Kalamazoo or New York, as long as it didn't say Youngstown. I had a hungry heart, ya know, hungry for something other than the life I had, the grand-fucking Museum of the Mundane," he laughs.

Abby clucks her tongue and hisses at his cursing.

"It wasn't just me," he rationalizes, wagging his head and waving his finger. "No, sir. It wasn't just me, you know. Everyone is always looking for some Oz, some magical place with a wizard far away."

Abby leans back and places a hand on her hip. "What are you going on about?"

"A dream, Nurse. The wizard, Buddha, riches, fame, Heaven—they are all one and the same. That bus will take anyone with a dream and a few bucks on a golden brick road to whatever it is they are seeking. The problem isn't the bus or even the wizard at the end," he states, letting out a small chuckle. "It's the monkeys and the witches on that road."

An unexpected, high-pitched giggle, like that of a bonobo, squeaks from her jiggling mass, drawing chuckles from the floor. "Danny, do you have any idea what you sound like? Oz, witches, golden brick roads?" She shakes her head and tucks the log sheet underneath a beefy bicep.

"That's a good part of your problem, Danny. You have no faith, or rather, your faith is relying on some wizard or magic beans to serve your needs. The true essence of faith has nothing to do with your self-interest, but instead how you may serve the Lord more effectively." Satisfied with her answer, Abby begins humming . Danny fidgets uncomfortably, twisting in his chair to face Abby.

"So, I don't believe I've ever asked you this…. Why, then, did you stop being a nun? I mean, it would seem to me you would be rather good at that," Danny states genuinely.

Abby softens momentarily, reflecting on a young girl some lifetime ago. "You know," she starts, as she looks out the window overlooking the vacant bus station. "It wasn't why you would think," she states. "It takes nine years to become a sister. All of the hardships—the joyful poverty, giving up personal freedoms, separation from family…I once used a newspaper to wipe my own bottom," she states, chuckling at the thought. "None of that pushed me to leave. What pushed me to leave was the absence of friendships. You were not able to establish friendships within the order."

Danny looks quizzically at Abby.

"I don't understand. What do you mean by 'no friendships'?"

"If any relationship began to root, the higher-ups forbade that and told us it would 'take away from the love required for the Order.'" Abby takes a deep breath, pushing the past from her mind and the present. Danny scoffs at the notion, dismissing it with a wave.

"See, that absurdity is exactly why I never bought into any of that religious stuff, like slinging snake oil. Wait, did you say nine years of *that*?" Danny hisses. And if that doesn't earn you *something*, how does—"

Abby hardens quickly. "Please go on about your witches, beans, and golden brick roads."

"Now, as I was saying, I got off of a bus in Cleveland. The only reason I stepped off that bus is because my transfer to Chicago told me I had to step off the bus in Cleveland." Danny hacks and winces in pain, spitting yesterday's blood on the floor, narrowly missing the fly.

"I never made it to Chicago. I walked to a liquor store a few blocks from the station because I needed something for the ride, you know? I just had to have something to get me to Chicago. If I had walked in any other direction but that direction, I swear, I wouldn't be sitting here today," he seethes, glaring skyward. "*THAT*, the goddamn curse to HAVE and to *NEED*, is the fucking monkeys lining my life's brick road—you see what I am saying?

"But just outside of that liquor store, a woman—or some devil in heels—asked if I wanted to try something better, unlike anything I had ever known. Now, by that point, I had done plenty in my time. I hadn't been wet behind the ears since grade school, and hell, I got drunk on wine we stole from the sacristy—no bullshit. So I figure, 'Show me what ya got.' I followed her behind the liquor store, where she pulled out a little thing of foil. I remember her telling me the first taste was free. Now, I had two hours before my next ride, so I took whatever she offered. When that bulldozer hit me, nothing else mattered—not alimony, birthdays, laws, health, or Chicago. That warmth—Jesus, that warmth just slithered around the inside of my body like a snake. I could feel it uncoil in my lungs and wind through every single vein, gently squeezing the breath in and out of me. Then, I felt that same slippery warmth all over my skin, like a naked woman, just sliding all over me, meshing into every nook of my body, like the most beautiful hug you will ever know."

He shuts his eyes and delicately traces his fingers, weaving them around his arms and neck, oblivious to the tube coming from him. "That warm body just melts into you, perfectly applied to every square inch of your body. Just soaked into me down to my bones, and I felt..." He sucks a long draw of air and shivers uncomfortably. "Ahhhhhhhhhh! You will never understand. That embrace snapped every chain I had wrapped around my body for thirty years. I sold my soul to play with that dragon. I stole, fucked people over, and shaved any edge I could for the next chance."

Abby recoils backwards as if pushed. "You know I'm not a lawyer, right? There's no client privilege thing going on here, Danny."

"Hell, Nurse—do you think I care either way? I would get better food in prison than here.

"I chased the dragon down every road, under every bridge, in every VA clinic I could work myself into, and after fifty years, I thought I'd reached the big curtain—you know, I would have some purpose for what I had been chasing. That freedom would lead me to understand what I was meant to do, to be. Some grand answer would come. You know what I realized when I got there?" Nurse Abby shakes her head and looks at Danny, who is fixed on the bus station. He raises his hands and clasps them together, as if holding a pair of dice, shaking briefly. He slowly opens them, revealing nothing.

"I realized there was nothing behind that curtain, no dream, no answers, no purpose, no family, not even an epitaph. There was just a quick flash of twenty-four frames, one long second, and then black." He shifts in his chair, in obvious discomfort, exposing a nip of black velvet near his hip. Abby fires a glare at the man beneath her. He waves his hand dismissively toward the nurse. "Does it really matter?" He closes his eyes and sips from the bottle. The swill stings his insides, as he grimaces to force the liquid down. His body folds in half.

"I do not want *that garbage* done around me! I've got a license, a job, and a responsibility over you. I have a purpose! Don't put me at risk with stupid, selfish choices," she fires, swiping the bottle from him. Abby scans the room for any curious eyes, but is met

62

with indifference. Danny grabs her arm with more force than he has mustered in all the years he has been here.

"I would give anything for my twenty-fourth frame, to simply know I have been forgiven, nothing more, nothing less." Abby wrenches her arm free and rolls the cart toward the cargo elevator. She pauses briefly before entering the cabin and peers back toward Danny.

"Honey, that's what God is for. He…"

"No, no, don't preach to me, Abby. Have you listened to anything I've been saying?" he whines, flailing his arms in exasperation. "I am not worried about God's forgiveness; I am talking about those I abandoned."

The cargo elevator slips shut as Abby shakes her head. Danny struggles but eventually sets in motion the wheelchair toward the bright sunlight poking through the window. As if magnetized, the wheels roll to a rest, covering two worn patches in the white tile floor. The light warms his skin, and for a moment issues a respite to incessant itching. He eyes the latest noonday bus arrival, the word "Youngstown" beaming above the windshield.

The pneumatic brakes whoosh and the doors retract, releasing several people onto the sidewalk. Danny watches each scatter cautiously, as if taking the first steps on a blindfolded treasure hunt. "Get back on that bus," he whispers to himself. "There isn't a damn thing in this city you couldn't leave behind." One by one, the people are swallowed by a convenience store, the YMCA, or a random alley, none of which appear as part of life's greater curriculum. He huffs at their naiveté. "That's how the witches will get you soon enough." But he notices a final passenger de-boarding, neatly dressed in khaki pants and a pressed, powder-blue Oxford as stiff as cardboard. He pauses briefly in front of the bus, snatching a small box from his pocket that flicks sunlight with each turn in his hand. Danny watches the man pull something from the shiny box, flip it into his mouth, and place it back inside the pocket. "What's your story?" Danny whispers, inspecting the man as he walks purposefully toward the Trumbull County Workforce commission, adjacent to the VA building. Not lured by a random alley or even the YMCA, the man passes through the doors with a conviction borne of past success. "You don't look like the others I've seen going there. You don't look like I did. You're gonna make it."

Chapter 6

Mayor Donnelly pumps and empties his lungs, as if blindfolded and awaiting the fatal bullet from a firing squad. But his breath crashes into a cement barrier within his gut, preventing it from reaching his lungs. He desperately leverages a ladder as a crutch, but the rhythm continues to misfire. "Damn it…. Just breathe," he instructs, while gently kneading his stomach.

The introductory town hall meeting, advertised for weeks, has been ripped by the locals with brutal candor. "Give us jobs, a decrease in crime, and a future fir Youngstown," they scrawled on banners and exposed bridge girders. Despite the curt demands, they were far gentler than the anonymous emails sent to the city's website. While Donnelly recalls being overly cautious detailing the Forca infrastructure bid, and in fact likening it to "a Hail Mary pass," it has morphed into a demand by the locals. *"It is a flea flicker—it hits, we score seven and get the prom queen...but,"* he thinks to himself, "they never understood we were on our own fifteen-yard line," he whispers.

He also recalls offering a progressive health care initiative to combat dementia. "Get us jobs and you will have a whole lot less crazy going around," they would retort.

"Just get through this," he whispers. He fires his plunger pen at a modest tempo, to which his lungs and heart begin to synchronize. His anxiety-primed stutter is restrained for the moment, penned up in his provisional pup tent of resoluteness. However, a squall threatens to dismantle that very shelter, sending it aloft like an untethered kite.

He peers from behind the Youngstown Elementary school gym curtain to see a mob gathering. They appear as motley shards, as if three decades of Youngstown misfortune fell ten stories onto the pavement. Donnelly's fingers flick the plunger haphazardly, sending his breathing off-kilter.

"Why the hell don't they use the chairs—what was the point of setting them up? Baby Jesus, it's like the Jets and Sharks out there. Half of these people didn't even show up to the polls."

His office manager, Dee Dee, a fiery redhead of thirty and never short on smartass quips, pats Donnelly's shoulder. "You know, Mayor, it could be worse." She smiles while placing a hand on her hip and cocking her head. "You *could have been* the mayor of Youngstown in 1916 giving his town hall," she references, citing the famous East Youngstown Plant Riot. Donnelly recalls few details other than the city being burned by mobs demanding improved working conditions. He shudders at the thought. "How 'bout them apples?" she singsongs, wagging her finger.

"S-stop, this isn't 1916. I didn't have a damn thing to do about that mill, conditions, or why it closed. And all that Little Joe D, Cadillac Charlie, Bomb-City mob-stuff...that sh-shit was before I was even born, for Lord's sake. Don't bring the mob—"

"Hey, Mayor, you are here now. Whether you were alive or even know about that history, you are now part of it. You are the person that is trying to fix this place, and understanding what happened might help," advises Dee Dee.

"Look on the bright side, Mayor," she adds. "What do you think they are gonna do, fire you? Ha, no one will do that. They just want someone to blame."

Donnelly shakes his head while second-guessing the decision to even run for the position. He had a comfortable and familiar council job two hundred miles west of Youngstown between cornstalks and barns, well insulated from the Jets, Sharks, and 1916's stain. However, Youngstown waved the "local resident rule" and extended the search beyond Carter County to any councilman with at least five years' experience, one Donnelly leapt at. Presently, he would give anything to be riding a bale of hay at a Fourth of July parade in Ada.

"All right, here goes something," Donnelly says to Dee, who fires back. "Hey, Mayor, I would tell ya to break a leg, but you might take that the wrong way," quips Dee Dee, sending him on his way with a wink.

Donnelly strides to the podium with surprising ambition, keeping the anxiety pangs at bay. His years navigating even the petite political pond of Ada have fashioned masks, like a masquerade party, which afford cover for broad circumstances. "Don't look at the individual—just find a spot to stare at," he thinks. His eyes settle on a blaze-orange basketball rim behind the bubbling sea of suspicion. As he draws tidy index cards and the pen from his pocket, his eyes pry free from the rim and descend like fog onto the disjointed mass below.

He *feels* an undertow tug beneath the gymnasium floor as arms begin to cross chests and heavy sighs sound like waves shuffling, the ebb and flow jostling for dominance. Penetrating eyes begin to pluck at his mask, and cynicism threatens to breach the levees. Donnelly stiffens against the tide and shields himself behind a modest podium, perhaps sufficient cover for a sixth-grader. Pressing his hands against either side of the podium, his eyes latch onto the blaze-orange life raft again. He grips the pen tightly and depresses the plunger *slowly*, feeling each click thump within his hand. His voice begins to fill the space.

"Good morning, everyone. I would like to begin by saying 'thank you' to each of you who have set aside the time to be here. I know all of you have other responsibilities an—"

"Let's cut to the chase, Donnelly," fires an abrading voice from somewhere.

Soon, a man wielding forearms of a lumberjack emerges from the mass, and points at Donnelly. "What other responsibilities do you mean? If we had jobs, we wouldn't be in a grade school gymnasium in the middle of the fucking day. If our kids didn't leave here for other opportunities, then they would be part of the drug and crime problem."

The group begins to unravel from within, as frustrated voices pan fate, God, and even certain families for their misfortune. Donnelly's pen begins to click like a rickety, wild mouse rollercoaster.

"I have reached out to our capable law enforcement organizations, both local and state, and they have renewed their commitment for—"

"Stop, Donnelly," fires the man. "You might hear me, but you aren't listening. The only thing you should be telling us here today is how and when you will be creating jobs. Your legacy will be judged by others on some spreadsheet, unemployment percentage, average household income, budgets, all that buffed-up horseshit that falls back to one root issue. Do we have jobs? You fix that issue and you will keep people in their homes, building tax revenue, and off the streets. Idle hands are the devil's playground, Donnelly, and this place is like Mardi Gras for idle hands and vices," he fires in an exasperated tone.

"Jesus Christ, how I wish I had old man McGuire's Funeral Home down on Pone Lane. Do you know that guy started that business *before* Black Friday? He must be a goddamn prophet, printing money off of this soul scrapyard," he huffs, pointing somewhere beyond the gymnasium. "You know *that* business—selling stones, burying bodies—is the only place in town that has grown since 1970. Oh, excuse me. *Legally* grown since 1970." The man finishes his soapbox tirade and turns to walk out of the gymnasium, followed by a few others equally cynical about the use of their time.

Donnelly shifts anxiously from behind the podium and places a new index card in front of him. "Okay, then," he mutters. "Let's t-talk about job creation. I have been following and lobbying for the governor's great bridge infrastructure rebuild, and we are closer now to understanding the potential ben—"

A new face from the masses begins eviscerating the mayor on the potential infrastructure rebuild, as the hot-topic can has been kicked down the road for a decade.

"Donnelly—stay away from that goddamn bridge rebuild," bellows a grizzly of a man, encased in a blaze-orange hunter's vest. As he trudges toward the stage, Donnelly stares at the man's vest, deep red streaks staining it from last year's deer harvest. His volume calibrated against the years of frustration in his voice. "Do you know the West Avenue bridge collapsed into the fucking river waiting for three mayors, governors, and whoever else to approve funding over the last decade? The girders and concrete have been at the bottom of the Mahoning River for five years now. You wanna know what the only saving grace is about that heap of rubble underwater?" The man is now slapping the top of the stage platform where Donnelly stands, a look of shock on the latter's face as he grips the podium. "Carp fishing." The crowd releases a booming cacophony of laughter, filling the gymnasium and underscoring the lunacy of it all. The man turns to face the audience and sarcastically announces, "Come to Youngstown, Ohio, where we have the best carp fishing hole in the tri-state area." As the crowd is feeding off their mouthpiece, the agitated man

70

turns back toward Donnelly and says, "Imagine that. The fish at the ass-end of the food chain are picking through the bones of a dead city. How fitting."

Donnelly winces as if they have sucker-punched *him, his legacy, his mismanagement*, and not the generations prior. He hangs on the podium, his jaw slack as if he is awaiting an eight-count, collecting his wits. The only resolution that awaits is whether or not the ref will allow one more defenseless punch to land, appeasing the blood-thirsty masses.

Donnelly gathers himself momentarily before one more looping hook concerning his integrity lands squarely on his jaw, knocking him on his wallet. "Even being in bed with those Brazilians didn't net us anything," barks a man from the far corner of the room. "What did you give up to them for nothing in return?" He feels the sting shoot straight from his head to his heart, chopping his breath in half. Before he can respond, he spots a distinctively attired figure approaching the stage. He recognizes the man as Cafferty.

"That's Bobby's boy," says one man. The crowd eases momentarily, recognizing one of their own approaching the stage. Cafferty climbs onstage and shakes the mayor's hand, a perplexing gesture for the easiest target in the city. Cafferty, sensing the chasm between the mayor and the audience, slowly drags the diminutive podium off the stage and approaches the mayor.

"You were elected because you were the best man for this job," he whispers to Donnelly. "Most of these folks, myself included,

71

haven't seen an engaged leader in their lives—they've had politicians and potholes for the last thirty years. I can understand their frustration, and I know you understand it as well." Donnelly nods, briefly scanning the eyes. Cafferty continues, "To understand *this* community, you have to be a part of it. That podium over there," Cafferty says as he points offstage to the discarded stump, "that thing has served as some shield for the five mayors before you, as if even they didn't believe what they were saying. Roll up your sleeves, step down off this stage, and walk among the group in front of you. Know their names, their stories, and above all else, tell them you are willing to fight for them." Donnelly takes a deep breath and acknowledges the sound guidance from a local man.

Cafferty rolls his sleeves and descends into the middle of the pit, momentarily catching curious eyes. "Folks, I would like to make this clear. The man in front of you," he says, motioning to Donnelly, who has followed suit from the stage, "is our elected leader and is one of us. I have heard people complaining high and low about how this man doesn't understand this and this man doesn't understand that. He is from Podunk, Ohio, where the only thing he had to worry about was not getting mashed by the Amish carriages sharing the same roads as his Buick." A smattering of giggles echo against the vaulted gym ceiling.

"Let me ask a question: Does it take more courage to stand in Youngstown for fifty years—the very same place where we were born, had kids, attended high school, watched the mill fold, Cadillac

72

Charlie, married and buried—while not once running for council to drive change? To make a difference *here*. I know I'm guilty of that. Worse yet, many of us *ran* from the problems here. The population in this town has gone from 177,000 people in our heyday to sixty-four thousand today. We own these generational issues, collectively choosing to instead run, cry, or simply die." The gymnasium hushes like a confessional on Saturday night, all eyes fixed on a man tossing a net of brutal candor around everyone.

"Or does it take more courage to see every scab we pick at— and the many demons that caused them—and run *toward* that very town? Bringing a wife and two kids to the same place we want ours to leave? Do you understand what I am saying?" A collective murmur bubbles throughout the gym, with subtle nods offering tacit acceptance of this view. "History will tell what type of leader Mayor Connelly was. However, in my humble opinion, he has the single greatest attribute in one's constitution, and that is courage."

Donnelly is emboldened by Cafferty's support and lets the words marinate within him—*something* beyond nothing allowed him to foster trust and win this election not many months ago. *It* was *courage,* he thinks to himself. *No one dragged me away from Ada and the cornfields. I've done this before and I will do this again.* His thoughts float like a buoy, jigging and bobbing in the harshest conditions, impossible to sink. Donnelly knows Cafferty doesn't offer support flippantly—he recognizes it will have a shelf life and will be one precious commodity he never intends on allowing to expire. He thumbs the index cards within his pocket while Cafferty continues.

"Most of you have heard of the Brazilians, Forca, the mill, etc. All of it has been anecdotal, speculation by everyone but those involved in the actual discussions. I don't fault anyone for that. It's natural to draw conclusions, particularly when one wants something so badly. So, let me give you some facts.

"First, Forca is the Brazilian conglomerate that has officially chosen this town—knowing its rise as one of the world's leaders in steel production and its subsequent fall, warts and all—to hedge its entire bet on its US steel production. I think it is important to understand Forca could have chosen anywhere. Pittsburgh, Cleveland…. Every city wanted this deal. But they didn't. I appreciate this because for the last two years, while I was employed by the Bain firm, we worked on this very deal and were often targets of rampant speculation—watercooler talk about what was going on behind the curtain. Often, the talk was at best misinformed and at worst malicious fabrication…bullshit to undermine the deal. This will be the new home for Forca Steel." Having spent decades dormant from cynicism and hopelessness, mouths clang open like knotted drawbridges around the auditorium. For moments, not a sound passes except a clamor of hope rushing headlong across a vast moat and smashing through a fortress gate.

"Second, Forca has committed $1 million to fund a memory care facility and program here in Youngstown. That initial investment from Forca has now grown to a little over two $2.7 million from matching organizations. We will build a self-sustaining program that cares for those afflicted with dementia. I know some of you have loved ones affected by this tragic disease. Millions of others in the US do as well. We will attract experts from around the country and will establish the facility and the care program, and importantly, we will train our own people in this specialty affording care and hope for those families afflicted."

A chatter stirs, like frost-laden leaves swirling against each other. The rush germinates and disperses a current of optimism across the group. Donnelly pushes the cards firmly within his pocket and clasps his hands together.

"Mr. Donnelly, would you care to add anything else?" Cafferty says.

"Yes, in fact, I do," he states firmly. "I am very excited to announce that Forca has won the initial bid for the 'Great Build Out' starting in March 2016. I have worked with Bobby, Forca, and the National Infrastructure Oversight Committee in ensuring our place at the table for this important rebuild."

"What does this mean?" booms one man, while another chimes in, "Does this mean the YSM will open back up?"

Cafferty raises a hand. "There will be a formal press release by Forca in the upcoming week, but for now, it's important to understand that if not for this man," he says as he points in Donnelly's direction, "we would not have had the influence at the state or federal level for any of that funding. It would have gone elsewhere."

Cafferty looks at Donnelly and nods, as if they both have jump-started a dead battery. "Thank you, I appreciate you," says Donnelly, absent of any stutter or panting.

Cafferty turns back to the crowd, which is now anxiously awaiting the formal announcement, a bubble of anticipation throughout. "Now, if you all will excuse me, I hear there is one helluva carp fishing hole down at the Mahoning River, and you never know when those just dry up."

Chapter 7

Richard surveys the dust flickering against the sunlight, slicing through his apartment blinds. The feathered dots appear to float as if suspended by some invisible crib mobile, frolicking for an audience of one. A faint smile traces his face as he recalls a memory long ago.

"Just like a billion stars," he whispers to himself. "Just beautiful." Richard runs his hand across the sunlight's blade, churning the boundless matter into a swirling eddy. The debris slows and falls atop the moving boxes like new snow. The smile wanes from his face as his eyes settle upon a cracked pair of Converse high-top sneakers he hasn't worn for over a year. He looks contrite, as if the shoes are glaring up at him, reminding him of the moment he cast them off in his trunk, instead opting for loafers.

Don't you recall? they seem to chide. The shoes, ravaged by months of temperature extremes, dole out retribution, choking his feet with a vice grip. His eyes dip back and forth, tracing the path of twine across a shoe, through the tongue, and lying limp along the sandstone carpet. "Ah—why do they all have to have these ties," he asks to no one. He breathes an inaudible rhyme. "Runner...runner..." He pulls the laces skyward, looping one end of the lace over and under, until he yanks it tight with an X. After some moments, the laces slacken like slippery worms crawling in different directions. He tucks them into the sides of the shoes.

His loafers collapsed prematurely while unloading his car at the apartment ten minutes from his mom in suburban Pottstown, Ohio. Shortly after his resignation, Richard told Skynnar it was "time to go home" and noted that he would reach out once he situated himself. Richard recalls that exact moment with rare lucidity. However, perhaps the sting was too fresh or he simply became too preoccupied with life, but Richard never called. It was only after he received a call from his sister, Maddie, that Richard realized weeks had become a month, plenty of time to situate in a small, one-bedroom apartment.

His rigid body struggles but rises, his feet acquiescing and crimping within the shoes. He initiates an arduous shuffle out his front door, cracking brittle, frosted leaves beneath his feet. "Hmm, what was I doing today?" he blurts skyward. The early morning sun hesitates, as if wishing to reply, but soon retreats behind a ponderous blanket of grayish-white clouds. Soon, the cold crouches from the sky, biting against his naked arms, painting them with streaks of pink.

The leaves begin to chatter, blurting a din and drawing Richard's eyes earthward. "What was I...," he presses as the congregation grows increasingly restless, blurting nonsense and tumbling about like children on a schoolyard. The leaves afford little help and Richard stomps at them, annoyed. "Goddamn it. Ahhh, the car," he says, finishing one of many questions he will have to answer today. His body, as if tethered, is being pulled toward the car if for no other reason than that it presents a natural obstacle in his path to the street. He pushes the door handle and awaits its release. Nothing, except the persistent frigid slap against his body. He pushes the handle again without success and spanks the window. "Please!" he spits at the handle. With a violent jerk, the door rips open, swinging past his leg and returning against him with a violent bang, cutting his shin. "Ugh," he whimpers. A fresh red stream seeps through his khakis while a tear traces his cheek. He enters the car, keys still in the ignition, and automatically twists the engine to life.

"Ah, Mom. I need to see Mom. Mail? Yes, mail."

He pulls a crinkled Post-it from his pocket and reads the instructions, which are in bright red bullet points, read. *Mail. Traps. Mom's House. Winterize. Be Careful, Love Mom.* Richard stares at the word "winterize" and begins wringing his hands, with anxiety coursing through his body. "Wh-what does winter have to do?" He looks outside the windshield, looking for something. "Snow? Why would I bring snow? I don't understand," he says, slapping the steering wheel, then banging his head.

"I am going to Mom's house," he says with conviction, dropping the note to the floor. With a plodding *thunk* of the transmission, the car begins rolling forward, sending a pleasing ripple through his barren hands. The car ambles through remote country lanes, unremarkably passing a mail truck and disinterested livestock foraging through frozen clumps of grass.

Soon, Richard spots a decorative windmill hugging the street, each fan blade and base laden in blue reflectors like garish beads. Richard's face cracks a smile as he observes the figure. Its wooden pegs resemble long legs, he thinks. And its blades plopped atop the lean body look like a head, he further guesses. Her long legs straddle the culvert, beckoning, almost demanding he turn down the gravel lane. "It looks like…a street girl!" he laughs, turning down the path.

As he approaches the house, Richard pumps the brakes a few times, dragging the gravel off the frozen dirt beneath. He settles the car with an abrupt stop, a few feet shy of the garage, car coughing and idling against the brake.

"Agh. What are those things that, oh, what do you call them? They hold them down, like bite them. Dammit. They bite the rats…. Traps!" Richard slams his hand against the steering wheel and follows that with a quick slap to his forehead. The impact fires a dose of electricity throughout his head, priming a mist in his eyes. He searches the vacant passenger seat, prodding the distant cloth, convincing himself he must have stopped.

"What did *you* do with them?" he chides the figure in the rearview mirror. His brain, insidiously feathered with lacquer each minute, is waning. Memories are gratuitous perks on good days, when cycling blood and breath consume his presence. Today is not a good day.

"Later," he promises as he tugs on the handle and steps onto the gravel. The car groans, tugging its handle away from Richard, slowly drifting and eventually punching into the cement foundation. A coarse hack bellows underneath the hood as if the car is fighting for breath, trying to dislodge a terminal clog. With a final grunt, the car convulses against the wall and dies. "Why did you move?" he asks. As he approaches the heap, he is whirled toward a boom behind him. A large garbage truck crawls down the road out front, positioning itself across the road. Mesmerized by the beast, he stares at the systemic lifting and dropping of cans in a violent but precise dance. He follows the truck until it sends a final bark at the top of the knoll, turning back toward the city.

Richard stands before an obstinate oak door, which refuses to give way. The foundation, through years of settling, grips the doorframe like a vice. With a heavy shoulder, the door squeals and reluctantly loosens, revealing an older woman asleep on the couch. Matted white hair, unkempt like a stray mongrel, pokes from beneath an afghan. Her body contorts around itself, locking into a stiff ball as if frozen in place. Richard's eyes poke around the room, spotting an ashtray resting on the lemon-washed windowsill. "Agh…. Again?" he huffs. The window is still ajar from last night, soaking the room in a chilly dew.

"Mom, hey. Mom, I am here," blurts Richard as he gently shakes the bundled figure. His mom begins stirring and fumbles for a pack of cigarettes left on the coffee table nearby. "No, no, not now, Mom," Richard says, looking at the cigarettes, one thing that he cannot learn to forget.

"Richard, honey. It's nice to see you. Are you feeling with it today?" she asks while pushing the cigarettes away and trying to right herself on the couch.

81

"Why didn't you sleep up there?" Richard motions toward the second floor beyond the steps.

"Honey, I told you, remember? When the cold sets in each year, the critters move into the attic and make a clatter. It makes me crazy. That old wood burner only fills the bottom floor with any worthwhile heat. It's not so bad, the couch." He stares at the ashtray intently, as if observing a fossil from a past era. "Honey, did you bring the traps and seals for the windows?"

"What traps? Oh, ahhh. Um, I got them, but t-they...I don't have them."

"Honey, that was the whole point. If we don't send them packing, they will chew the whole house down, wires and all. I will write it down for you, and can you make sure to bring them tomorrow?" says his mom, disappointed but heartbroken.

"Sure. I will remember."

"Do you ever feel it coming on, you know, the good days and bad?" asks his mom, motioning to his head. "Maybe we should get you checked out again and they can give you something for it."

"Give what?" says Richard. "It's just...I—I forget things."

"Honey, it's not forgetting things like a birthday. Look at your arm," she says, pointing to a chafed and red appendage resting lifelessly against his body. "Baby, it's late November in Ohio. People don't forget to cover *that*. That's what I want them to help you with."

"Forget what?" he huffs. Richard's eyes drift back toward the open window. "Rats in the attic? The window is open—they could come through here."

He forces the window shut, the old, wooden frame screeching in revolt but eventually submitting. A machine gun clatters from above, followed by shrill squeaks.

"What was that?" says Richard.

"The rats, honey. You woke them up too."

Richard spends the rest of the day dragging stiff, hairy corpses from the attic and wandering the basement, goosing a cast-iron wood burner. He eventually loads the burner and slams it shut with an authoritative *clank*.

The sun dips beneath a horizon of oaks, dragging any light and facade of warmth with it. Richard begins to sag, having chased sleep for months.

"It's strange how much more I look forward to sleeping in the winter," his mom responds. "It's like the wood burner, the short days, bundling up on the couch sends me into hibernation."

"Yep," Richard says, distracted by the old wooden coat hanger near the front door. "Did I bring—"

"No, honey, you didn't," she fires as she tugs a single stick from her cigarette pack. "You see? I wish you would go to the doctors, see if they have anything to give you."

"Mum, it's just what happens when you get older," he says, motioning to white medicine bottles strewn about the coffee table.

She places the cigarette in her mouth and lights it, emitting a violent hack and a hazy plume. Both observe the cloud lose steam and sink into the carpet below. She pulls the cigarette from her lips and tamps it out.

"I will tell you what. I won't light another one of these things if you promise to see a doctor."

Richard's mind fires with clarity, as it often does, regarding smoking. The hot cherry flame pulsing with each breath. The rolling wave of dusty silver, uncoiling and slithering. Stench seeping as deep as your bones.... But the cough. The cough is what he remembers with perfect clarity. Like a demon choking the soul, he remembers how the body would convulse trying to undo its own harm. He remembers watching that penance and it being so severe that he would say: *Why can't you stop?*

"Sure, Mom. Yes. So you won't smoke tonight?" Richard asks with cautious optimism.

His mom bubbles with optimism and sets the cigarette on the coffee table. "I love you, Richard, you know? I cannot promise to quit forever but will quit tonight. How does that sound?"

Richard smiles.

"Plus, you have already shut the window. I don't want you jiggling that and stirring those rats again." He kisses his mom's forehead, and before walking into the black country evening, she scrawls a list again. "Here you go, honey. This will help you remember."

As he shuffles toward the car, he fumbles through his pockets, searching for the keys. However, he only finds some stray lint and grasps at the inner seams of the fabric. "Where did I leave—oh, um." As he reaches the driver's side door, moonlight flickers against the keys still dangling from the steering column. Richard twists the key, but the engine fails to turn. Instead, an orange light pulses from within the panel. He pokes at the deep-set flare, then knuckles it harder, if trying to wake it from a coma.

"Jesus, what? I can't do this!" he screams, banging the steering wheel with a fury. His breathing hastens and every puff into the frigid cabin appears like a cloud, further obscuring his perspective. "I don't want this any—" Richard's foot depresses the brake and the transmission clangs into park. With a twist of the key, a chunky rumble springs the engine to life and begins to thaw the man.

The next morning, Richard untangles wadded bills and drops them on a counter at the local hardware store. "Just take what—h-how much are these?" asks Richard, eyeing rattraps, duct tape, and a forty-eight-piece socket set labeled in a "20% Off Sale, Today Only."

"Did you want to purchase this too?" asks the cashier.

"No, I don't think so—just these here." He pushes the materials toward the cashier, a wiry and jittery specimen who vibrates with energy.

"Perfect. That will cost twenty-one dollars and fifty-three cents. Would you like to pay with cash, orrrrr..." His words spew forth as if they are fleeing a fire, tripping over the other. "...perhaps you would like to save ten percent off of today's purchase if you open a line—"

"Ummm. Can you—do I have what you need?" asks Richard.

"Sure, we just need one of these and two of these," the cashier notes, plucking a twenty and two ones from the counter. Richard doesn't move, leaving the remaining pile untouched. The cashier recoils from the counter, cocking his head.

"Ah, I get it," the cashier says. "Are you from the corporate security team? I hear they are doing these undercover audits and stuff, like cashiers are ripping credit card numbers, shorting the drawers. Are you a cop?" the man whispers, casting a finger at Richard. "Don't you have to say if you are? Do you have a badge or something?"

Richard stares blankly at the man, while fingering the leftover crumpled bills.

"Hey, none of that stuff goes on here, man…er, sir. And make sure you tell them you put like two hundred dollars on the table. And I counted the exact change in front of you. Can you at least tell them *that*?" the cashier asks.

"Tell who?" says Richard, grabbing the traps and duct tape while avoiding the change.

"Wait!" the cashier pleads. "Take this—don't leave this here. I didn't touch it!" he cries, his voice netting curious gazes. "I need this job, man!"

Richard scoops the bills, cramming them into his pocket as he finds his way to the exit.

Days and nights pass before he pumps the brakes in a staccato fashion, skinning the gravel from the hardened brown mud below. He observes the house, not quite sure what is different. The living room window is secured just as he wished to find it.

"No smoking," he thinks to himself as a rare presence washes over him. He smiles.

Richard raps the front door and then delivers a sharp shoulder, dislodging it from a warped frame. He enters the house, but immediately feels *something* wrong. The room sits eerily placid, clutched in a frigid grip. "Th-this is…" His frame twists toward the window and he senses a quiver above his stomach, as if pushed from a cliff. The sensation presses gooseflesh at the base of his neck, then races the length of his arms to the fingertips.

"The fire—where's the wood fire, Mum?" he blurts nervously. Richard approaches the couch and pokes the stiff ball of flesh underneath an afghan. "Hi, Mom—you didn't smoke last night?"

He nudges hard, pushing the ball into the couch and watches as it returns with equal force. "Your nails—why are they pink?" he quizzes. He never remembered his mom painting her nails, especially a garish pink. A loud clanging and banging startles Richard in front of the house, the obnoxious garbage truck riling everyone within miles.

Richard spins back toward the couch and sees a heavy ball unwilling to rise. His face contorts, constricted by fear. "Mom! Why aren't you answering me? Please—ah." With heavy chops, he shuffles hard to the front of the house and frantically waves at the garbagemen.

"I—help me," Richard says, with one of the men following him to the house.

When the dingy man enters, his color drains. "We need to call help."

Richard slides against the couch, collapsing like a heavy bag of sand on the floor. He stares out the window at the ball in the sky while little streams tickle his face. The never-ending days of frustration and grief stain his white T-shirt gray.

Figures cloaked in uniforms scatter about him as chatter pecks away at the surrounding countryside. The staff manipulate a stiff body and examine blushed fingernails that radiate against the pale couch. One assistant approaches the window, tugging it ajar, and briskly continues the same practice with each window. Another EMT enters from the kitchen, scrunching his shoulders while his head wobbles back and forth. A police officer, fashioned from decades of tragedy and graveyard shifts, listens to an EMT. His hand clutches a simple notepad and pen, yet fails to scratch a single letter. Without a word, he rubs the bags beneath his eyes and moves toward Richard. His hand rests upon Richard's shoulder.

"I am sorry. Sir, what's your name?" the officer asks.

"What?" Richard responds, confused by the question.

"Yes, for our report and for notification to family members. Can you tell me your name, are you related to the deceased?" the officer asks.

"Um, yes. That's my mom. I'm Richard," he says, while looking at the medical personnel covering the body.

"Thanks, Richard. What is your last name, date of birth, and address?" asks the officer impassively.

"Um, ahhh.... What do you—I don't know what," says Richard, quickly spiraling from the delicate perch of a good day into a sea of confusion. The officer observes the man.

"Do you have your ID on you?" asks the officer, words thudding on the cold, bare wooden floor below. "Is that your car out front? Let's see if I can find your registration or wallet in the car. Can you walk with me for a moment?" the officer says while helping Richard up from the floor. His choppy shuffle follows the man outside, while catching concerned stares.

As the officer approaches the car, he observes a large dent on the bumper and brittle paint chips clinging to the marred piece. His eyes trace the muddy scars, leading to where they stand. He fingers a large, baseball-sized hole in the foundation and the resulting debris from the ground beneath. "Jesus, Mary, and Joseph," he whispers. He continues tracing the various cracks emanating from the hole and follows one around the back side of the house to the chimney.

"Must have been a helluva force, cracking all the way to the ass-end." He looks at Richard skeptically and says, "How long ago did you hit the house?" Richard pauses for a moment, thoughts and feelings sifting through a damaged colander, until nothing remains.

"What? Hit what?" he says with bother.

"The house—your car has the dent, and that foundation has your paint still stuck in it. I have to ask this, but…did you have any drinks last night?"

"Drink? Um, I don't know. Drink what?" he fires, unsure how this solves the issue of his mom being dead.

The officer sags as the sequence of events begins to interlock within his mind. "You really don't remember hitting this, do you?" he mutters apologetically. "You weren't drinking at all," he whispers.

"Drink what? Hit what?! What—aggh, I don't know what happened to her."

"Well, we hope to have those answers for you soon. Do you know if your mom kept a wood burner going at all during the nights?" asked the officer.

"Yes. It's c-cold. She sleeps on the couch during the winter months too."

"Okay, Richard. I think that's enough of this for now. By the way, do you have a coat in your car or the house? It's freezing out here."

"No—I—I can't remember," says Richard.

"Come on, we've got to get you back inside," the officer states, his voice softening. Gently, he guides the man back to the house.

After some discussion with the EMT staff, the officer returns to Richard, who is seated at the kitchen table, head in hands.

"Richard, do you have any other family who needs to know about your mom?" asks the policeman.

"Um—yes, I have a sister."

"Can you tell me her name?"

Richard pauses. He feels like he is detached, as if watching a TV show unfold around him. Nameless characters parrot scenes as if holding cue cards, impassively playing a part before dipping out. Each line and movement is choreographed by someone or something. He is not sure what role he is to play, or if he is merely a prop in the grand scheme of it all.

"Uh, Ma—Mo—M—Goddamn it!" he spits, while looking around the room for his cue card. Richard's eyes settle on the refrigerator in front of him, one index card with three numbers, each highlighted separately by bright orange, yellow, and green streaks.

One number says "St. Stanislaus," another "Richard," and a third "Maddie." Richard's eyes scramble for the officer. "Maddie-May." My sister's name is Maddie-May," he says with a flicker in his eyes. Richard's heart leaps for a moment, as he observes a grainy reel flicker within his mind.

Two ragged children giggle, tossing leaves in the air as rain pours down upon them. Yellow, orange, and red paintbrushes tickle their faces as they stomp, roll, and sing. *Maddie-May, oh Maddie-May, where do we go with skies so gray? To oaks and maples who let us play. Let's stay forever, or until there's no more gray. That's what we'll do, oh Maddie-May.*

Richard exhales softly as the vision quivers violently, as if being masticated by a cheap projector. "She went where there are no more gray skies," Richard mumbles.

"What?"

"Nothing," says Richard.

"Thank you, Richard. I will contact Maddie, and I would like to see if we can get you the answers to what happened and get you the help you need. For now, I would ask you to stay with the medical team until we have next steps." The officer scans behind Richard, settling on a contorted pile of faded metal keys lying on the countertop. He thinks hard before words spill out.

"Richard, I would like to get your car into a shop before it goes back out on the road. Is that okay with you?"

Richard sits motionless. "No more gray skies."

Two days later, Maddie arrives from South Carolina and meets Richard at the cold and empty house, along with an EMT and social worker. The workers remain outside, puffing dirty gray plumes against a tree. Having left Ohio two decades ago and tethered only by family birthdays, she scoffs at how scant the surroundings and life have become here.

"God, I forgot how much I hated this place," snaps Maddie, shivering in her leather coat and needlessly steep designer jeans. She ogles the room as if it were a mongrel walking down her gated community back in Ferris Estates, South Carolina. While she feels some loss with her mom—she is supposed to feel something—she sees this as the last time she will be dragged to Ohio.

"Did you forget your jacket? I wish I understood that disease of yours. I mean, forgetting a name or how to balance checkbooks, I kinda get that. But how doesn't the freezing cold *tell* you what to do? It's…not even you," she says while pointing at his head, recoiling from the unseen force within. "I mean, can't you even feel anymore?" she pleads.

"Umm, yeah—I don't know. I can feel cold. I mean. I am cold. So—"

"That's exactly my point," snaps Maddie. "If you *feel* it, why don't you do something about it? When Mom told me you had some disease that attacked your mind, I thought the worst—like cancer or something. But she assured me, 'No, Maddie, not cancer.' She kept saying you 'forgot things.'" She huffs at the floor while Richard stares blankly ahead.

"When Skynnar told me the Board of Education needed to let you go, I got mad at *you*. I told Skynnar—and forgive my French—how the fuck does one lose a teaching job in inner-city Pittsburgh?" she lobs, in a biting judgment. "I mean, no one wants to deal with most of those kids," Maddie spits.

The vitriol slips around Richard like oil in water as he ogles two tattered cardboard boxes.

"Here," says Maddie. "I found these in her room." She toes a box toward Richard's feet with some gaudy footwear. "I am afraid to go up there," she says, pointing above them. "You can have anything in there. The rats have eaten and shat in that attic for God knows how long."

"What is in it?" says Richard.

"Your yearbooks, some baseball stuff, and an old caboose. I think that's the same one from when Dad was with us," she states. "That was, like, forty-some years ago. You should see if it's worth something, sell it. Maybe worth decent money."

Richard places the boxes in the same spot where he found his mom two days prior. He looks around, unsure of what to do next.

"Richie. I am having this house cleaned and readied for the market as soon as I can." She softens momentarily. "When you began having this trouble, Mom transferred the estate to my name." Maddie pauses, rubbing her temples and washing her hand over her face. "She transferred your care to me as well—
do you remember?"

Richard's shoulders shrug, as if details are gratuitous fodder. "She was unsure where you might be mentally when the time came." Maddie cracks a smile.

"The woman was always smart like that, planning and all— not so much with men—but..." Her voice trails off, chasing the smile. "Richie, I don't want any money from whatever we get, which might not be much, I suppose, with a damaged foundation. But no matter what comes, you will need it more than I will." The words fall harmlessly to the ground.

"Also—I met with the police when I first got here. They asked about your shuffle, like if you had any history with drugs or drink, whatever. I laughed at them—I told them you probably hadn't touched a drink in your life, with Dad and all. Maybe I am wrong, but I would put my house on it. No vices, just…forgetting things. You know what they told me? They told me it is highly likely Mom died of carbon monoxide. She was weak and all, the heart thing, smoking since birth, that whole bit. She could've died tomorrow walking to the kitchen for a glass of water. But maybe not—we'll never know. What I do know is you don't even remember hitting the house hard enough that it broke the foundation." She smacks her fist into her hand, sending a scatter of claws above them. She stiffens as if the claws tickled her neck.

She whispers. "Richie, I want to get you help—I can't do *this*," she states, pointing at his head. "Social services connected me with a new program starting in town. St. Stanislaus Memory Care. Have you heard of it?" He looks back at the boxes on the couch. "The social services group will manage all aspects of your care, residence, all that stuff. You will eventually have people that can *help*."

The word sends a charge through the man, as if someone pinched him from within. "I want help."

"Thank you, Richie…for understanding. Can you tell me where you want me to send the check when this sells?"

95

Richard plucks a small keychain from his pocket with the name "Arbor Walk" scrawled across an outline of a large maple. "This is where I live."

A deep sigh escapes Maddie. "Do you know what this reminds me of?" Maddie blurts. "It reminds me—"

"Oaks and maple who let us play," Richard finishes with an off-key singsong whisper. 'That's why I wanted to live there…the oaks and maples and no more grays." Maddie brushes the back of her hand against her face, smearing the small, trickling stream from her eye. She walks slowly toward the front door. Her head shakes as she absorbs the reality of lifetimes that have drifted continents apart.

"Richie," she says, looking at the untied shoelaces and muddy marks slapped across the bottom portion of his jeans. "Do you know your shoes are untied? You might end up tripping on those."

Richard stares at the shoelaces as if presented with wires tied to some unknown device, ticking away. "I'm not sure how—" He jams the wet, dirty ends into the shoes' sides.

"No, no, Richie—let me help," she quivers as her breath is chopped short. She kneels before him and ties the shoes before rushing out the front door. She slams a stubborn door shut and begins a scramble back to palmettos and peaches. A sudden clatter races within the walls as a game of Klinko is played by the last beings standing. Then silence, and Richard stands alone.

Chapter 8

Cafferty studies a twenty-something realtor furiously pounding a "SOLD" sign in front of a remote, "Coming Soon, Mid-Cities Phase 1" outlet billboard. A smirk forms on his lips as the agent struggles against frostbitten ground. He observes the hammer, which he surmises is suited for cuts of meat, ricocheting off the steel post. "I don't think this will do—hang on," he says, bounding for his car.

As Cafferty's eyes unfasten from the man, they hit upon barren, rust-tinged hills to his east and pale-yellow fields to his west. He ponders the stark contrast, a mere twenty-five miles from Youngstown, yet a world apart in terms of pace, complexity, and people. It occurs to him that the Grebe brothers, a slick property development duo from Philadelphia, simply didn't fully appreciate the circumstance of this spot.

"Bringing value to the heartland," he whispers to himself. "How would they have known?" he continues, chewing on the ill-conceived plan. The ruthless Grebe brothers made a fortune picking through terminal businesses, eviscerating dreams, and fabricating homogenized micro-cities in the middle of nowhere. But it was as if the dream victims cursed this spot, their ghosts chasing the brothers back to Philadelphia. Two concrete and steel building shells remain, cast off and forgotten like orphaned twins.

"Even hyenas starve, gents." No stranger to sound timing himself, Cafferty recalls the careful consideration afforded before seizing the opportunity. The major interstate out front, the flood-prone creek behind the buildings, and continents of empty space swallowing the rest—only two naked oaks and a massive maple rise against the wall of blue. He remembers the maple the most, in the throes of early autumn, its massive shock of colors as loud as a bomb. "Beautiful," he whispers.

"Mother of Jesus," the young man blurts, as he searches the ground for a more forgiving spot. Cafferty doesn't budge, his eyes settling deep into the area surrounding the maple. *Perfect resting spot for livestock...or simply just being,* he thinks. His mind races. *They sat in these very same wide-open spaces, and certainly some farmer had his livelihood dependent upon addressing the same concerns. The cattle wandered aimlessly, grazing with heads tucked low, oblivious to eighteen-wheelers roaring by, creeks flooding, or miles of empty space. They lived without consideration of obesity, scarcity of food, elections, or whether or not the farmer's land had been foreclosed. They lived because time only passed by the sun rising and the sun setting, nothing more. They followed that same path until one day they stopped living, be it from the unimaginable brute force of a truck, a lightning strike, or a tired heart. They never stopped to think about when, why, or how that day would come. They just lived through the day until they didn't.*

Cafferty catches himself, and is momentarily wracked with guilt, the, unconscious connection of ungulates to lives occupied by dementia. "Jesus, please forgive me," he whispers to himself.

He scrawls down the same note he had written when he acquired the land: "Review single point entry/exit design, GPS, fencing, barriers to the creek."

"Whoooowee!" the young man exclaims, slapping the top of the sign. "It's now official. These, sir, are yours," he states while jangling the keys. "I want to wish you the very best luck with your new facility."

The following morning, a harsh wind rips through the empty shell as denim- and duck cloth-clad men huddle around a blueprint labeled "St. Stanislaus MCF." Cafferty listens intently, ignoring the paper flapping violently against the floor as if throwing a tantrum. A man in a white hard hat points to various spots within the sea of blue lines.

"Right here, that's the entrance. Here's your front desk, and this spot right here is the first room."

Cafferty purses his lips and nods. "Now, it looks real," he states as one man breathes air into his clasped hands.

"Good morning, gents," Mayor Donnelly chimes with an ease off-putting to the wind.

"Good? It's freezing out this way!" grumbles a man in a hard hat, his face tucked beneath his collar.

"Ah, it's not so bad—if you go another hundred miles west..."

"Yeah, yeah, I know," he fires to the mayor. "Bigger fields, even less hills to break the wind. Still doesn't help me now," he gripes. The mayor simply smiles to the group as he continues toward Cafferty.

"Congratulations to you, Bobby. I am very happy to see your dream gathering its legs."

"Thanks. Lots of work, obviously, but getting the money and property was a big first step. Forca and Bain came through as they committed. I might need some help in making sure you keep the building permits, etcetera, moving through the system quickly." Connelly nods while dutifully scratching the request in his portfolio.

Cafferty cocks his head, smiling at the mayor. "Did the city have some cutbacks on your fancy pens?" he asks, pointing at the basic instrument.

"Ah, this. No, I suppose I will always use a crutch if it's there. It's a silly habit, anyway." He pauses a moment as the contractors slowly trudge away for cigarettes and coffee. "Besides, the ever-so-gentle Dee Dee suggested I grow a set of stones and stop clickety-clacking through meetings.

" Assuming all goes on schedule, when will you start receiving patients?"

"Well, we will onboard the first set of certified MC attendants—one nurse, one doctor—over the next week. They will help us establish some realistic goals for our mission, get familiar with the site, etcetera. While they have done similar programs in larger cities, they have not done one from scratch with a focus of training new staff to ultimately be self-sustaining. It is brand new here."

"Yes, it is an entirely different animal when you can walk away from something," the mayor chimes. "We need to teach our own workforce how to attract, train, and retain our people for years to come."

"One of the main objectives, as you know, is to utilize the veterans' workforce for even a few roles. The federal incentives through the SEI program and the number of incoming veterans to this area make it a no-brainer, financially. But we need to, and should, target this segment of the workforce for more reasons than just 'manpower' and 'financial incentives.'" Cafferty pauses momentarily, the picture within his mother's house appearing and disappearing like an apparition in the mist. The mayor nods automatically.

"You know this statewide infrastructure rebuild?" the mayor continues. "These projects require massive amounts of labor—all kinds, from blue collar to white collar to no collar. Upwards of thirty to fifty percent of a veteran's salary, expenses, hell, even their equipment, can be reimbursed through federal support. Financially, it is a low-risk investment for a high return," he adds.

"Eight hundred thousand veterans in Ohio," Cafferty utters, each syllable pinching the air. The gravity and scale slips around Donnelly like an iceberg under a blackened sky.

"Obviously, there are additional benefits for the city—additional tax bases, attracting younger workforce, and lower unemployment," Donnelly continues. "Ugh, I am digressing here. When will you be able to receive patients?"

101

"Not soon enough," Cafferty affirms.

"Well, this is partly why I wanted to drop by and speak with you today. I have one gentleman who might benefit from a program like this." The mayor continues, "Richard was a history teacher in Pittsburgh for thirty-something years. He retired—well, was encouraged to retire early—and came back to Youngstown to help his eighty-something mom, who wasn't in the greatest of health. But turns out, she was in better shape than her son."

"How old is he?"

"Ah, he's younger, younger than what you would think—like, early sixties? Well, he's at a point now that he doesn't remember leaving his car in drive. He stepped out of his car, wrecked into his mom's house, cracking the foundation, split the flue, the whole thing. Chief Marshall said she most likely passed from carbon monoxide. They still have his keys. The guy is now living alone over in the efficiencies off of Big Oak Drive."

Cafferty exhales. "This story, unfortunately, is not that atypical. It's heartbreaking, but… You've seen all the silver alerts on the highway marquis and texts on your cell, right? And that's with seventy-, eighty-, even ninety-year-olds—now imagine a guy with the same disease who doesn't *look* 'old.'"

"Jesus, that scares the hell out of me—I mean…"

"He simply slipped through the cracks. Just brutal. Does he have any other family?"

"Sister in South Carolina—after she got word from the police, they all contacted Social Services and they've been handling it ever since. He might have a father out there somewhere. The dad left them fifty-some years ago. Was in the military and living in and out of VA clinics for years. Could be dead."

Cafferty deliberates quietly.

"Well, the timing could be better, but…it always could. This is my life now. Do you think there's any way I might be able to meet him?"

"Well, I can certainly reach out to Captain Marshall and see who from Social Services might be in contact with him. Yeah, let me give it a shot," replies Donnelly.

"Perfect. Oh, hell, almost forgot to mention. It's still not formally announced as of yet, but…from what I have heard—and it's a pretty good source—Forca not only won the initial 'Great Rebuild' for Trumbull County, they received word they won fifty percent of the Western PA designated 'critical status' bridges. That's like sticking a defibrillator on the old mill and the entire town. Can you believe it?" Cafferty smiles, and for the first time, he sees the proud Youngstown getting up off the canvas. "The mill and your MCF will come to life together. That's great news for sure, Mayor. I do appreciate everything you have done behind the scenes. If you are not careful, they will never let you leave this place," he offers with a wink.

"This is home now, for me. I don't ever want to leave."

A few days later, Cafferty sits alone inside a cafe, staring at steaming black mud flowing from a coffeepot. As the last drop splashes into his mug, a ripple ebbs from the sides and dives into an invisible black hole. He stares at the still liquid as if it is a block of black ice.

"Thank you," he states, without looking up, as the waitress has already slipped away. His eyes drift across the Formica tabletop and settle on a vintage Seeburg Wall-O-Matic jukebox serving double duty as a menu holder. He stretches toward the diminutive glass housing, peering inside at the selections. As he pokes the letters and numbers, he spots "The Everly Brothers" and cracks a smile.

"Ah, Mom, you would be so happy," he whispers to the yellowed song label. Taking a strong pull from his mug, he scans the muck-spattered parking lot outside. He spots Donnelly carefully navigating the mocha slush while walking alongside a tortuously frumpy woman. Her bob haircut embellishes a globular face while her stringy bangs nearly cover her eyes. *If she didn't have an ID badge hanging from her neck,* Cafferty thinks, *she could pass for Donnelly's mom.* He smirks.

Just behind the woman trudges a stony-eyed man, one shoelace flogging his khaki pants with each heavy step. He makes no effort to alter his course, as if locked onto rails, staring ahead at the café.

The trio enters the café, and Donnelly immediately spots Cafferty, guiding the group to the table.

104

"Sorry, Bobby. We had a little issue finding Richard's coat. This is Lizzie Moeller, from the Trumbull County Social Workers office."

"Hello, Lizzie, nice to meet you."

"Same to you," says Lizzie, removing a heavy coat.

"No worries at all," Cafferty says.

Cafferty extends his hand toward the figure, sagging against the deep booth bench. "Hello, Richard, my name is Bobby Cafferty."

Richard looks at the extended hand and lays his into Cafferty's palm, cold and stiff.

"H-Hello, Bobby, have we met before?" Richard replies.

"No, Richard. First time for both of us. Did you notice your shoe's untied?" asks Cafferty. "It's brutal outside and I don't want anyone to fall."

"Um, yes. They—sometimes they are…I put them here," he says, motioning to worn leather, just beneath the wet, stained pair of khakis. Bobby leans down and watches Richard's fingers poke at the shoelace until they disappear into the shoe.

"Thank you," says Richard, seemingly relieved.

"So, Lizzie, I understand your group has established assistance for Richard at home—the laundry services, benefits processes, meals?"

"Yes, we've taken the initial steps to ensure Richard has the day-to-day care he needs. Obviously, our goal is to get the appropriate short-term and long-term assistance which will be necessary."

105

Richard observes the waitress pouring a viscous black liquid into his mug, rippling with bubbles and life. The steam escapes like an untethered ghost.

"It is a challenge balancing quality in home care against the number of medical practitioners available—as the cases have increased, the region has not adequately met the services necessary. Your memory care facility will be a welcomed addition to the region." Donnelly leans behind Lizzie, motioning for the waitress. "It's all the little things—paying bills, managing money, laundry, medications, meals, but—"

"Yes, the challenge to the caretakers as well," Cafferty finishes, with Lizzie nodding in agreement.

Cafferty turns his attention to Richard. "Would you like a hamburger, or shall we order something different?"

"Sure, I like hamburgers."

"Richard, our new place—St. Stanislaus—will have a bunch of people to help with everything—laundry, cafeteria, exercise facilities. But most importantly, they will have staff dedicated to helping folks like *me* as well."

Donnelly sinks against the booth chair, confused by Cafferty's statement.

"You see, Richard, dementia impacts everyone—the patient, for sure. That's a painful reality and one I know you understand."

Richard nods while staring into his now still mug, not a trace of life or breath within.

106

"But it's also a tough roll for the family as well." Donnelly nods, now grasping the swath of the storm. "My mom has Alzheimer's, Richard. I cannot care for the single most important person in my life, despite searching and paying for help. It isn't working for her and it is not working for me. If I could roll back a year, maybe two of her life, I am certain, on one of her good days, she would have wanted the help for me as much as for her." Richard huffs as an uncontrolled rush of emotion empties his lungs.

"We will have a facility dedicated to helping address both the patient and the families, for those that have them. But one part of this program which I feel is unique—and where I believe it will be especially helpful for you—is addressing the care for patients who have no one."

Richard places his head in his hands, failing to hide from a committed and precise hunter, dogging his escape for years. Richard's nebulous reality hardens momentarily like concrete, affording a snapshot to the only path on which to pass.

"No one wants to help you more than I do, Richard. Will you allow me to do that for you?" Cafferty states, opening his hand toward Richard. Richard presses his hand within and grips the flesh like a lifesaver bobbing within a vast sea. The waitress arrives and plops overloaded plates in front of the group.

Donnelly jams the leaky mass into his mouth, while his breathing labors. "I guess that's our cue, right?" chides Cafferty. A muffled *mea culpa* strains from Donnelly's mouth. Richard gropes the mass and removes the bun. He begins nibbling the bland cap while fingering the lettuce beneath. Cafferty notes the approach, one he saw with his mom.

"It is a rather peculiar meal; so many individual pieces you have to clamp together," Cafferty muses with a faint smile. "Actually, it probably makes a whole helluva lot of more sense to eat this thing in layers instead of jamming couch cushions in your mouth," he says, pointing in Donnelly's direction. "You know what? I am going to try it your way one time," he offers, neatly cutting his burger in bites, a random collection of contents within each. Cafferty observes Richard and ponders if he himself would have accepted the same news as Richard had just done. Cafferty's mind ticks fast...

That very moment when you realize you've had the last piece of freedom taken—a car, your own home, your choice of making whatever meal you want, work, relationships. But most importantly, the realization you are not "you" and will continue wandering farther away from what "you" were. And one day, perhaps overnight while sleeping, perhaps while staring into a blackened mug, perhaps while multicolored pills are being served to you, a moment will pass, faster than a bullet, which will forever disconnect the comprehension from the reality. You will never again even recognize the movie playing out around you, the actors, the props, or the point. You will simply "be," until you won't.

Cafferty watches the man, one who could pass *physically* as his brother. Yet he has been sentenced, as if a crime was committed, to the same fate as his mom, with no opportunity for pardon. His mind ticks again. *I want you to have dignity, Richard, through it all. I wish you to have one single moment on this journey where you have complete clarity, control, and reward from your actions. I wish this more than anything.* His mom's life is gone and it's unfair, perhaps abusive, to keep captive a soul wishing to roam without fences. It's only a matter of time before she just stops living.

Cafferty's phone vibrates hard within his pocket, snapping him back to the present. A message from Helio burns bright.

"My friend, it is time to awaken the sleeping giant."

Chapter 9

"It's such a sturdy structure, fantastic bones in this place," Helio chimes, pointing at massive steel spines and counties of concrete situated throughout the mill. "It was built to handle far heavier machines and the headcount of yesteryear…. Times have changed, machines lighter and fewer men. But these bones wouldn't have cared what machines or people worked here; it would have outlasted them all," he surmises. "Actually, it has."

Cafferty's eyes trace the spines to the walls, across support beams and into the floor, stirring a sense of pride. "Of course it has great bones," he states. "They were made for Youngstown, by people from Youngstown." The two men continue their march through the deserted cave as streams of light jab through shattered windows, spotlighting a section marred by graffiti and broken glass.

"You know what this reminds me of?" states Helio. "It's like a vagrant—see the missing teeth right there?" he asks, pointing skyward. "And these are his tattoos." Cafferty quietly observes the graffiti, the letters sagging and fading as if the skin has slipped from beneath.

"He needs a cover-up, and we will give him one," states Helio proudly. Cafferty's lips are pressed tightly together, contemplating the day men were evicted and which souls perhaps later returned to the only home they knew.

"Hell," says Cafferty. "I only hope we don't disturb them." A whoosh of wings thrash the silence, sending vermin clattering.

"Them?" says Helio. "I hate rats," he hisses. "And birds have plenty of other buildings to nest in. Soon this hotel will be closed," he booms, wagging a finger above.

"No, not them," says Cafferty. "I mean the men that returned after this place closed."

"Bobby, there's been nobody here for maybe forty years. It smells like we are in a dank castle cellar, only with wet ash everywhere. There's moss *on* the moss here," he quips.

Cafferty halts before timeworn charred logs and murky bottles, a provisional campsite for gypsies. Cafferty stares into the faint glimpse of life and begins.

"I remember the day. The men's faces were clean, far too clean for any man that ever lived in this town. Before that moment, I never saw any of those men, not once, without 'Hell's flour' pasted all over their faces. You only ever saw gleaming white eyes—like flashlights—and teeth, like pearls, against their smooth, ebony faces. When they would smile, you could see it from a football field away!" he muses.

"But then, the furnace was snuffed, and the air brightened. They were *clean*, for the first time in forty or fifty years. It was the first time I could see their faces, every fracture, every torched pockmark, every weeping blister on their skin. You know what I never saw again? I never saw their eyes or teeth. Their chins sagged, like

111

they were sewn to their chests. They stared at their shoes all day long, just smoking…overcome and hushed.

"They left the mill looking like they had been orphaned. And how else should they have looked? When that final whistle blew, they had absolutely nothing." Bobby smacks his fist into his palm with a violent burst, dispatching a crack past a startled Helio. "They were too old for life anywhere except here, but too young to die. But they still had families, obligations, and pride to contend with but…no more of this," Cafferty states, his hand tracing the steel spines from afar.

"But a few of those men kept showing up, as if they were sleepwalking. Weeks went by and became months. Those men continued bringing lunchboxes, their uniforms, repeating stale jokes, but mostly betting which customer would place the grandest order in the history of the mill. An order so big that it would force double shifts until even the strongest grunt dropped from exhaustion." Cafferty shakes his head, turning toward Helio, his blue eyes piercing the distance between them.

"There was a newspaper photo that showed those men moving liquidated machinery out of the building. Loading the trucks *for free*. Can you imagine that?" Helio recoils at the thought. "Is that fear or blind loyalty?"

"No, I cannot imagine helping anyone who sold my fate. The gall of management. Why would one—"

"Christ, they were too numb to even realize or accept what was going on. They pledged blind faith to the life they knew," fires Cafferty. A mad scatter of rats somewhere echoes and startles Helio.

"When the new tenants began moving in," Cafferty says, motioning back to the rats, "only then did the men realize this was the end. Fewer and fewer men returned each day. The rats began fighting, staking their claims to every nook in this building. Soon, the men who kept showing up started bringing booze instead of lunch. Pistols instead of playing cards—waging some misguided war against those filthy bastards, like they were scabs coming to take their jobs." Cafferty shakes his head. "They would spend their pennies on booze and bullets, drinking and shooting, at walls, windows, whatever moved.

"But not one solitary rat stopped coming. Hell, they built nests all over the place." He chuckles to himself. "Anyway, one day a local named Bobby, a guy that put in years of blood, sweat, and a marriage in this mill, realized it wasn't the rats' fault. They weren't there for jobs, they didn't snuff out the furnace, and, oddly, they would still gather near the guys, despite the vitriol and bullets thrown their way," Cafferty continues. "They are so nonjudgmental, like they've seen it all before. Certainly, they don't give a damn what you think of them and wear their universal hatred like a badge." Helio shifts, pondering the point, but remains quiet. "Above all, those rats were so loyal, never leaving the place or those few workers who remained. More loyal than the management who shook their hands, looked them in the eyes, and lied."

113

"Bobby, I would never—"

"No, no, Helio. You are a man of your word. I trust you, which is why I am telling you this.

"So one day, this Bobby stopped shooting at the creatures. He arrived for his shift like he always did, with the three other men, and sent the first five of those bullets piercing the mill—shooting out lights, windows, whatever machinery even the most parasitic scrappers wouldn't take.

"He shot at *them*, the management that stole pensions, copped buyouts, and scurried off into some safe place, leaving the mill to die."

Helio looks down at the floor, toeing a faded Rolling Rock beer bottle, contemplating that scene from forty years ago.

"He sat down with his shift-mates, the rats, and ate one bologna sandwich, dressed in spicy mustard and a slab of cheese, French fries, and Heinz ketchup, washed it down with soda…not an RC, not a Pepsi, but the *best*." Cafferty's voice trails, his eyes pinching shut as he reflects on a meal so vivid, his heart jabs at his throat. "Have you ever had O-So grape soda, Helio?" Cafferty smiles, his eyes still wired shut.

"It stains your lips purple. Half of the sandlot ballfields in Ohio had pasty white kids running around with purple lips, like they had been frozen in the middle of summer…but you just knew it was O-So. Then it paints your throat with a sugar lacquer so heavy, you still *taste* grapes three days later." Cafferty chuckles and smacks his lips, as if savoring a sip from only a few moments prior.

"But the thing I remember most about O-so is *that smell* when you first pop the cap. The sweetest smell you'll ever know, like Easter Sunday at the Vatican. Hundreds of fresh-cut lilies saturating the air. Me and my sandlot teammates would drink three or four of those apiece under the stifling summer sun. We couldn't get enough of that stuff. By the end of the day, those empty cans were like little ovens, just baking that O-so into a gummy paste. That delicious smell we encountered just hours prior now made us nauseous and swear to never go near it again." Helio doesn't budge, his eyes fixed on his friend. Cafferty's smile evaporates, and with it his blue eyes split the air.

"Anyway, my father washed that meal down with his O-So. He then bit the muzzle and drove the last bullet through what was left of him. Boom." The words clang the air like rocks in a coffee can. Helio's shoulders slump forward.

"A couple days later, I remember going to the funeral home. I remember looking for any sign—anything—that gave me an answer to 'why.' No one, not even the priest, made sense of why. So when I approached the casket and knelt—I have no idea why other than that you're supposed to—I sputtered a few sentences to a shiny wooden box. 'Why did you leave, where are you now, what happens next?' And there was silence. Nothing.

"You know how those homes are sealed like a vacuum, no air moving and eerily quiet? It's like a large coffin, ironically. Anyway, after a few moments, I gave up on anything or anyone telling me 'why' and rose to my feet. At that very moment, I heard the door at the back of the funeral home open, not where guests come in, but rather where the workers enter. Who knows who it was. But a gulp of crisp winter air dashed throughout the home, tickling the flowers, the casket, everything. And you know what smell blanketed the entire funeral home?" Cafferty asks.

"O-So grape soda," Helio states softly.

"When everyone else told me it was a sign from Jesus, lilies, or perfume, I smelled O-So grape soda. And *that* grape soda is as close as I have come to an answer." He kicks the blanched bottle and watches it bounce, violently spinning a few feet from them. They watch the bottle slow, with each revolution of the barrel passing them, sighting its muzzle on some final target. The bottle screeches abruptly, halting squarely on Cafferty. He glowers at the barrel, his shoulders swelling, daring the bottle to discharge. Only a clatter of claws breaches the silence.

"Bobby, I am so sorry about your father. I mean I—I had no idea ab—"

Cafferty retrieves the faded bottle and approaches Helio. "It's okay, Helio, I have learned to simply accept the unknown. Would you like to christen this ol' ship now?" he asks, motioning around to the empty mill. Helio nods quietly, still mindful of the memory on his

116

friend's mind. "Okay then, Helio." Cafferty chuckles, handing the bottle over to Helio. Helio smiles politely and, burdened by his tightly fitted suit, heaves an awkward throw, smashing green shards about the ashtray-colored mill floor.

Out in front of the mill, a bright red ribbon stretches in front of a makeshift platform, a few wooden pallets stacked upon one another, a single bullhorn laying on top. Hundreds of locals mill about, crisp air nipping at their faces. Donnelly arrives, parking his truck in the far end of a sprawling, sparsely populated parking lot. He strides alongside other townspeople, regularly stopping to face people, gripping their shoulders with one hand and pressing his flesh into theirs with another. Gone is the ostentatious trench coat and impractical loafers, and in its place are jeans and work boots. He has spent weeks canvassing neighborhoods and engaging locals with dialogue. He is becoming one of them, a fact not lost on Cafferty.

"Hello, Mayor," says Cafferty, shaking his hand. "Look at you. You've more than settled in." He winks at Donnelly.

"Well, Bobby, I might continue running for office until they ask me to leave," he responds, smiling at the compliment.

"You remember Helio, I am certain."

"Of course. He's the headliner of this show," muses Donnelly.

"It is good for everyone," agrees Helio. "Now, let's see if we can bring this beautiful creature back to life."

Donnelly ascends the crates, steadying himself before watchful eyes. "A big thank you to Mother Nature for the clear sky today.

She can be cranky in the middle of winter, yet here we are, under the bluest skies all year," he chimes, his breath puffing with each syllable. "Most importantly, thank you to those who have gathered to hear what we believe to be some pretty exciting news. So, without further ado, I'd like to introduce Mr. Helio Pee-rera, chairman of Forca Steel." Donnelly chews on the last name, generating a smile from Helio. A smattering of chuckles and subdued clapping nips the air.

"Good morning, Youngstonians. I know many folks have awaited some update as to how a federal initiative, known as 'The Great Rebuild,' would ever impact this town, these people, and quite literally, this very spot. I'm delighted to announce that Forca Steel—of Youngstown—will be an important supplier of steel to America's future focus on infrastructure development." The words blare from the bullhorn and leave a trail of high-pitched squelches streaming from the small cone. The parking lot simmers with chatter.

"We have contractual commitments for four hundred of the seventeen hundred bridges deemed 'critical' throughout greater Ohio. There are an additional thirty-five hundred bridges in Pennsylvania, one thousand in West Virginia, and two thousand in New York as part of a second bid which has commenced." The words ascend as if unencumbered by local history and shine brighter than the midday star.

"This does not yet factor in steel for roadways, critical support facilities such as water treatment plants, etcetera. From our best estimates, upwards of two hundred *billion* dollars could be spent on

118

national infrastructure by the year 2020. Soon the entire country will be rebuilding its skeleton, if you will, with steel. I will make sure we do everything in our power to not only have the brand 'Forca' on the underside of every bridge in Youngstown, but also every bridge, road, and critical facility in the US. Let's own this together."

The parking lot simmers yet again, random voices spattering against one another. "My friends, I share your optimism." His voice patient and controlled, he awaits a gap in the air. "We have a great deal of work to do beyond making steel. What I mean is we will be judged—Forca and Youngstown—on everything, from our ability to execute our contractual commitments all the way down to our land-scaping out front. Business is as much about what we are producing as it is the manner in which we are producing it and at what cost. Not financially, but cost in terms of how we appropriately manage impact to the environment, how safely we employ our workforce, and finally, how we care for our employees, not only while they work for Forca, but also once they have left our team. My commitment to you is to 'do the right thing.' That's it." Voices settle, affording the moment both space and time. "What does this mean?" Helio states rhetorically.

A pesky zap vibrates within Cafferty's pocket. "9-1-1, Mom en route to St. Stanislaus."

He stares at the screen and numbness washes over him—first his fingertips, then his feet. Soon, his legs deaden as if he plunged through ice, his legs trapped in frigid water beneath. His face stings

119

like his vessels are pumping electricity, and words appear mangled. He stares at the symbols again. A powerful jerk thrusts him, as if his car has cast a cargo net around him, reeling him against his will. The steady movement dumps the electricity from his veins and numbness from his body.

"Mom," he mutters. His mind fires as he is dragged ahead. He recalls the moment she was diagnosed and how he vowed to stay vigilant in their fight. He would tell the doctors, "No, you are mistaken. The fight is woven into our DNA—
we are different than anyone you have seen." And the doctors, all of them, spilled hundreds of sentences, with only one that stuck: "Be there for her." He remembers each night standing watch, like a sentinel, awaiting Alzheimer's, that bumbling, conspicuous pest. He would confront this *thing* and knock *it* down. Then he would scream, "Stand up!" He would do this over and over until *it* never came back. But days would pass as he awaited *its* arrival and his eyes grew heavy, sealing shut. He would awake each day, bent awkwardly on a bedside chair, and sense *something* had been there. She had changed.

Initially, cousins' names would evade her and she couldn't remember her last meal. But it would slide further, frustration would germinate, and she would lash out at him or at herself if another target was unavailable, begging for an end but lacking the faculties to do it. Cafferty remembers doctors citing the last example of the ultimate sleight of hand, the exact moment Alzheimer's permanently slips beyond awareness into a permanent sea of madness. "Just be there for her," he mutters, shaking his head. "That's it."

Cafferty slams the car door and stares at the ignition, drawing a deep breath from the frigid interior. He holds his breath for a moment and exhales, observing the steam slither like mercury into the air before vanishing. "Just. Be. There."

Chapter 10

Cafferty slips past an impromptu crush of nurses savoring assorted pastries at the St. Stanislaus entrance. Holiday music ripples the first floor and fetches smiles from even the most haggard members pulling double shifts. In moments, he exits the third floor and is stalled by overwhelming silence and an arresting wooden Virgin Mary stationed atop the wing's door frame. She exhibits a listless and pallid semblance, her mantle and gown having shed their luster, like collateral scars from death's carousel. Cafferty avoids her unbending gaze as he did decades prior, instead drawn to the gilded wooden frames aligning the hallway.

He pushes past stoic patron saints standing watch over each door, as if their vigil would buy time. One by one, a swirl of colors and pious figures lags behind as Cafferty blows past each, preoccupied with the grave reality of why he is here. Room 336. "This is it," he whispers, the words ricocheting off an authoritative painting of St. Dymphna, pricking a demon's neck. He fills his lungs as if he will be submerged, the fear of the unknown nips at his breath.

The latch depresses with a sturdy metallic clank, immediately exposing a singular and unexplained world. His feet sturdy themselves, as if crossing the precipice will send him tumbling. He recalls uncomplicated pamphlets and doctors preparing him for this voyage of unknown duration, unknown course, but certain arrival. "This is…so different," he mutters.

Death germinates in front of him, its reach widening, rendering him awestruck yet curious. *It* is alive and fluid, saturating and viscous, like quicksand swallowing every bend and nook on his body. *It* is not as he imagined some byproduct of life; rather, he *senses death co-opting life for its own duration of being.* But death is utterly lonely. Its presence is not surrounded by doctors and hope but instead by bouncing LEDs and mechanical bleats.

His eyes bounce about the room, seeking not an answer but a splinter of character and dignity. He is affronted by white cotton, white blinds, and fluorescent lights casting upon a waxen face, stripped bare and taxed by each fissure life has born. His eyes settle upon the white linens.

Those sheets, he thinks, *are mere seconds from becoming winding cloths. It's all so...clinical.* He hesitates again and continues pondering if this is what Father Sistak got wrong, pitching faith to him as a youth. He mulls over Catholic grade school stories hawked, and cemented for years by sobering nuns. Valiant men slaying giants, being fed to lions, burning at stakes, whales—it was all so grandiose, so intrepid, so inspiring. Even his modern-day brush with faith, documentaries reenacting near-death experiences, the white tunnel, hands reaching out for the dying soul, flashes of lightning, inspiring those to believe in something beyond now. He huffs and words empty from his mouth. "Fuck, of course they are going to see white!

"But this," he gestures while shaking his head, "this…" The words trail to nothing, and his hand falls limp to his side. Moments pass before suddenly, he is reined in by erratic beeps and a racking surge from his mother's sunken chest. A young woman approaches the bed from the corner of the room with a steady, purposeful movement.

"I didn't even see you," Cafferty blurts, puzzled by her presence and unassuming clothes. "What is your name, Nurse—?" Cafferty says with a quiet but subtle slip in his voice, scanning her for a name.

"I'm Nurse Christina. But all of my friends call me Mira—"

He interrupts her and, for the first time, enters the room and approaches the foot of the bed. "Nurse Christina…. That's about all I might remember from this point forward."

"Honey, please go hold your mom's hand and talk to her," the diminutive woman responds, as she navigates a series of IV hoses. Her hands and arms appear smooth and delicate, almost fragile. Their milky white hue matches her impossibly youthful face, one lacking blemishes and free from a hectic pace. Thick brown curls frolic with each of her movements.

"You should crack the window a tiny bit as well, this always helps."

Obediently, Cafferty cracks the window, and a stream of frigid air crawls about the room. Mildred's chest gargles again, like a cement mixer grinding and mixing to stave a coalescence within. Cafferty situates himself along his mom's side and strokes the straw-like tufts of silver.

"What can you do—does she feel any of this?" Cafferty's heart throbs against his ribs as he observes the scene, a body gasping from an invisible constrictor, stealing breath inch by inch.

"Honey, we gave your mom medicine for that gunk you see here, and also for the pain. She is not feeling any of this."

The body stiffens again and the chest rises, as if a current surges within. "How can you know that?" asks Cafferty, his eyes not moving from his mom's chest. "This is not pain-free—I can't see her suffer like this."

"I do know," responds the nurse, with utter conviction, "we have to have faith in God, and even at the darkest hour, God gets us through this." Cafferty winces at the answer and squares up to the diminutive but dauntless figure.

"Can you tell me something, Nurse? Did you believe in God before you were a nurse, or did you find faith as some sort of convenience—you know, some coping mechanism for what I assume you are now numb to? I don't want to say 'shallow' because that—"

The nurse catches him mid-sentence. "Mr. Cafferty—have you ever run a marathon?"

The words jolt Cafferty, leaving him defenseless. Slowly, he shakes his head.

"Well, over the course of twenty-six and some odd miles, do you think anyone cares about what you did at mile two, or mile ten, or even mile twenty-six? Or more importantly, what obstacles you overcame to reach mile two, or ten? No one will care about the weather that day, how you altered your diet, what shoes you wore, or anything else. The only thing that will matter is: Did...you...finish? Because if you did, *something* bigger than the weather, the hunger, the pain in your feet, the fear of not having done enough to complete it, something pushed you to believe...and you arrived."

Her words inexplicably ease the labor within his chest and a surge of air fills his lungs. "Maybe God put me in front of hundreds of dying people to help me understand faith I otherwise would have been too dull to have figured out on my own. It's the rarest occasion that some sign is offered like proof to validate what you have always hoped the most to be true. For the rest of us? That is true faith." She smiles as the words ring, with a conviction stronger than steel.

Cafferty contemplates her response, as he notices a slight smile suggesting a secret deep within. Mildred's chest dwindles beneath an overwhelming squeeze, a whistle of life evacuating in haste. "What about the oxygen mask or something?" mutters Cafferty, resigned. "I wish I could have done more."

"Honey, she doesn't need what the Earth gives anymore." As the two sit quietly, watching the woman, the cold Youngstown air has filled the room. Cafferty shifts his eyes from his mom's stalling chest to her lips, pursed and pulsing with each breath. Suddenly, the unseen constrictor releases its grip. Her chest soars, absorbing every ounce of raw Youngstown air, and produces a faint mist from her lips. Cafferty recoils violently against his chair, toppling in the process. He is unable to speak, and his breath is misfiring, sputtering like a flooded engine.

The woman slips out of the room, gently shutting the door behind her without a sound. Cafferty, puzzled by the mist, twists to where the woman once stood. "Are your seeing this, Jesus Chr—" His breath shunts as he realized he is alone. Focusing again on his mom's chest, he lays horizontal to her, searching for the rise and fall of her breath. "Breathe, Mom…. Just breathe." He cannot detect movement and the gurgle has departed; only the unmistakable flatline drone pierces the air. He rises in his chair, cocking his head, and stares at the gaping mouth below.

A white fog slithers from her lips and rises through the placid room. He reaches a hand toward the mist but stops just shy of touching it, as if not to disrupt a fragile seedling. The subtle motion of his hand propels the mist, causing a gentle eddy, which is drawn toward the open window. He is mesmerized as a crest of peace washes over him. Just shy of the window, the mist pauses like a chick preparing for its first flight, independence a mere foot beyond the window ledge.

The mist swirls, overlapping itself, hatching a sparkle that is striking. It hangs, waiting for a cue. "I love you, Mom. Never stop dancing," he whispers. At once, the eddy shoots past the third-story ledge and disappears into the vast sky.

Cafferty gazes upon the body, a shell merely occupying space. He touches his mom's hand, and simultaneously, the door suddenly opens.

"Hello, Mr. Cafferty," says a woman, wearing nurse scrubs and a lanyard identifying her as "Rose Simpson, RN." "I am so sorry for your loss. As difficult as this was, it is so important that you were able to be here for her. She was not alone. I was your mom's attending nurse over the last few hours."

"Thank you…. Can you tell me where Nurse Christina— ummm, she never gave her last name. It, uh, it began with an 'M,' I think," Cafferty states as he dabs his misty eyes.

"I don't believe we even have a Christina on the ICU ward," says the nurse with a soft voice. "But then again, you have gone through a most stressful experience today. Sometimes that can impact our ability to—"

Cafferty stops her. "No, no. it was *definitely* Christina. She stood right where you are, talking about faith…. She had a nickname—I can't remember it, but it started with an M."

"Mr. Cafferty, I promise to look for anyone named 'Christina' on our team. If I find her, would you like me to pass along any words?" she offers.

"Yes, please. Please just let her know I've begun that marathon."

A few days later, Cafferty stands before a podium within the Patton Funeral Home in Youngstown. He strokes a hideous tie, as if the effort and occasion will at last defeat the permanent creases. He gazes over a modest gathering, offering a brief nod to Helio, his ever-faithful friend, the mayor, and still others who have known him for decades.

However, his eyes are magnetized to a little girl in the far corner, alone, outfitted in her First Communion dress. She doesn't appear lost, but rather interested in what Cafferty has to say. Cafferty sends a brief smile to the little girl. She approaches toward a surprised Cafferty, carrying an ivory envelope wrapped within a striking olive-wood-cord rosary. Quiet immerses the room.

"I wanted to give this to you for your loss," a hushed voice offers.

"Well, I appreciate that. May I open this after the service?"

"Yes, please." She spins and initiates the walk to the back of the room, leaving Cafferty perplexed.

"Thank you, Miss—" His words trail off.

Cafferty eulogizes his mom and recounts his fondest memories of his youth, his maturation into a man, his first girlfriend, and years he spent ascending the corporate ladder. He pauses briefly and looks down at his tie, pulling the ever-present crease without success.

"In closing, I wanted to apologize to you, Mom," he offers, while intercepting a smile peeking from his lips. "I lied to you—you never knew this, but now is the best time to fess up." He draws a breath, his hands no longer fighting the creases. He loosens the tie, while eyeing Helio and a few Bain partners scattered throughout.

"Mom, I told you how much I *loved* this tie and, as you know, wore this to my very first gig with Bain." Chuckles smolder from the seats occupied by the Bain contingency while the rest nod graciously at the compliment. "Well, that tie has been with me for the better part of thirty-some-odd years, through thick and thin." He giggles to himself as if the absurdity of its history could never be fully understood.

"Do you know I once left this very same tie on a New York subway? It was my very first trip to the city, and, wanting to be prepared, I was very early for my meeting. So I had the tie folded on the seat next to me, had a bagel in one hand and notes for a meeting in the other. The train finally made it to my stop and I stepped off into the maddening crowd, leaving the tie neatly folded on the seat. Now, I don't know if that was on purpose or not.

"I got halfway into the building before I even realized the tie was still sightseeing somewhere in Manhattan." The room churns with more laughter. "A few hours later, I took the same subway back toward the airport, and wouldn't you know it: the damn thing *still* was still sitting on the exact same seat! No one would claim that thing, not even Goodwill!" Laughter erupts throughout as Cafferty sheepishly looks over his shoulder, smiling at his mom's photo.

"Oh, and I hate to admit this. Not too long ago, maybe a few years, I hit a deer on old Rouseville Road. Now, I had that tie sitting in the fold of my briefcase forever. I had decided one day I would give it away or toss it…but couldn't follow through. So here I am on Rouseville Road, my bumper is a mess hanging just a few inches above the blacktop, and you know what I did? I wrapped that tie around the bumper, up through the hood, and drove ten miles back to old man Binder's shop. I untied it and the damn thing did not have a single rip, drop of blood, or anything on it. It was as if that thing was supernatural."

The place comes alive again, Cafferty smiling at the sheer lunacy but truth of such actions. "So, Mom, I lied to you about liking this tie. It's absolutely hideous, made of some professional-grade polyester, and it's loud as hell." The room buckles with laughter as Cafferty approaches the open casket where his mom lies. The room stills, silence now engulfing every nook and lung, all awaiting Cafferty. "But this tie is a part of you, and I promise you, I will never wear this again, at least not until I see you next." He slips the folded tie into his mom's hand and quietly turns around to face the room. "Thank you all for your support and understanding."

As Cafferty shakes the last hand of the day, he is alone with the closed casket. The last ray from beyond the door is hustling low, as if privy to the billable rate. The flowers' fragrance too acquiesces to undiluted Murphy's Oil ascending from century-old oak slats. He studies the pile of high-wrought stationery, the pink letters, like ribbons, softening death's vocabulary. "Sympathy. Grief. Loss. God. Peace," he reads quietly to himself. The voice halts as his eyes are drawn to misshapen printed block letters. An olivewood rosary wraps around the envelope, and he remembers the girl in the Communion dress.

He plucks the envelope from the pile, slides a finger between the seal, and forces a perfect separation along the crease. He peers inside and sees an elaborate pencil-drawn image on an ivory card. Her features appear to reach from the card, like a hologram, causing his hand to twist for further inspection.

There in bold red letters, the name bounds forth and pierces his chest: "Christina Mirabellis (the Astonishing)—the Patron Saint of Mental Illness."

Chapter 11

As daybreak unveils a mortally frigid December morning, the city hibernates beneath a cloak of unblemished white. Not a single jagged feature remains, as if nature has spent an evening sanding anything that could present a hazard or point of demarcation. Traffic signs pose as freshly formed lollipops, still hardening in their Styrofoam bases. Houses present as billowy confections, as if an amateur patissier iced them, spilling white over the sidewalks out front. Liberty Street, the wrinkled generational pass for commuters and industries alike, is presently speck-less, almost begging for a horse-drawn carriage. Even the VA clinic, a brownish-red stained facade and bruised history, has a fresh frosting of makeup for the holiday season.

Every facet of the building appears delicate and untarnished, with the exception of the third-story window. Irregular gashes streak the window, as if a frantic hand once clawed for freedom on a sinking hulk.

Inside, Danny shivers as choppy wisps of air spit from a clenched jaw. A plastic bottle cap oscillates wildly as he shaves thin strips of ice from the window, exposing the bus station below. "Jesus, Mary, and Joseph—it's freezing from the *inside*," he grunts over his shoulder, looking for anyone who will listen. With a final gash, he watches the crystals fall onto his arm and melt into tiny beads.

"Better," he says as he retreats and positions his wheelchair just beyond December's fingertips. His hand dives into a crinkled lunch bag, and at once a soupçon of lavender teases the air. He sniffs inside the bag, releasing a smile kept captive for too long.

For the moment, he is rapt by a woman's scent and oblivious to the lumbering cargo elevator arriving from the first floor medical wing. Only the unmistakable odor of germicidal lather and latex gloves slaps him back to reality. "Goddammit," Danny groans, as he comes to terms with a likely scolding.

"So you make me come fetch ya again, do ya, Danny?" chides Abby, her double shifts eroding her patience with each missed feeding. "I need you to pay attention to the clock. If we miss more of these, Dr. McGuire will require you to stay down there until after dinner. He's got very little patience anymore."

Danny scoffs at the suggestion while thumbing through assorted holiday cards lying about on his lap. Stray glitter flakes twinkle with merriment above his brow, sapping his bitter veneer. "How am I supposed to see the bus station with all that construction down there? Ol' Dawson probably has us all breathing asbestos and lead from this dump," he says, pointing indiscriminately.

"Think about it—I'll bet ten bucks." He twists in his chair, stabbing a hand into his pockets but locating seams and lint. "Wait, I've got it here—somewhere.... When I find it, I'll bet ten dollars I've received more harm being here, breathing whatever toxic shit's in these walls, than I ever did while out there," he fires, fingering the desolate bus platform.

"Somehow I doubt that. Now, if you will sit still, I have a whole bunch of other folks needing my help too." Danny briskly surveys the floor, as if searching for a hidden tunnel that would dump him beyond thirty-foot-high, stone prison walls.

"Don't even think about *that*." Her hand tugs a latex glove impossibly far and releases it with a *thwack*. "We're both too old for that business."

"I'm *not* going anywhere, for Chrissake," Danny huffs.

She wraps a jellied, lemon cord around his arm and pats at a dormant vein. "Hmm, sometimes this little guy can be shy," she says, ignoring the minefield of pockmarks and blotches. She briskly scrubs the skin with a cold solution and pricks at a bluish hue buried deep.

"Jesus Chrrrrrrrrrrrrrrist, Abby—I will ask again: You do this for a living, don't you?" Danny whines sarcastically while recoiling from the misfire. "I haven't quite figured if your eyesight is that shitty or if you enjoy treating me like a pincushion?"

Abby scoffs at the suggestion. "Danny, you try poking around this empty bag of bones and see what you can do."

"As sick as I ever was, I never missed…anything. You'd be shit with horseshoes or hand grenades," he says with a vile glare.

"Ah, Danny. Perhaps…. But as long as I am drawing blood, I am the only marksman you have.

135

"What are all these cards for? Do you have some friends out-side of here?" Abby presses the needle against his skin as it resists like an ossified tree branch. With a quick jab, the silver flash disappears beneath, creating a gristly pop within. Danny's frame eases as blood begins to collect in the tube along his arm.

He glances at the shimmering pile of green and red cards, and spots a bloated St. Nick pointing a sooty finger directly at him. "Have YOU been Naughty or Nice?" the figure seems to admonish Danny, a twinkle suggesting insider knowledge. He forces a deep breath.

"Each year, we get holiday cards from the local schools. All the kids—probably hundreds—sign their names to something their teacher wrote. They're never addressed to anyone in particular, just 'the men who served'…no one ever goes to read them. They just collect dust until January 2nd, when the fairytale ends. But I don't play checkers or chess, and they haven't changed out the books since last summer," he grouses, pointing at the bookshelf, "so I read these." Abby stills and focuses on the man, not as a patient but as a person.

He hesitates, peeks at St. Nick's face again, and slowly cracks the card open. "…Because Santa Claus is coming to *YOUR* town!" the card threatens as his eyes snipe from beneath a red cap. He snaps the card shut and rubs the glitter from between his thumb and forefinger.

"A couple of years ago, I wrote back to one school. Can't say exactly why. Maybe they deserved to know that *someone is* listening to them, you know, here for them…they can't all be living rainbows and butterflies, ya know." His voice softens.

"*Really*? That is so—"

"But…I didn't even end up sending the card. Stamped, addressed, but when I looked down at the return address"—he hacks while laughing—"I could see them saying, 'Who in the fuck is *that creep* sending jollies to our kids.'"

"It was still beautiful, Danny. Your good intentions are what mattered. That *is* the spirit of life."

"Perhaps," he mutters.

"So does this mean God is taking root inside you?"

Danny slaps his forehead and sputters incoherently as if punch-drunk. "No—why, what the…. How does everything have to be about some 'finding God' moment?" he bristles. "It wasn't for God then, now, even at my darkest hour," Danny finishes, hissing at an imaginary crucifix.

Abby recoils from the feeding bags as if a bolt of lightning would zero in on blasphemy. "Careful, Danny. God's got his eye on you," she cautions.

"I'm serious as a heart attack," shoots Danny. "Back when I lived out there," he says, motioning to the bus station, "the holidays would stoke these 'prayer warriors,' carolers, closet Christians. You know what I would do? I would run. Buy the biggest vat of sauce I could, grab the cheapest company, and wouldn't wake up until the carolers were gone and the decorations were all packed away. Hell, it was an entirely different *year* when I woke up, and nothing was there reminding me about 'my self-imposed doom.'" His voice falters for a moment as if he has flooded an engine, too much too soon. But soon, his engine catches fire again and his entire body shakes with energy.

"The whole façade—you know, half the town getting oiled up and stumbling into a church because geriatric songbirds are warbling through 'Oh Come All Ye Faithful,' or whatever God wants spun on his jukebox.

"Some priest blazing a guilt trip on the people about how they are going to hell for not coming *allllll the time*," he fumes, smacking his wheel and earning a pained squawk of support. "And don't even get me started about priests, altar boys, and…. Holy shit, do you ever *hear* yourselves justifying the sins of the Vatican?!" His voice raises into a preadolescent timbre. "Why is it that you people are so intent about protecting *that* institution, like you earn some credit for being so blindly naive or so brainwashed, you would fucking march off a cliff just the same? No, not me!"

Abby folds at the waist as if punched in the gut. She steals a peek over her shoulder as if Father Polakowski's body would rise from the grave, splintered ruler in hand, and well-rested for throttling the demons lurking within.

"You hush your mouth, Danny, you are gonna get us all thrown into the fire with that talk! God ain't done a thing to you. You leave him be and focus on yourself," she says, poking into Danny's bony frame.

"Think about it," continues Danny. "Jesus wasn't even born on the twenty-fifth. Do you know the church didn't even celebrate that date until centuries after he was dead? It was based on the sun god's feast! How twisted is that? The church has a patent on hypocrisy, for fuck's sake," Danny says, while gasping for more air. "You cannot have false idols, yet let's rob the pagans' day and label it as Christmas."

Abby purses her lips, intently staring at the tray in front of her as if trying to avoid collateral judgment. He cranes his neck above the makeshift gurney and labors to see his target. "And nothing makes it worse than being pressured into buying shit, going into debt, all in the name of 'God' and 'giving.' Have you—hang on, I'm not done yet, Abby, don't you leave yet. They pass the tithing plate twice during the mass! The balls on those people, goddamn leeches. Why twice? Then you feel guilty for not having tithed the right amount in the first place! You know what 'tithing' means, Abby? It means ten percent may have fooled a fool back in whenever they dreamed it up, but ten percent twice is twenty, even for a shit-heel like me. Guilt. The church has a monopoly on guilt, and even the government couldn't bust up that boon."

"Have you finished yet, Danny?" she censures, as if observing a child's meltdown.

"Yeah, whatever. You just march along now, you little sheep, bah bah bahhhh bahhhh…"

139

Abby's eyes curse the angry man beneath her. They scroll over his body as if trying to pinpoint Satan's engine and rip the rusted metal block from its frame. Inch by inch they seek until soon, her eyes reach his feet, without an engine to be found. She is drawn to the Christmas cards scattered about him, flecks of glitter catching the midday sun, and leaping from the bland recycled cardboard. They sparkle with a ferocity, highlighting the words inscribed, and fortify her convictions like a white-hot brand searing within. "Love, Hope, Forgiveness." One word beckons her, however, more than any other: "Reason."

"Be the reason," she whispers to herself, reading the card. Abby steps in front of Danny for the first time, squaring her frame and blocking the view beyond his world.

"What are you doing—I can't see the—"

"Danny, I know why you wrote back to those kids...I was wrong. It doesn't have anything to do with faith or God." Her mass leans in closer, affording no space to look at anything but her. Danny's mouth parts as he notices her formidable width, a feature he couldn't have fully appreciated otherwise. She looks as if she is immovable, reinforced with sandbags and concrete. For a moment, Danny regrets ever criticizing her finesse. *Of course she pokes hard*, he thinks.

Without an escape, he leans against the chair, bowing the worn material to its limit. "I believe you wrote that letter because *you* hoped for someone to listen. You hoped to be heard, Danny. Everyone has a reason—faith, guilt, or in your case, you want someone to know there is more to you than *this*," she says, poking the engine of hate directly in his chest.

The finger immobilizes Danny, like he is nailed to a board, any slight movement only increasing the pressure. "I hope you send a letter someday, Danny, and perhaps you will be heard," the voice finishes, as she retreats from the chair. Danny cautiously eyes the figure as it navigates behind the tray and obscures her scale.

"Abby." His voice pricks the uncomfortable silence.

"Yes."

"I, ah...I'm sorry for what I said about this," he says as he motions to the fresh splotch from an errant strike. "That was unfair to you. I—um, I—so... thank you for what you have done for me— you're a kind woman." The words fling from his mouth as if a sling-shot loosed. Its contents scatter about her, startling her.

"Well, thank you, Danny—I know that was tough to say. Now, I'll let you get back to your view." As the minutes pass, Otis huffs floors beneath. His breath is choppy, as if December's hands fight to keep irreverence at bay. Cables creak and squeal, however, announcing his stubborn resolve. Abruptly, a hoarse giggle rips the air, garnering laughter and curious eyes to drift toward his drab doors. Otis expels one final breath and fires a ting for the third floor. He pauses just for a moment, as if savoring the punchline. Then he delivers his masterpiece.

141

"Watch this lip right there, Richard—it stopped a little shy of the floor," motions Cafferty. The high-top sneakers lift and fall beyond the hazard, and settle as the metal doors crawl shut behind him. Immediately, Richard's eyes are drawn to the set of twelve-foot windows, frosted white along the wall.

"That re-reminds me of my mom's house." Richard smiles, gazing at the untouched sheets. "But she always has the windows open, even when it's cold—it makes them...ah, the—"

"They ice over, don't they, Richard," interjects Cafferty. "They remind me of a whiteboard when I see them."

"Not that one," motions Richard, pointing to the distant corner where claw marks have torn apart the sheet, exposing the world below. Richard shuffles toward the nearest window as Cafferty spots Dawson gesturing at contractors, clad in blue hard hats, at a makeshift table.

"I will just be a moment, Richard." As Cafferty approaches, the group scatters, leaving Dawson alone.

"Hi, Bobby. I am very sorry to hear of your mom's passing. Did you receive our flowers?" asks Dawson.

"I did," responds Cafferty soberly, still numb from the confluence of life, death, and a young girl. "It was a pleasant surprise, and I appreciate your kindness."

"How are things otherwise?" asks Dawson, his tone snake-bitten from their initial encounter.

"Things are moving along. The funding, getting the facility properly outfitted, and receiving the first group of medical practitioners."

"Well, I know nothing about that industry, but if there is something I can do—"

"Actually, there is something, which is why I wanted to drop by. I would like to interview vets for our memory care staff."

Dawson hunches his shoulders and ducks his head as if dodging beads of dirty rain, and a whistle leaks from his lips. "Bobby. I am not sure how much experience you have had working in a VA clinic. I mean, some of these folks," he says as his voice hushes, "are a bit…long in the tooth. Many of them have other, ummm, complicating issues." He thumbs toward the distant blight in the farthest corner.

Undeterred, Cafferty presses. "There are positions in addition to attendants—maintenance, housekeeping, cafeteria. Obviously, there is some investment with each function—training, equipment, testing, etcetera, and that is the part I am sponsoring on behalf of St. Stanislaus Memory Care. What I am asking you to do is to help facilitate the program approval within the VA Administration. Communicate it. Cooperate on the vetting process."

"I would love to help, but the—"

"I am not interested in why you don't think this will work—I am requesting your support in allowing us to find qualified people...people *here*."

The words puzzle Dawson as if he stands atop an abandoned map, leading to some treasure far away. "Bobby—can I ask why you are so interested in this group *here*? With the unemployment rate where it's at—even with the mill—I would think you would have little trouble finding people."

Cafferty draws a breath as his eyes scan the space, resting on each figure for a moment. A swirl of distressed parts, canvassed in fatigues and patches, simply exists, idling on fumes. The image stokes a still-smoldering ember within, men simply waiting, deemed too broken for use elsewhere but too young to die. "I knew a man once...and he wasn't unlike the men in this room. He deserved better."

"Bobby—I'll do whatever I can," mutters Dawson, still perplexed.

"Okay then."

An arm rises and falls just behind Cafferty, leaving a wake of symbols and numbers on the frosted white windowpane. Dawson cranes his neck and squints his eyes as if trying to decipher a code. "T-206, SS, kernels 33.... What is *that*.... Who is he?" asks Dawson.

"His name is Richard and he will be one of our first residents at St. Stanislaus," hushes Cafferty.

"You mean he's—he's too young, isn't he?"

Cafferty turns and observes Richard standing in front of the pane and briefly wonders what he is thinking.

Perhaps he is in front of a large class, teaching kids about some ancient civilization in Persia. Or any one piece of history that made him what he is, that gave him purpose. He looks content. "He's not much older than you or me," laments Cafferty. "That's the complexity of the disease and one reason why we need to raise awareness. Smaller towns, places like Ball Grove, are hit especially hard because of the lack of facilities and people specializing in it. They can fall through the cracks." Dawson ogles the figure, as if searching for scars, as the words float beyond him.

"Okay, then," says Cafferty. "I think we have a plan." Cafferty approaches Richard, whose fingertips now rest against the glass, the heat forming clear islands that reveal the street below. "Ooooh, look," he says, pressing his eyes against the makeshift peephole. Tiny beads of moisture collect along the brink of the islands until the weight forms a stream, trickling earthward.

"Like he's umm, crying."

"Are you ready, Richard?"

"Okay." He turns from his work and begins shuffling behind Cafferty as Dawson stares. Soon, Otis belches, announcing his arrival, eliciting giggles from the residents scattered about the third floor. Danny scowls. "Doesn't that shit ever get old to you?" he fires at the residents, finally settling his eyes on the departing pair. He glares at

145

the man who shuffles, staring at his shoes as if they have sandpaper for soles. *Ch-ch-ch-ch*, the sound rhythmically brushes the air.

"Pick your feet *up*," Danny spouts as Richard turns, his vacant eyes poking out from inside Otis. Danny's scowl retreats as he stares at the eyes, hollow and indifferent, pointing back at him. At once, Danny leans and squints hard at Richard as if searching for a keepsake at the bottom of a pond, the murky water clinging to a secret. He presses against the chair, reaching closer yet to the eyes, and observes a soft brown hue against the black holes. They flicker against the midday sun streaming through the clear little islands along the wall.

"Who *are* you?" he whispers, as the wheelchair bleats a pained squawk against Danny's body weight, nearly toppling. As the door slides shut, Danny drifts toward Dawson, pausing briefly before crossing the imaginary boundary neither has crossed. At once, he is struck by symbols, flashing like neon signs on a deserted highway. T-206, 4-5-4, and a backwards K leap from the pane, along with the fingertips of the creator. Just above the sill, lying like castoff parts, is a collection of letters: MEZHURE MANN.

"Hey, Dawsie," Danny blurts, his eyes affixed to the message in front of him.

"What do you want? You've never crossed over to this side of the floor since I have been here. Your new diet giving you a second wind, huh?" pans Dawson, his sarcasm atypically bland.

"Yeah, something like that. That nurse of yours has me springing leaks all over your floor with that right hand of hers."

146

Dawson, disinterested, ambles away from Danny.

"Hey—who was that group that just left?"

"Why do you give a shit?"

"Is he part of that new group off of Route Eight—the Alzheimer's thing?" Danny continues.

Dawson feigns a look of astonishment on his face. "So you *do* hear of things beyond your bubble, huh? Yeah, somewhere off of Route Eight."

"Who was the guy—the one that was drawing on the windows?"

"I have no idea, some guy—a young guy—I think his name was Richard something-or-other," says Dawson, now scurrying away from Danny, toward Otis.

"Jesus H. Christ," Danny whispers, staring at the very space occupied only moments earlier. "I don't even think he noticed me. He couldn't have, could he?" The voice breaks against the crush of uncertainty. As his mind races, his eyes flit about the room before turning upon himself. He examines his clothes, his arms, and his feet, as if he has been awakened from a coma and is uncertain of their state. Abruptly, he twists the wheels, shooting his being directly at the base of the symbol-laden sheet. He observes what, to any other, could masquerade as a desperate plea from an abandoned soul, washed ashore on a deserted island, counting sunrises and water rations as the sea taunts, its mist nipping at the sun-cracked face beneath. His eyes slip shut as his finger traces each, locked onto each angle and curve, as if rolling upon steel rails. As his eyes spring wide, he whispers. "Four-five-four...the Golden Egg." He claws at the castoff letters beneath, MEZHURE MANN, like it's dissonant babbling muddying a masterpiece until each is no longer visible. "There," he states. "Perfect."

Chapter 13

The following morning, Danny fidgets within his chair as if needled by burrs. "What are you doing? You look like you are a dog skidding his rump across the floor," she laughs.

"I'm tired of being so low in this goddamn seat...I want to be higher," he blurts.

"I've never seen you with this energy, at least not in years," Trixie marvels. She reaches into her faded denim coat as a muffled crackle tempts within.

"No, no more," he blurts. His hand presses across her breast-bone, trapping her arm within. "Listen, I want you to do something for me tonight."

"Honey, last time we tried, you couldn't do nothing. You just sat there, broke dick dog with your head slung low.... Then you wouldn't even pay—"

"Jesus, no," fires Danny with a glare, the audacity biting at his core.

He hisses. "I don't want none of that. And no booze either."

The woman looks dumbfounded. "Honey...what do you want then?"

"Well...you got a date tonight?"

"You aren't making a bit of sense. I always have dates and Christmas Eve is always big. Lots of men ain't got a Jesus or a Jessica giving them faith or fucking on Christmas Eve. It's funny—"

"Okay," he interrupts. "I just want you here with me. I don't want to be alone. Not tonight."

She looks at him, perplexed. "It's still gonna cost you the full time, I mean I ain't cutting no deals just because we ain't doin' nothin'."

"I know," says Danny. "But the other part of the deal is you don't say another goddamn thing about money. Just be *you, not this*," he states, as if pointing to a lewd costume. "Do you understand?"

She cocks her head and furrows her brow. "I think I do, Danny."

Later that night, the bus station lights buzz anxiously and fix a steely glare against the sheet beneath. The platform is deserted, scrubbed of its usual ilk and instead painted clean, if but for one evening. Red, yellow, and green traffic lights sprinkle the black sky as snowflakes gently lap the third-story window. Inside the VA, a skeleton crew mills about the first floor. They wear their greens and reds with a holiday cheer, but faces that suggest they'd rather be elsewhere.

Otis, sensing a change is in order, chirps and draws his metal curtain wide, releasing an unfamiliar face within. As she slips effortlessly across the tiles, Danny studies the woman. He is struck by the simplicity of her, a pleasantness that could not have been grasped previously. Her skin is vanilla-plain and neckline-free. The fire engine-red paste and faux gold chains, as prevalent as her DNA, gone.

White tennis shoes ease her feet instead of plastic red pumps choking her toes. Ankle socks suggest weekends of tennis rather than hustling.

But it's her hair, curly and buoyant, which causes him to stare. It no longer clings to her neck, adhered by sweat and tangled by violent throes. Rather, it breathes freely, dancing with her movement.

"Hey, Danny," she offers, pulling a chair from the nearby checkerboard table.

"Hello?" His voice peaks as he wears a dumb smile. "You look, um…normal, you know, very nice."

"That's very kind, Danny."

"You should stay just like that," he says.

The smile evaporates as she laughs sarcastically.

"You don't want to talk money and I don't want advice. Hey, if I had a nickel for every single time some daddy figure suggested I quit doing this—literally ten seconds after they choked me, slapped me, treated me as an object…" Danny slinks in his chair as she continues. "You know, right after they kissed their daughter's forehead and waved bye-bye at the Catholic school, all butterflies and rainbows—I would be wealthy."

"Touché."

"Throw your moral compass in the river," she finishes, robotically.

"Okay, okay, I got it. I promise you, never again. You do look beautiful, though." The words pacify her as she lofts a simple smile in his direction.

151

"Well, there is something I've always wanted to ask you: Can you at least tell me your real name? It's not Trixie…right?" he quips. They both giggle at the cliché.

"Trisa, my name is Trisa. You don't get the last name. Not even the cops have it," she sneers.

"Thank you, Trisa." The words trail off as the Christmas music wafts through the third-story vents. Minutes peck away at the hour as silence interrupts their space, hovering like a worrisome parent. Only the St. Stanislaus church bell, clanging an early mass chime, chases the silence for good. Trisa cranes her neck and stares at the window, obtuse symbols shrouded in white, nearly extinct.

"What are all those things over there?"

Danny fixes his gaze upon the window, third from his left, mindful of the art.

"I mean, they cannot be yours…you've never been over that way, right?" she inquires.

"You see that symbol right there?" he asks, pointing to the warrior homecoming sign. "Well, not sure what you know about the transcontinental railroad, but when the Burlington Santa Fe began building it, they disrupted many Native American tribes in the process. That sign right there is the Indian sign for 'homecoming' after a warrior made it back safely."

The woman looks perplexed by the drawing, and equally so by Danny's knowledge of what it means.

"Okay, so what about that funky-looking K."

"Yeah, that is the sign for a strikeout in baseball, one that the batter doesn't swing."

She laughs nervously. "Bullshit, you're making this up, right? Did you draw that?"

"I swear, I did not draw it," he responds, looking at another set of symbols.

"Okay, what about the four-five-four thing?"

"That is the Golden Egg right there," he beams. "That's magic, like Copperfield or something. It's when the baseball gods have aligned and granted a once-in-a-generation sighting. Kinda like a Haley's Comet, ya know?"

"What does it mean?" she says.

"Well, my son and I once—"

"Wait, you have a son? Are you married, you sicko? I asked you—"

"Jesus Christ, do I look married?" he rips, as a mist spatters the floor between them. "I told you how many years ago I wasn't married."

"Well, you never told me you had a kid," she retorts, as if a street rule has been shattered.

"I never told you because I left him—left them when he was eleven or so—I haven't seen or heard from them in three or four decades. They don't even know if I am alive," says Danny wistfully, rubbing his hands through greasy strands of hair.

"Anyway, I used to listen to Bob Prince, the play-by-play announcer for the Pirates. My son and I would score games together from the radio broadcast—you know, enter all the symbols, signs, for each play. It was our thing.

"One day, he got this big old grin on his face and asked me what was one play I had never seen or heard of in baseball. In my forty years of living, to that point, thousands of games, I thought I had seen just about everything. There had been perfect games—an amazing feat of poetry, and one that has to have a whole bunch of things happen right for nine innings."

He revs up, thinking of the feat, slamming his arm pad, and startling his companion. "Do you know a guy named Harvey Haddix threw twelve perfect innings—*twelve*…and still fucking lost! Can you imagine *that*? Talk about having bad luck…. Must have broken the goddamn mirror that morning!" he hoots.

"It doesn't sound perfect to me," she pans. "How does someone throw a perfect game and lose?" she groans. "Sounds kind of stupid." Danny ignores the jab and instead savors the paradox.

"But perfect games don't sneak up on ya. You can see them forming. All the little bounces go your way—you're coming up aces. It sounds stupid, but baseball is so much like the *game of life*," he states. "Both games start as nothing, just pure as can be. You got no errors, no hits, no at-bats, nothing…but over the course of that game, you're making catches, you're making errors. One day you're seeing

154

beach balls floating to home and the next, the ball looks like a god-damn Bayer aspirin, you know?"

The woman stares cluelessly.

"There has been a walk-off Game Seven home run. I mean, Maz's shot, even today, is still better than any drug, sex, lottery high! You had to have seen it, didn't you?" he blurts. "And beating the Yankees, oh God, beating those flashy bastards. The whole city went crazy!" he yells, inciting graveled hacks from his chest...

"But fairytales are funny like that. There's almost a deeper connection to the pursuit of the fairytale, that magical thing just beyond your reach that keeps you going, wrapped around the game's finger. I suppose it's like faith in some weird way. But that homer was one more fairytale that became reality.

"So, I was stumped when my son said again, 'Tell me a play you have never seen, something so crazy that we could experience it together for the first time, and if it happened, it would be more magical than Maz—it would be our fairytale.'

"I thought to myself for days and I came back with the most random, unlikely event. The 4-5-4 triple play. If you know anything about baseball, to even have the opportunity of making that magical play, your team has got to be in a world of shit, just flirting with disaster. Baserunners on second and third, no outs. One crack of the bat and it's a guaranteed two runs crossing that plate. But..." he pauses and shuts his eyes. "But instead, the batter *crushes* the ball and every person in the stands knows the ball is on its way to the deepest

155

gap in the outfield. Hell, those baserunners could *walk* home safely. Everybody in the park, that is, except for that second baseman. See, he shifted to the perfect spot on the infield, like he was born to stand in that spot. The ball is just sizzling to him like someone dumped a bucket of water on a grease fire. With one flick of that glove, he nabs that ball, and instantly the sizzle and fire disappear. Poof. Everyone in the stadium, including the baserunners, can only watch. They watch that second baseman toss it to third and the third baseman toss it right back to second, like they are little boys playing catch for the first time. 4-5-4. So damn simple, like a can o' corn." His eyes open and a simple smile hangs across his face.

"It was so dumb in hindsight. Such an impossible play that it will never happen in my next three lifetimes. Baseball has been around a *long* fucking time, Trisa. Zillions of games over the years so almost all of what could ever happen has happened. Stars have to align for that play to transpire, but unlike the perfect games, Maz's shot, this play would be quick, like lightning. No buildup, like in a perfect game, no anticipation and finality like on Maz's shot. It would just 'happen.' Some middle-inning, regular-season, Tuesday after-noon event, buried in a Buffalo Bisons game.

"But the very idea of it happening when you least expect it would have made it magical." Danny's eyes have drifted beyond the window, romanticizing a magical kingdom in a world beyond.

"That sounds kinda neat, I guess," says Trisa, the words lack-ing oomph.

"Anyway, that was our litmus test for truth—you never lied on the four-five-four swear. If he got in trouble and I had the slightest inkling he was lying, I would make him swear on the four-five-four."

She looks amused for a moment. "Like a pinky swear, right?" she says.

"Yeah, something like that."

"The day I called him in from the front yard—he and the neighbor boy were throwing the football—the day I got down on a knee and told him I was leaving the family, I swore I would never stop visiting, being a dad, watching him grow and play baseball. This was complete bullshit on my part. I knew I was running away from all of them for good. He had these awful big tears rolling down his face and he stuck out his hand and said, 'You swear on the four-five-four you mean that?'"

She looks at him and, after a pause, says, "Well, what did you tell him?"

"I told him yes, I swear on the four-five-four. I couldn't even look him in the eye, and as soon as I closed the car door, I never looked back."

Both sit in the quiet, watching the pitch-black night spit wafts of white at the window. Her brow creases as she looks back at the man.

"So, if you didn't write that, who put those on the window?"

Danny pulls his face away, huffing quietly down upon the bus station below. As he looks back, a fresh tear traces a path to the bottom of his chin. "Just a boy whose mind is sick," he says almost inaudibly, "but one who hasn't forgotten the truth."

Chapter 13

Herb Benson drags a thumbnail along the taut cellophane of an Altoids tin, unleashing a wintergreen current as frigid as the Ohio morning. He plucks a dusty mint and shoots it into his mouth, while surveying the orchestrated chaos in front of him. The mint pricks against his tongue, lashing the lingering remnants of stale brew. He twirls the caplet, channeling air through pursed lips, until the froth forces him to swallow. His mouth doesn't feel just clean, but *sanitized*. "Now, I am ready," he states with a conviction.

He shines like a diamond against the muddy slush, pulsing with contractors and heavy machinery. He slips by pods of men, toiling in work coveralls, until he reaches a flatbed burdened by shrink-wrapped windows. He cinches his tie and smiles straight against his reflection through a gash in the plastic. With a shiny black Tumi briefcase in hand, he patiently bides his time while grinding through more mints, awaiting Cafferty.

Soon, he is tapped on the shoulder by a man wearing a heavy peacoat. The top button is left undone, revealing a fresh pineapple ring around his collar. "Hi, I am Bobby. And you are either a lost or brave man," he states, nodding at the coat draped under the man's arm. "Spring's not revved up quite yet, at least not in Ohio."

"Hello, Bobby. My name is Herb Benson, and I am interested in your attendant positions," he states matter-of-factly.

"Well, that's great to hear, Herb, but we haven't even—"

"Yes, I understand, Mr. Cafferty." He slips his hand in the black Tumi briefcase, deftly plucking an ivory white resume, revealing his life's score.

"I understand you haven't started interviewing, but perhaps if I can borrow five minutes of your time.... Hope my name is fresh on your mind when you sort through half of the valley's resumes. I wouldn't take the initiative, and perhaps risk my chances, if I didn't believe I had something to offer *in person* rather than on paper."

Cafferty observes the slender man before him, noting the eagerness, the presentation, and the attention to detail. After all, he contemplates, the traits are the foundation for everything he has obtained. He notices the rich brown hair, its conservative styling, molded in place with what he surmises is pomade. His face is clean-shaven, almost slick in appearance, as if a barber removed a hot towel just moments prior. But it's the man's aura, the upward lift of his chin, that suggests a confidence destined for boardroom success, not a slop-laden construction yard.

"Not many folks are walking around Youngstown, job hunting, looking like you do," says Cafferty.

"Well, to be brutally candid, I don't necessarily want to blend in with the competition, if that makes any sense," he chuckles. "I arrived in Youngstown a couple of months ago, committed to finding the right opportunity. I have always been busy working. Pretty much done it all—welding, construction, mailroom sorter...hell, I even shoveled horseshit for the Detroit Fourth of July Parade," he states, his head nodding in affirmation. "But this time, it has to be different, not just taking anything that comes along." He extends a resume to Cafferty, who glances at the life's summary.

"You know you misspelled Saginaw on here?" says Cafferty, offering a slight smile at the faux pas.

"Ah, the coup de grâce of resumes," Herb moans. "The finesse of a farm animal at times, that's what my mom would always say. My apologies—the Kinkos on Gurney Road only has one computer, and half the town was lined up to use it."

"It's okay," offers Cafferty. "We all make mistakes."

"Indeed we do," offers Herb, settling again.

"I actually do have some time before the architects arrive today—you can walk with me and look at what we have done." Cafferty digs deeper into the resume, which is spattered with random jobs. An acronym flickers halfway down the page, arresting his eyes. L-M-C-A.

"Licensed memory care attendant—when did you receive the certification?" Cafferty asks, his voice now more businesslike.

"Well, I might as well give you the unabridged version, so to speak, as you will get the *Reader's Digest* version in the background check. I got canned from a welding job in Biloxi."

Cafferty hesitates, squaring to the younger man, his eyes rooted upon his. "You ever hear of an elevator pitch?" pans Cafferty. "Well, so far, you are stuck somewhere between the basement and the first floor."

The man budges, as if pinched, but steadies himself dead. He draws a lungful of crisp air and slowly releases breath colder than a ghost. Like a fleeting mirage, his shoulders unbuckle and erase any vision of doubt.

"When I got back from the war, me and the boys would go on these six-week gigs, you know, welding massive tanks. We would work sixteen-hour days, sweating every bit our body weight and then drinking every bit of that back on at night. And that's just the culture on the road; we all did it. Well, the foreman cut us loose early one day—we had a couple of fire-watchers not show up, so we couldn't weld. What else is there to do in Biloxi but drink or gamble?"

Cafferty observes the man, his composure *flourishing* under duress, his voice pastoral and grounded. He retrieves his Altoids tin and offers a mint to Cafferty. But Cafferty declines with a single wave as he searches for any fractures in the story. Without hesitating, the man flicks a mint and then swiftly tucks the metal box from sight.

"Of all the vices that changed otherwise good folks to scrap-heaps of themselves, so to speak, gambling never got its hooks in me. I don't gamble, Mr. Cafferty. I only take risks I *know* I can win," he says, wrapped in a wink.

"Herb, I want to hear you, but you still haven't gotten past the first floor," shoots Cafferty, a seriousness hanging in the air.

"Okay, I went on a pretty good tear one day and it was approaching five o'clock anyway. I was thinking the day was done. But I got called back to work. The fire-watchers had some engine problems, or something, but they did show back up. The foreman caught me wobbling on a ladder with the torch in my hand, which happens a hundred times a day on construction sites. I can spot-weld fillings in your molars even on my worst day. But this day, he was upset because we were behind on the schedule, so he came over and gave us some grief, asked a few questions, and the next thing I knew, I was giving blood at some clinic.

"Now he had a *serious* case of the ass with me, and two days later, I had no job."

The words distress Cafferty, but still, he wonders. "Okay, so why memory care?"

"Losing that job was a slap to the face, a wakeup call for me," says Herb, toeing the ground in front of him. "It's not easy admitting you have a problem. Not just any problem, but *that* one. If I didn't get that wakeup call, there's no telling where I would have ended up, maybe dead. I swore that off forever, and for the first time I realized how much empty space was in here." He thumps against his chest.

"Memory care was a way for me to help others, while at the same time pursuing something that could repair this," he says, again tapping his chest. "How do I say it?" A smile forms. "Enrichment."

"I think I understand the rationale," says Cafferty.

Herb continues, "I had no idea how prevalent dementia was until I started studying to ready myself for the certification. God knows this facility will be filled in no time. When you have time,

163

please look at my rehab program in Arizona, references and all." He fans the papers, various fonts and letterhead flapping by.

Cafferty waves at the papers. "Not for now, Herb. All in due time," he mentions, offering a nod.

"Tell me, have you ever had any loved ones impacted by dementia? Not as an attendant, but as a son or a nephew?"

Herb clears his throat. "Bobby, I left my house far too early to know what happened to any of my relatives. Heart attack, cancer, a bolt of lightning? Maybe one day I will research my family tree and piece together what became of them. Because people *should* know what happened to 'family.' Then again, sometimes fate's arc dictates whether you should overturn a rock or not," Herb offers, a hint of sting in his voice.

"What I do know is I spent the better part of seven years changing sheets, bathing, playing checkers, sharing dinner and holidays with residents. In some cases, I was the last person they saw in a sea of confusion, creatures of the murkiest deep circling around them. I want to believe—have to believe—they died with some degree of comfort, with me around them when no one else was."

Cafferty surveys Herb as if searching for marks, like scars, bearing veracity of such claims. "Do you feel like you provide them some dignity in death?" Cafferty asks.

"Dignity?" offers Herb. "You mean like in validation therapy?" Herb peers at the ground and grinds the last mint into a frigid dust. "I don't think dignity, Mr. Cafferty. Compassion, for sure, and I do believe they sensed that, they were *comforted* by that. But in some peculiar way, I think something else happens: Empathy. Empathy of the disease which stole the very people they once were." Herb gently nods as he mulls over his own theory.

Herb continues, "I watched a beautiful, talented musician— she was a cellist in the Detroit Philharmonic—morph into a caricature of one of those monkeys playing the cymbals. Do you remember that toy, that eerie, frozen smile on its face, the unblinking eyes?"

Cafferty nods. "I do remember it."

"Well, I had breakfast with her for about a year and we spent her last birthday listening to her recording at the Kennedy Center. Just the two of us.

"This was the same woman people paid small fortunes to see perform for years. She was invited to play at *royal* ceremonies, and not because she posted the online video of the week," he pans with air quotes. "She got invited because she was the best. Hell, she even had a coffee drink named after her in the Michigan market. Imagine a cellist being hip enough for the twenty-somethings." He laughs.

"Everyone wanted to be around her, until one morning, they didn't. She became a senile bat, crazy loon. Some said she was on drugs. They would do a parody on those night shows after she started cussing during interviews. Do you remember Kaitlyn Folger?"

Cafferty nods his head. "Yes, Cuckoo Katy. I do," he says, with a hint of regret in his voice.

"She was *finally* diagnosed in early 2000. No one ever came to see her again—not her brother, not the media that had once dubbed her 'the Debussy Darling.' I would take my guitar and play for her each night before bedtime, even learned one of her compositions. Er, at least a dumbed-down version. Took me six weeks, and a ton of struggle, that piece of hers on a beat-up Gibson, strings as high as telephone wires. She watched me fail and work, just like she had done writing it.

"But one night, I made it through its entirety, not a bum note. She nodded to me and squeezed my hand and smiled, like she *did* recognize *that*," he gushes, bubbling within, pushing mist into his eyes. "I believe that was the final moment of 'the Debussy Darling,' her soul, spirit, being, whatever you call it, leaving this world.... She turned toward the window, staring off into the black beyond. Do you know what became of her?" he asks, his voice slipping. "She wandered off and froze to death. She was found two days later behind a paper recycling plant in Detroit.

"I honestly believe those experiences, the last moments of empathy during death, are not found on a resume or in an interview. Empathy, Mr. Cafferty, is what I try to provide. So dignity? I hope to witness that someday." The candor and emotion tug at Cafferty, his heart leaning hard against his chest. Cafferty rubs his square jaw as he considers Herb's statements.

He recalls the moment his mom's health absconded, pneumonia commandeering life's course, and ponders what it would have

166

been like to die alone. Would the soul still have slipped forth, dancing freely atop the wind? Or would it have remained trapped within her body, like smoke swirling within a bottle, banging against the glass until it simply faded away?

Cafferty's heart soothes as his mind cues that final moment again. *I was there*, he thinks, so hard that the words almost break the seal of his lips. "Thank you, Herb. We will likely begin hiring in the next few weeks and I am sure one of our staff will set aside a more formal interview." He extends his hand to Herb, embracing a surprisingly delicate shake, one suggesting finesse rather than brute force.

"Thanks, Bobby. Any openings you have, I can start anywhere—construction gopher—until the positions are open." Cafferty walks Herb out the door and offers a quick wave as he focuses on pressing tasks and timelines.

Chapter 14

Cafferty peeks at Richard as his hands snare a trifold pamphlet entitled "Global Deterioration Scale—Dementia, Know the Stages." He worries about the sudden shift in Richard's personality, a Jekyll and Hyde assortment of delusions and frustration. The threadbare filter, once marginally effective, is leaky.

Words, charged by the silent conflict within, now chamber and discharge indiscriminately, tearing at the wrong target. "It's the anger," Richard whispers to Lizzie, who clinically observes Richard. "My mom had frustration, but…I don't know if it was the medication or her age." He pauses, struggling to understand. "I don't know, this is different," he whispers.

"As far as the stages, home health support is no longer adequate. He needs the full-care assisted living, your facility, Bobby."

Cafferty nods while pondering the figure across the room, what he even knows about his current state.

It's as if he's standing in the middle of a rickety old bridge, strung across this long canyon, and it's being tossed about by a gale-force wind. One side of the bridge is on fire. The flames consume the rope, the wooden slats, the land at the end of the bridge. They inch closer and closer to him, ashes falling like snow into the valley so far below…but behind him, in the opposite direction, there is no fire, the rope is taut, the slats are untouched, and most interestingly, there are familiar faces beckoning him to run to the land's edge. But he doesn't know how to turn around; he only knows "to be." He curses and slaps at his head. What is it? The slats, the fire, the height? Is it recognition of the rope sizzling in the inferno, millions of threads hissing as they snap, foretelling his certain doom and that he still comprehends fear? Or is it that he cannot remember how to step just high enough to clear the rope handles, pitching himself into the gorge below? He doesn't move; only waits as the ashes fall.

Cafferty hears a phone ring behind the office desk, snapping him back to the present. "Richard, would you like to use the restroom before we meet the doctors?"

Richard fumbles an oversized Magic 8 ball, chirping at the unmoving die within. "Fuck—stop!" booms Richard, twisting his head away from the ball as if that will shake the die loose. Stares focus on his struggle. One woman can't be bothered and conceals her face with a newspaper spread wide.

He slams the ball on a heavy oak coffee table, sending cracks across the window of fortune. Cafferty dabs at tiny dots of blue plasma, spattered from the blow, as if covering a crime scene. "May I give it a try?" says Cafferty. He plucks the ball and gives it a gentle shake. Bubbles jumble against the fractured window, obscuring the die within. As he places the ball on the table, the black soothsayer is noncommittal: "Hazy, try again."

"Hmm. Well, Richard, this toy knows more than I do about where this all goes." He gently shakes the ball again.

"What would you like to ask it?"

169

"Wha-what do I what?" snipes Richard, confused by the request.

"Did you want to ask the ball a question?"

"A ball? But why? No! He won't stop looking at me," says Richard crossly.

"Who won't stop looking at you?" whispers Cafferty, scanning the room. Richard turns his head away and glares sideways at the ball. He shoots his finger against the glass as if trying to poke the eye of a beast.

"There! In there!" he spits, nearly knocking the ball from Cafferty's hand.

"Oh. It's no one, Richard. It's just a toy that says different things when you shake it. See, watch."

He shakes it again, revealing "Ask again later" from the cloudy, blue liquid, now staining his fingers. "Sounds about right," whispers Cafferty. He reaches past an anxious Richard, setting the ball on the bookshelf. "Okay, that's enough of this for now."

"I just don't want to be here anymore," whimpers Richard, the words marinating in the silence.

A nurse peeps out from behind the sliding glass window. "Hello, Richard?" Her voice is decorous, a soft chime in contrast to the anxious current that buzzes like a frayed circuit. Cafferty rises and extends his hand, cueing the man to follow. Richard stands and lurches with each step. *Ch-ch-ch-ch.* His feet chisel at the tile as if speed bumps litter his path. Soon, a shoelace slithers free and drags behind.

A doctor, carrying a clipboard and swallowed by a white lab coat, greets the group as Lizzie secures the lace with a firm tug. Richard stands listlessly, observing the man.

"Good morning, everyone, I am Dr. Bowden. I have the full workup on Richard here—brain imaging, MMSE, and general wellness." His voice is instinctive as his eyes squint and pore over the data in front of him. "I'll discuss these results in a second, but I'd like to run a few brief tests first." He slides a chair toward his patient and slips a blank piece of paper upon the desk. "Hello, Richard. Would you mind if we tried something? I would like you to remember three words for me, okay? Pencil. Street. Train. Did you get that? Pencil. Street. Train. Keep those words right here"—he motions to the front of his head—"while we complete an exercise, okay?

"Now, would you please take this pen and draw three o' clock for me?"

Cafferty braces himself as he recalls Richard's last attempt. *It looked like a ball of ice cream, plopped on a sidewalk, melting underneath the midday sun. No structure, just a flabby ball being consumed by a swelling pond of itself, symbols sprinkled in for good measure.* His fingers grope the pen as if fighting a giant monkey wrench. As the three await, he pushes hard against the desk's surface and tears the paper beneath.

"Whoa, sorry about that," the doctor offers, snaring the pen. He depresses the plunger, exposing the shiny, silver barb. "Here, let's try that again. This is the tip—"

"I know!" snaps Richard. "I am retarded, a fff-fucking retard," he screams, the blunt self-assessment assailing both men across the brow.

"Richard, you are not retarded, and I hope you believe me when I say that," Bowden assures, his voice measured. "From what I understand, you were a tremendous teacher. You have a disease that makes these tasks tough. Even so, nothing—not this disease, or any other—will ever tarnish those great things you have accomplished, because—"

"I'm a teacher?" interrupts Richard.

"You weren't just a teacher, you were a *history* teacher," the strange voice reaffirms. "I simply want to make sure we can get the right path forward for you. Now, can you try and draw it for me?"

"What? Draw what?"

"Can you draw a clock, and place the time at three o'clock? This dot." He fetches a felt tip pen and etches a large, black dot in the middle. "This is where the hands will come from. Now, can you draw the other numbers around the clock?"

As his eyes bore into the dot, Richard grips the pen. His fingers slowly blanch as the blood ebbs like a drought-stricken riverbed. Panic courses through his face along a cobweb of striations, carved by the enduring hands of anxiety. Frustration simmers as he strangles the tool, as if its death is his only chance of survival. The black dot mirrors him, goading him to fight. While the room is silent, a splitting clamor ricochets within his mind, causing him to wince.

The black dot prods again. A gnarled finger extends from within, fixing Richard's back against the chair. "Think of a clock, Richard," the voice drones. The words shatter between his ears and tear at his mind.

"That's right, Richard, ten…eleven…. Take your time, but use numbers, in order." This time, the words fade as they are consumed by a hidden din. The black dot smirks as it feeds on the struggle, siphoning every drop of resistance and transforming it into a wave of fear. Soon, soot-blackened hands slither around his throat and constrict until air whooshes from his lungs.

I'm dying! I…can't…breathe, he screams silently within, his pulse bleating against an unmovable force.

"Take your time, Richard. Just start at the black dot and make…" The voice fades again. The black dot pulses, mirroring the fading heartbeat, slower, then slower yet. The clamor within wanes, until there is nothingness, no pulse, no senses, just a void as if floating in space.

A voice breaks the air with a static so dissonant and corroded, it sounds as if lashed by demons and crushed glass.

"You. Can't…do it…can you? You will never know time again." Gooseflesh erupts on the back of Richard's neck and trickles along his spine, like a current, pricking the flesh numb. "Just as you will never tie your shoes again."

"Who ARE YOU!" Richard screams in his mind.

"Who am *I*," the voices hisses. "I...am...you. I have crept within every nook of your body since the beginning. Every night you slept, every breath you drew, I *took pieces* of you. Every memory you had, your job, your family, and your legacy. I fashioned you into *us*," the voice spits.

"And for as long as you breathe, I will take from you. I will take until your only desire is for the end to come. And yet the world will use every desperate deed—drugs, service animals, prayer warriors, and denial—to prolong *their* hope. They will do all this against your will, and do you know why? You...can't...tell them!" The voice quivers with excitement and gasps for breath.

"*That's* the pearl! Not death itself, no, no, no. But the journey of decay, every episode of your life smoldering in front of you until you have nothing but ashes. That very moment before you lose recognition of *you*!" jabs the little voice. Richard trembles. Tears trace otherwise lifeless features as they roll down his chin. His lungs suck and hands combust, scoring the paper's surface with violence. He glares at the nameless bully, now wearing white instead of black. The little black dot shrieks at him from the paper.

"That's it, Richard! Fucking do it. *They* will never let it end!"

The pen shoots toward the ceiling as if yanked by marionette strings and plunges into the outstretched hand he shook moments earlier. The skin explodes, painting the table black and red.

"Goddamn it!" howls the doctor, as he retracts his hand moments before the second spike lands. Cafferty bursts from his chair and restrains a tremulous hand against the table.

"Jesus, Richard—are you okay?" begs Cafferty, ignoring the doctor's groaning.

"Maybe that's enough for now?" offers Lizzie. Richard quivers and sobs, his tears mixing with the black and red speckles on the tattered page. The blood flickers against the fluorescent rays from above, like callous eyes chastising the condemned.

"It's going to be okay, Richard," the doctor groans, dabbing at his wound. He nods toward the remote corner of the room, where the three go to huddle.

"So, this won't come as a surprise to you," he whispers, "but Richard's scores—both the MMSE and the FAST scores—are concerning. Those tests, the wandering, incontinence, sleep disturbances, anxiety, outbursts, would likely place him in the latter portion of stage six on the GDS. He still has some verbal ability, although this will fade as well. The delusions and outbursts," Bowden says, offering a bloody hand wrapped in gauze, "can be quite complicated, dicey. He will—"

"Yes, I think I understand," utters Cafferty. "I lost my mom to this not long ago. She caught pneumonia before she lost the rest of her speech. I don't know, maybe that was for the better," Cafferty says wistfully.

175

As Cafferty contemplates the road ahead, he stares at the man in white. The doctor's lips ripple with a mechanical process borne of familiarity and acceptance. Pharmacuetic cocktails and subsequent hangovers leak from his lips and compete for the highest ground in a flooding valley. "The hallucinations, diarrhea, hostility, Haloperidol, Risperidone, anti-psychotic, strokes, Clozpine…" The deluge continues as prescriptive corks barter for time with an overwhelmed dyke. All the while, Richard sits quietly, staring at an ink-wash rendering of the human brain.

"Death," says Bowden, snapping Cafferty back to the present.

"What?" shoots Cafferty.

"Death. While uncommon, it is a side effect with some treatments."

"Isn't that the shittiest irony," snips Cafferty. "You fight like hell to live, and this thing, this parasite, sucks the soul from you. You cannot even remember how to die." He pauses for a moment, eyeing Richard, transfixed by the art. "Well, that's exactly why I want to fight this thing. I suppose that's any disease, to an extent, but this one"—his voice hesitates, stabbing at the struggle—"this one is different."

Dr. Bowden nods while contemplating the path forward. "We will send the prescriptions over, but I also would like to move forward with additional, nonpharmacologic behavioral management initiatives. Does he have any photo albums, personal items?"

"I have a box from his sister, has a few things in there. An old Lionel train," says Cafferty.

"Well, does he ever pull the items out or speak of them?"

"The home assistance staff said he pulls out a few old magazines, but generally wanders off not too long after. He plays with an old radio I gave him, but not for music. Just kinda flips around on the AM static, never settling on anything but ballgames if they are on."

"How is your facility coming along?"

"It's moving. The staff have relocated here and are basically awaiting the facility opening."

"Well, perhaps you should start some of the work with Richard now. It certainly won't hurt him."

Cafferty nods. "That will be my first request of the team. We will get him the best help we can." Cafferty avoids the wrapped hand and pats the doctor's shoulder instead. He spins to collect Richard, but instead finds the door gaping wide.

"Richard?" Cafferty rushes to the waiting area, nearly tripping over Richard, who sits peacefully, crisscross style just past the door. A *Sports Illustrated* rests in his lap, as his breathing is long and even. He slips next to Richard, careful not to startle. "Hey, buddy, what are you reading?" A lush green canvas greets his eyes, an idyllic green acreage befitting a king's estate. However, no castle exists, just the lushest of bright green earth. One golden fleck bursts from the page, like the sun fallen from the sky. As Cafferty fixes his stare on the gold, he realizes he is viewing a baseball player's cap. The figure

177

stands in the outfield, anticipating the thunderous crack of an ash. Cafferty gently thumbs the cover and whispers the title: "America's Game: Opening Day Countdown." Cafferty is mystified at the paradox, as if the gods are playing a game. *Words escape this man. He is consumed by anxiety as he fights to remember...yet, a simple painting of grass and a ballplayer speaks volumes, stories so clearly. It is as if the world hit a reset button, went back thousands of years, and spoke the same universal language. Uncomplicated, nothing lost in translation.*

Cafferty observes Richard intently. The incessant striations scoring his jaw have retreated, leaving his face momentarily unruffled. "What are you thinking, buddy?" Cafferty whispers to the silent man.

Richard traces the foul lines on the page, completely immersed in the green. His eyes have slipped shut, as he has settled his feet in an imaginary batter's box, his right foot carving a valley so deep, nothing could ever topple him again. His hands are glued to the bat, and intoxicating pine tar nips at his nose as a smile forms against his face. Five-point-two-five ounces of rawhide. "That's it...I don't need anything else." The words echo within him. "Richard, can you hear me?"

Silently, he tracks his finger around the base path, savoring every inch of maroon clay. His finger pushes a wide arc around third base and adjusts a beeline for home. He taps home plate and stands erect, chest puffed in front of forty-five thousand people. He exhales.

Cafferty is taken by the moment and awaits patiently, imagining. Minutes pass. "What did you see?"

As the scene fades within his mind, his eyes crack wide. His voice is clear... "My dad."

"I want this thing lookin' pretty—buff her up like it's her wedding day," fires Dawson. A set of eyes far above peers down from behind fogged goggles. The young man turns as if standing atop a house of cards; the slightest movement would send him plummeting to the pavement below. Carefully, he flips the compressor's switch, priming a throaty growl, labored as if awakened from hibernation.

Soon, the reluctant machine settles into a steady purr, ripping the morning air with a punch. *Ch-ch-ch-ch-psssssss. Ch-ch-ch-ch-pssssssss.* The man offers a nod and points the silver-tipped muzzle at the awaiting target. Instantly, an angry hiss lashes the facade, flicking pieces of worn brick into the sky as a rust-colored mist falls on the sidewalk beneath.

"Hey!" booms Dawson. "Not too close—you'll carve the goddamn thing, not clean it."

"Can you turn down the pressure?" begs the man over the growl.

"Nope, this thing is older than you are. You're gonna have to make do—

just use some finesse."

The worker leans heavily against the scaffolding, affording the silver tip more distance from the building's face. He releases the surge again, this time unmasking a fire-red and gray latticework. The rebirth pastes a lustful smile across Dawson's face. "This is my favorite part," he mutters, hypnotized by the muzzle's methodical sway back and forth against the surface. "Eighty-some years of grit and shit rolling down the face of that building. It will look brand new, even alive, by the end of today," he vows with a mortician's flair.

"You have done good work," offers Cafferty. He peeks at the man above and reflects on the bright red swaths, aglow as if they just arrived from the kiln. His eyes follow the cascade of ripples tumbling over each imperfection, coursing its path along the building wall, waning to a slow trickle against the base. Soon, a gritty cinnamon stream winds along the curb and disappears into a nearby drain.

"That's eighty years of history that shaped its character, both the good and, well, some not," Cafferty states. "I guess watching it wash away in the time it takes to drink a coffee seems kind of—" He struggles for the word. "I don't know—too fast, in some weird way?"

Dawson mulls over the comment. "Jesus, Bobby. I didn't mean it like that, but I got to clean the thing, right?" he laments with a scent of a martyr. "Now you got me feeling all weird about it, you standing here and all. What am I supposed t—"

"What are you going to do with this part?" Cafferty shifts, motioning to a corner piece that looks as if an animal has bitten it in a fit of rage.

Dawson approaches and reads the steel girder stamping: "YS—How the hell have I walked into this building for months and not seen that? Better yet, how did my foreman not see it? I've got to patch it up somehow."

Cafferty thumbs the insignia, its precise edges still discernible after so many years. "Girders like these were built by my granddad, my father, along with a few thousand others, right there," he says, pointing beyond, toward the mill. In an instant, the discussion is halted by a screech and a thunderous boom from a nearby flatbed. "Holy good God, Nixon," yells Dawson at the laborer. Chalk-white drywall rests in a heap on the blacktop, shattered from the fall. "Let's go. Let's get this shit picked up and get a new load. Jesus."

Dawson ignores Cafferty and the girder as he assesses the damage. Cafferty rubs the cinnamon grit between his fingers as his eyes observe the stilled figure occupying his truck. Richard sits, un-blinking, ogling the dingy stream trickling from the structure above him and disappearing into the netherworld below.

Inside, Otis huffs and deposits a squeaking wheelchair onto the first floor. "Danny, is that you? Oh my gosh, write this day down," pans Abby. "You've made it to your appointment, and on time—actually *early*. If they'd let me hand out golden stars, I'd give you one."

Danny offers a smile, one unburdened.

"Thank you, Abby. I'm trying."

"You look, um…something is different." Abby eyes the figure and settles on his head. "Your hair—it's, uh, puffier or something."

"You know that soap in the bathroom—at least I think it's soap…I got tired of the hair sticking to me and gave it a scrub." The hair is frayed and dry, like fibers in an old rope falling apart. Errant

182

strands oscillate, pushed about by the subtle furnace current. Abby gently presses the strands against his head as if hurriedly readying a child for school pictures.

"You are passable for someone who gives a damn," she states with admiration.

"Yeah, yeah," he snips. "Maybe I am here interviewing nurses with better aim." Before the comment can stick, Danny's mouth opens. "Listen, that wasn't fair. Didn't mean it at all, Nurse."

She cocks her head and squints her eyes. "What can I do for you, Danny."

"Look. I'm shit with words." He pauses. "I don't know if it was our talk the other day or if someone placed you in my life. You know, like they talk about guardian angels and stuff? Like a lifeline to whatever good I have left?" he offers as Abby's squint disappears. "You know I am not religious."

"Ah, yes," she sighs with disappointment. "You and that street urchin that drops by to see you when your Social Security hits. When are you going to give that stuff up, Danny?"

Danny takes a deep breath and fingers errant strands of white, wispy hair into order. "Yes, she does visit, and I like when she does. But I can still do good. That new memory care facility, you know the one off of Rouseville Road? They are looking for employees this whole week, for entry-level tasks. Like the kitchen, maintenance, laundry, etc. Stuff like that. You have to get pre-qualified, though, meet with the administration, HR. Like..." He pauses and closes his

183

eyes. "Interview," he grumbles. "You know I don't move around well, have these special care needs…but I really want to give it a shot." His voice fades as he looks at the ground. "I think I have some good left in me, and I can't take it where I'm going when the ride's over."

Abby appears stunned. "What made you decide this? You know what? Who cares? I think it's a fantastic idea. This is the most energy I have seen from you since I met you. And you want to do *good*! Of course, this"—she motions to his rickety carriage—"there would be some stuff we would have to work around. So what do you need from me?" she responds, her astonishment fleeing.

"Well, they have these courses to prepare for a licensed attendant of some sort, like a practitioner. That will take a lot of time, studying…but I figure, if I *start* them, it would be one better than the other folks in here." He pats the chair's handle, as if convincing himself of the strategy. "But I need access to a computer to sign up, do the video training and all. Hell, I need a resume or something. You know we have no computers up there," he says, motioning to the third floor. "Dawson would shit a Volkswagen laughing if I told him about this."

"We do have two visitors' cubes here for VA personnel," she chimes in. "But no one from the administration even comes here. You know Dawson can be a—"

"Dick," Danny chimes in.

"Yes, he can be quite tough. So no one comes here anyway. I can set aside an hour or so, maybe even tie it into your feeding time just to be safe," she says smugly, as if planning a coup.

"Thank you kindly, Nurse. This means a great deal to me, you trying to help me." He offers a hand. "Deal?"

She presses her hand within his and offers a firm shake.

"By the way, that woman—the one I hear people call a street urchin or dog? She hasn't brought me anything stronger than a Coke since before Christmas."

The words perplex the woman before him, causing her brow to bunch up.

"And I didn't give up drinking, not by a long shot...I love the *process* of losing control, that deconstruction. That total absolution of self, responsibility, and what life has not become. No one spoon-fed me mantras to repeat, like some parrot, until one day, I convinced myself to stop. No, not at all. The drinking gave up on *me*, man. Like *it* woke up one day, descended the same dungeon steps it had for fifty years, stepped over yellowed photos of my family, and observed me chained to a cold, stone wall. *It* looked at the cuffs hanging so loosely around my wrists, like big old rusted hula hoops. They were sliding off of me, clanging onto the floor. I kept trying to put them back on, trying to bend the metal around my wrists, digging them into my skin until they bled. But they kept slipping off.

"I begged *it* to tighten the screws, nail me to the wall, anything to keep me where I was, like some little pet in a box. It just looked at me and said, 'I'm *tired* of watching you die.' And that was it: drinking quit me."

He draws a breath and rubs fading blotches on his forearms. "And you know that street urchin? She hasn't touched me for over two years. You know what she does? She listens to me, like you. That's it. You know what I love about her?" His words are stunning the nurse.

"She will never lie to me, doesn't pretend to be anything but what she is. A lawyer, a priest, teachers…hell, parents lie to their kids all the time. I did for seventy-eight years and here I am, a twelve-step recovering liar," he huffs, teasing stray fibers from his arm pad.

"Have you ever fed a lie to a patient that deep down you knew was dying—like an IV drip of bullshit? You knew they would never see the sun come up again, and they were begging you to tell them everything was gonna be okay? Have you ever?" says Danny, looking her straight in the eyes.

"Yes, Danny, I have. You don't understand what it's like to have that fear, the greatest fear, running through someone, and you are responsible for the last words they hear. It's real tough, you know, so I—I have told them they would make it through the night. Some-times"—she looks out the window—"when I walk down Liberty Street, I apologize to ghosts that pass me."

"It's okay," Danny soothes. "I will never know how hard your job is, especially dealing with someone like me. But you are one of two women in my life. She has been very good to me when no one

186

would. So have you. You have helped me in more ways than I will ever know how to say." He pats her hand and whispers, "Thank you." A boom fills the first floor as Danny laughs at the absurdity of his thought.

"If you would have told me at seventy-eight years old I would end up with a nurse on one arm and a hooker on the other, I would have written a far more interesting story." She looses her bonobo giggle while slapping Danny's shoulder. A glint flicks about Danny's eyes as he motions for the nurse to lean in. "Now, show me how shitty you are with your aim again—I'm feeling pretty tired."

A few blocks from the clinic, a little girl with a sketchpad sits beneath a venerable oak in front of the steel mill. The oak towers over her, affording a safe haven, like a gratified grandparent admiring the steady strokes appearing on the page. Its crooked fingers pitch in each direction, carefully navigating thick cables while reaching for the sky. Stocky, withered roots have muscled the heavy concrete, now fragmented and formed into dangerous crags. At the cusp of its figure stands a single, bright green shoot, lapping the midmorning rays with vigor.

Off in the distance, a rolling thunder builds, harassing a car alarm until it finally barks. Soon, silver tubes flicker against the sun as they break the hill's crest, exhaling puffs of black exhaust against the blue sky. Others break the crest one by one while their silver tubes puff a cadence to the engine's grumble. A smattering of curious eyes follow the commotion and soon trail behind the no-frills parade of metal.

Unsteady materials rise from the truck beds and thrust against the cargo straps, blanching the yellow ties white. Soon, the rumble cuts and a man descends the lead semi, wearing a hard hat and carrying tubes of blueprints. A smile flashes about his face as he spots Cafferty approaching.

"*Bom dia*, my friend," states Helio.

"Hello, Helio. Today is a pretty big day for you?"

"It is a big day for us, and I'd like to think for Youngstown as well."

"I would like to introduce you to a friend of mine, Richard." Richard's eyes survey the payload, mirroring a small city sitting atop the mobile units. "Richard, this is my friend Helio."

"Hello," mumbles Richard, his eyes still tracking the ridges.

"Hello, Richard. I have heard a great deal about you and am pleased to meet you. I have a special favor to ask you." Richard shuffles against the thawed ground as he seeks the source of the request. "We have to break ground on our new site, and I would love for you to help me. Would you like to do that?" Helio asks, handing the shovel to Richard.

"Ummm, wh-what do I do?"

Helio unlocks a padlock on the outer gate and the men follow him onto the mill proper, a local beat writer lagging behind. A scatter of eyes peer through the chain-link fence as the men form a small circle.

"I did not want to make the groundbreaking a big deal—to me, it's more important when we produce our first order. Here, this spot is as good as any," offers Helio, motioning to a chasm in the pavement that reveals muddied earth below. He pauses, patiently awaiting the writer, who fidgets with a smartphone camera and small notepad, unworried by the significance.

Helio cites the Youngstown rebirth, occasionally citing his colleague's assistance. Richard wrings his hands as his body sways back and forth to some unseen catalyst, prodding him to move. The shovel slips from against his body and slaps the ground below. Images and sounds course over him like a bloated river, as his brain sifts the contents for anything of value. Lost, he sinks to his knees with a heavy thud, ogling the split in the pavement. At once, the dissonant tension hushes, as if he has plummeted through the surface into a world of his own.

His fingers grapple the cold earth, scooping gobs and placing it on the shovel, blind to the world circling around him. The men observe Richard as if watching a child play at the beach rather than an adult digging in filth. The pyramid inches skyward with each scrape of the fingertips, spellbinding the men who hover above.

Helio squints at the man beneath him, as if trying to locate the puppeteer commanding the movements. But there are no cables, no platforms, or smiling children nearby to shed light on this grand ruse, only a man rolling mud through his fingers. For the first time, Helio encounters the veiled tormentor of which Cafferty spoke. He clears his throat against a silent backdrop.

"That's it, perfect, Richard. Your work ethic and hands are the very reason why we will succeed here."

Richard sinks backwards, like a turtle preparing for the unknown hand upon its back. "Who are you?" murmurs Richard, as his hands dip back into the soggy terra. Helio sinks to a knee next to Richard, eventually sitting on the cold muck.

"May I help, Richard?"

"Yes," says Richard, smiling at the stranger. The men sit alongside each other, silently, working toward some collective epilogue of realization. Cafferty can't help but think about generations of immigrants landing in the same spot many decades ago, chasms of cultures and skin types between them. Languages and lunches as different as night and day, but each steelworker showing up alongside the other to work, to live, and to build a hope for tomorrow. He smiles at the site, and the thoughts he tucks away inside his mind.

A few days later, the *Youngstown Press*, the last surviving newspaper in the city, readies its trucks for delivery. The once-heavy stack is now gaunt, wracked by cheaper mediums and the inability to adapt for the new generation. For months prior, persistent rumors of a closure chased writers, photographers, floor workers, even meter engineers into retirement, a fact not lost upon management or the community. With a last-gasp effort, the paper launched a "YOU

Make the News" campaign, pandering to children and amateur artists alike, the successful submission garnering a front-page spotlight. As the first delivery slaps the liquor store sidewalk, bold type spits the sign of the times in a staccato bark: "Hedging the future, teachers prepare to strike." "Baseball is finally here—Indians and Pirates head to Spring Training."

Occupying the entire lower half, thick black font spreads about the empty white like an oil slick. "YOU Make the News" beams forth, dwarfing the headlines above. A sketch hangs beneath the font, one man attired in blue jeans and a white shirt sitting across another in khakis, a pair of shoelaces sinewy and limp against the ground. They both are gazing into a chasm, as if from the mezzanine, as they observe the final act playing out from the obscured depths below. Their hands, calloused and muddied from the work, rest atop their knees. There, almost indiscernible, lies a message buried within the freshly stacked dirt: "He is one of us"…signed, "A girl who cares."

All about the city, sunlight pokes through clouds of spun silk, gently lapping the faces below. Children's laughter fills the sky, as the final bell clangs and ushers in the start of spring break. Window blinds begin a measured retreat, inching higher and higher into the window frames until they settle for their annual hibernation. The cardinal warmth coaxes smiles from almost everyone, except, that is, for Otis.

As the warmth penetrates his shaft, he begins to bloat. His recesses catch against themselves like displaced bones, forcing grunts, gasps, and a bitter refusal to share in revelry. His fondness for clowning is gone, even at the most inappropriate time, and instead he groans with each passing second.

Across town, Cafferty studies a vast fish tank, set within a two-story entry wall of the St. Stanislaus MCF. He cocks his head, scanning the entirety for any stray blemish on the glass or bubbles within, any tip-off that the fish indeed are not artificial, suspended by a razor-thin filament. "Doesn't even look possible," he whispers to himself as he strains to see the water line obscured by the flush mounted wall.

As a figure approaches, a tetra caroms wildly, rippling the sandy bottom beneath and firing a shockwave through the crystal-clear space. "Good morning, Mr. Cafferty," the voice bubbles, reeling him back to the present. Cafferty twists to find a youthful man, his face beaming and quivering with excitement. Nearby, a small pack of workers chat, their voices buoyant.

"Good morning, Mr. Moeller. How are things?" Cafferty observes the young architect's wardrobe and a slight smile cracks the corner of his mouth. He can't decide if he admires Moeller's ability to piece such a collage together or rather the architect's lack of giving a shit who judges his sense of fashion. His red low-top tennis shoes, or as he once explained, "bull's blood in color," somehow coexist with olive trousers so thin that they resemble compression leggings. *Like Robin Hood,* Cafferty muses to himself. The navy blazer he wears appears crinkled as if forgotten in the washer. But Cafferty recalls, as the architect once informed him, "this is a purposeful 'distressed' design, quite popular in European clubs." But it's the golden hair, chopped and teased high, that screams rock star chic.

"Mr. Cafferty, I must say. Your commitment for the best, and the creative latitude you afforded, brought this to life…made it *special*," he oozes. "Of course, we took some functional cues from the leading MCFs around the country, but your dream, it is alive. While each detail might not be obvious now, they'll take shape as the years pass. Let me show you an example of the subtlety," he affirms, motioning for Cafferty to stand in front of him.

"I want you to look down this hallway," he whispers, gently steering Cafferty's shoulder into position, as if guiding the man to an elusive prey. Slowly, as if not to disturb, Moeller's hand traces the length of the hallway in a smooth arc; he closes his eyes and relishes

193

the nuance. "Can you see *that*?" he whispers, tracing the entirety back toward his face.

"Yes, I do. I can only see half of the artwork hanging on the walls, like they are staggered, like an illusion," responds Cafferty.

"Yes, exactly," purrs Moeller. "To see the full sequence, you must continue walking the hallway, each step revealing more. This encourages safe wandering by the residents, no dead-end walls." The young man turns toward Cafferty, his brow suddenly notched from reflection within.

"You see, my designs must live, breathe, and inspire. They must have purpose. In this case, the design *is* life! The residents will be curious, the sequences will inspire exploration," he fires, smacking his hands together for effect.

"Mr. Moeller, you do know we have already paid for this, correct?" muses Cafferty.

"Oh, and the wandering I spoke of?" he blurts. "This causes hunger, and of course eating. It is functional. This is purpose," chimes Moeller, patting Cafferty on the back. "I know I can get a little excited." He pauses, shaking his head. "But this is what we dream of in our field."

"Thank you, Mr. Moeller. You know, I had that same passion when I was your age. I hope you keep this forever."

The architect smiles, offering to explain the benefits of the color-coded themed wings.

"No, no, that's okay. I had the full rundown on the benefits before we made the purchase," he responds with a wink.

"Gotcha, Mr. Cafferty. Okay, then, your punch list will be done today—

simple touchup paint, a few bushes out front yet."

Cafferty nods and shakes the man's hand. "Now if you'll excuse me, I have my medical staff awaiting me."

As Cafferty enters the conference room, greetings volley from around the table. "Good morning, everyone. So how about our new home?" he asks as his eyes connect with each. The room bubbles, stoked by the annual confluence of warmth and greenery and the start of a new journey.

"I know it has not been easy, sitting for weeks in Youngstown, awaiting work. But the time has arrived. We are here now and I'm excited to begin the in-processing of our first residents." Last-minute tasks are sorted, and as the team breaks, Cafferty glances down at a thin, plain file folder labeled "Final Interviews—Support Staff." Retrieving the papers within, he encounters a single application, its front page sprinkled with green checkmarks. The green ticks continue, like a breadcrumb trail, to the final page, where two signature lines have been signed. A third line is obscured by a bright yellow sticky note and red letters: "Needs your review." Without hesitation, he rises and moves toward the lobby.

"Good morning, Mr. Cafferty," offers the man, his hand stretching urgently.

195

"Hello, Herb. Come with me—let's grab a seat in the conference room."

Upon entering, Herb scans the area and is struck by both the vastness and the unobstructed miles of pasture land greeting him beyond a wall of glass. "Wow, it seems so much bigger from this vantage point, like it's all connected. Looking outside in doesn't really do it justice...so beautiful on the inside," he notes. "Any seat you prefer me to take?"

"No, feel free to grab whichever you prefer."

"This will do perfectly," says Herb, situating his belongings.

Cafferty ignores the vacant seats elsewhere, and instead chooses a chair next to the man. He shifts his chair, as if shaving space in a boxing ring, narrowing options and calibrating his reach. Herb's eyes glance at the door, as if cueing others to occupy the empty space. The door stares back, indifferent and sealed. Cafferty tests the aspirant, lobbing a soft jab.

"So, the rehab program you entered in Arizona, you did tell me you completed it, correct?"

Herb presses his back against the stiff wood, surprised but unruffled by Cafferty's directness and precision. He draws an even breath, and, like a heavy truss, steadies his posture.

"Mr. Cafferty, I did indeed get clean in Arizona, at the rehab center listed on my application. When we spoke, I mentioned the recommendations from the director, staff, even fellow residents," he recounts, his hand delicately aligning papers upon the tabletop. Cafferty glances at the signatures on each, with one displaying a happy face and red block letters clamoring, "One day at a time—carpe diem!"

"However, I never graduated, and respectfully, this is a point I'm always quite clear about when discussing my past."

Cafferty senses his hands loosen momentarily. "Am I missing something here?" he asks.

"Mr. Cafferty, I have not touched a drink since I left there, years ago. Heck, I don't even eat *chocolate*," he states, shuddering. "This program had a final requirement—steps to complete—to be awarded a 'certificate.' The final steps have a 'religious' lean to them—and I certainly don't want to trivialize that, but in my eyes, it had little bearing on my sobriety. You were asked to make amends to those you hurt, lied to, stole from. And absolutely, I wished to have done that. Once that step was done, you had to make amends with God or spirituality, with whatever you believed in. Some folks bought into that, but what gave me the biggest hang-up was the pressure to 'fish' other troubled souls. Like a door-to-door religious salesman. That process of knocking on doors and selling your life's story reminded me of selling vacuum cleaners, not developing my spirituality. I still don't know what I believe in now; surely didn't then."

Cafferty's fingers rub his jaw, perplexed by the intersection of Hoover vacuum cleaners and God, but ultimately grasping the point. He recalls his own struggle with beliefs, despite decades of encouragement and guilt administered by families, nuns, and events he

197

cannot explain. Even now, he ponders, *What is faith?* Herb presses forward.

"My boss, the same guy that fired me for drinking, died in a gas tank explosion about three months after I left Biloxi. It could have been me in that tank—who knows? In any event, he was gone. Those same guys I welded with? They are more transient than gypsies, moving from project to project, city to city. I couldn't locate them to apologize, make amends or whatever if my life, or a certificate, depended on it. My parents? I haven't seen or spoken to them since I was seven. I did not graduate, Mr. Cafferty, and I have neither shame nor anything to hide," he says as he gently taps the papers in front of him. "But I can give blood, hair, whatever you want at any moment and guarantee I am clean, and *that* is the accomplishment I am most proud of."

Cafferty leans against his chair, his mind now wrestling faith more than the exact words during their introduction. Semantics trip his footing as he observes the clean, confident man before him. He rationalizes in silence. *Addiction is an inherited weakness, like a boxer's woeful reach or cumbersome footwork.* He acknowledges his penchant to forgive, almost to a fault, a lack of skills. His father would scold him for not dispatching less skilled boxers, and instead pinpointing more restrained ways of winning without disgracing.

"Make him give up the sport, forever," he would hear his dad snarl from his corner. He recalls deliberately spiting his father, rejecting healthy blows to a porcelain chin, or worse, a weak heart. Leaving it to judges "was for pretenders," he recalls. "You are too nice, Bobby. Not a thread of killer instinct. *That* is how you lose; get played for a fool. You let the weak hang around, survive. The rest of this world doesn't give a shit about the weak. *Everyone* gets one lucky punch, Bobby. Everyone. Don't be the sucker kayoed by the lucky puncher..." *POW!* A fist to the hand would rip the air, and a disgusted father would saunter away, leaving him to marinate in guilt.

Cafferty examines Herb. *Just another weak chin*, he reasons, for not completing the course. *Addiction is a hand dealt, not chosen.* It would irk his dad again to hear this rationale, but then again, it can't and never will again. *God dammit*, he thinks to himself.

Cafferty looks up from the pages before him and trains his eyes on the figure before him. "Your LMCA expired some four years ago and in Ohio, which means we would need you to start fresh like the others."

Herb exhales with a crisp, steady stream. "I understand, Mr. Cafferty. I will do any of the jobs while I pursue the training and licensing like everyone else. I am only asking for a job while I work toward the training and certifications."

Cafferty nods, and for a fleeting moment, hears the snarl of his father's voice.

"We have an opening in Facilities, Herb. You can start by moving patients in, garbage removal, lawncare, etcetera."

"Thank you, Mr. Cafferty. I'm certain you won't be disappointed," he states.

199

"Call me Bobby, Herb. Welcome to our home."

Chapter 16

Danny's head swivels about, scanning the first floor topography as if on a reconnaissance mission. His jalopy, however, squawks, revealing his position to anyone who might do him harm. He peers over the side of his carriage and delivers a desperate fist into the wheel, eliciting a bitter shriek.

"Goddamn thing. Every time I move...," he huffs as he spies random strangers loitering beyond the cubicles. "You see, this is what I am worried about," he fires to Abby, who is prying the sphygmomanometer from a squirming arm. "Can you make sure one of these is open on Friday?" asks Danny, pointing to the computer space on the first floor. "Remember, it's four hours. It doesn't have to be confessional quiet in here, but I have to be able to hear the presentation. They will have tests too, you know."

"Danny, I got it. Dawson is up in Cleveland for the next week, shutting down the VA. And you know what? I don't even think he would care one way or the other," Abby retorts. "He's got his deadlines creeping up now, and the last thing he needs is another distraction."

"Yeah, I got that, but it doesn't take him but a second to send his IT goons in here to block the access. Petty torments are like house money to him," says Danny, shuddering at the thought. Abby emits a cackle, but her thick torso smothers her voice like a wet blanket.

"IT goons? You think this place has an IT department? And them worrying about an online test? You just focus on preparing for it and I will worry about having a cube open, okay?"

Danny offers a quick nod while taking a final survey of the unfamiliar space. He plucks a sweat-stained, three-by-five card from within his pocket and slowly traces his finger beneath meticulous penmanship. His voice barely audible, his lips annunciate each syllable as if he is willing himself through the commands.

"By my estimation, I can complete the first block of the Assistance Dementia Care training by the end of the month, twenty-eight days from now. That means—" He flips the card and his lips begin to ripple again without the slightest trace of sound. His fingers move with a remarkable finesse, as if detached from the rigid man guiding them.

"By my account, I can request the program interview on the fifth week. I will need proper clothes before then, convince them I can actually *get t*o the worksite each day." His voice begins to lose steam as self-doubt weighs him like an anchor. "Even a resume...fuck." He slams the idle wheel, rocking the heap precariously.

"What do I put for work? I know a number of guys in here with more recent work experience, have transportation, aren't chained to a wheelchair, and aren't on Dawson's shit list," he booms, generating a few glares from afar. His brutal self-assessment ricochets against the walls and comes to rest in his gut.

"I mean, they are gonna at least ask for references or feedback from the staff, right?"

"Listen, honey, you don't know what you don't know," she states. "You have not been the easiest person in this place for me. But it almost feels like the distant past, like I didn't really *know* you. You have, umm, changed. Less bitter, er, you know…um, kinder? And you've been on time for your medicine."

"Well, I *am* trying."

"But the best thing about you? You are the only guy I know that is not using a hooker for hookering," she giggles, wagging her finger.

"Goddammit, this is serious, do you hear me?" he growls. "I don't want this job; I *need* this job." His voice trembles. "If you don't want to help me, just don't hurt me? Okay? Can you do that for me?" pleads Danny.

"Danny, yes. I am not going to hurt you. If you get that job, I will make certain we can get you to the site. The bus doesn't run out that far, but we'll manage. That's my commitment to you."

"Okay then. I just need to get through the training first, and then worry about the next step." He retrieves a book from his pouch and arranges it on his lap. He squints hard through the cover, as if the answer is locked inside, sealed as tightly as the fate he has sown. A mist forms across his eyes as he senses the sting of another man's journey.

Do you hurt? he thinks as the letters leap from the cover: "Dementia—The Invisible Journey." He folds in half, his body bent awkwardly with his head nearly touching the book. He cracks the tacky pages and an ethereal crisp scent, like a newly minted bill, awakens his senses. He consumes the words, then pages, and finishes each with a heavy dab of his finger against his tongue. As the chapters pass, the foreign specter begins to materialize beneath his now-chafed fingers. Like a skeleton, the ghastly image hardens in front of him and is unescapable.

His eyes draw shut as his imagination colors the structure with precision. With a heavy gasp, his papier-mâché is complete and its presence absolute. Danny no longer gropes a lifeless textbook. Instead, he cradles his son's nemesis, and its pulse twitches beneath his fingertips.

"That's it, Danny, that's the first time I hit the vein on the first try," a voice chimes.

"Hit what? Are you ready to begin?" he asks, as his eyes chase after a fleeting image.

"Danny. We're done, honey. You didn't flinch at all."

"Oh. Okay. Um, you did a great job, Abby." His eyes scour the pages, twisting the textbook as he examines the back cover, as if the apparition seeped through and escaped.

"Okay, Danny, I will let you be now."

The next day, Trixie sneaks about the third floor wing. Her movements are labored, anchored in trepidation and weariness. "Hey, do you know where he is?" She asks no one in particular.

"Where who is?" garbles a faceless man, covered beneath an army green blanket. She points to Danny's corner of the room, where a strip of faded floor tiles is unoccupied.

"That guy," she whispers as if afraid of his answer. A wrinkled hand surfaces from beneath the blanket, dragging a grotesque appendage with it. Trixie lurches at the sight. The man's marred arm resembles a burning pillar candle, its wax drooling in long streaks toward its base . The vet's hand balls into a fist, with an index finger pointing to the floor.

"Oh my God, he's dead?" Trixie gasps, placing her hands over her gaping lips.

"Jesus Christ, lady. Downstairs, first floor," he grumbles from beneath the fleece. "He ain't dead yet, or wasn't at sunrise. Either way, he's down there." Trixie shakes her head, squealing at her own misunderstanding, and skitters over to a groaning Otis.

The first floor is abuzz as an army of contractors scurries about, one nearly dumping paint. An errant ladder gouges the newly hung drywall, releasing a deluge of epithets. Danny sits in a make-shift cube, wearing a headset as distractions are drowned out.

"Jesus, honey. I thought you died last night. What are you doing here?" she says, pulling the earphones off a startled and annoyed Danny.

"Huh?"

"I said I thought you died last—"

"Yes, I got that. Thanks for the vote of confidence."

"What are you doing?" she says, peering over his shoulder as if trying to read a diary. "Module One: Dementia and Palliative Care," she announces aloud, butchering the pronunciation. "What is pal-lal-itive-whatever care? Dementia? Wait, is this what you have? Is that all the tubes and stuff you are always hooked up to?" offers the woman, a desultory diagnosis that scrapes Danny. He powers off the screen with a thud and twists his chair, banging her thigh with the rusted arm.

"Goddammit, Trixie, stick to what you know," he fires. The barb halts the floor's activity, eliciting wolf whistles and brazen offers.

She smothers his mouth with a tenacious grip and lashes into him. "Don't you *ever* treat me like that, here or anywhere." Danny wrestles her hand free and begins frantically wiping his lips and cheeks.

"Christ, I'm sorry—grab a chair." He motions to the neighboring unoccupied cube. She yanks the chair and, after a moment of posturing, slumps into it as a seething heap.

"Trixie, listen to me. I haven't told anyone this and will most certainly hate myself for telling you this." Trixie perks up, the majority of her anger fleeing. "If you haven't figured it out by now, you are

206

the only person I trust. Well, you and that nurse, the one hooking my veins up like a fucking Jiffy Lube."

Trixie bursts out laughing at the thought, random hoses pumping high mileage oil and a prayer into a terminally ill Chevy Nova.

"Seriously, though. That stuff you saw? I am studying it. But it's not because I got dementia or anything. I am working on an interview in two weeks."

Trixie's face morphs serious for a moment and delivers a brutal candor.

"Danny, you are a dinosaur. I don't give a shit about employment laws or whatever, but they don't hire old people. Even if they did, they wouldn't hire *this* old person," she says, motioning to his jalopy of a chair. "Honey, I love ya and all, but I never bullshit."

Undeterred, Danny scans the area for prying eyes and points back up toward the third floor.

"Have you seen my competition? Ol' Charlie has been buried under that field blanket for four months. That cocksucker can't even—" Danny stops abruptly, recoiling at his insensitive barb. "Sorry, no offense. But one time, Dawson stuck a mirror under his nose just to prove he was still breathing! Took a photo of it and twittered it."

"Tweeted it," states Trixie, with minor annoyance.

"Whatever. And the checkers twins? Neither one of them has even completed a game without pissing or shitting themselves. Christ, half the time they are playing each other's pieces and fight over who gets to marry the queen!"

She laughs hysterically, like a pack of hyenas during a feeding frenzy.

"Seriously, man," he continues, "I know I don't look real good, but my mind is still sharp. They have this new pilot program with vets for that memory care facility. They are going to train and place us over there—facilities, maintenance—and even some to mirror the licensed attendants. Maybe even get a full-time job after that," he says, his voice less confident, fading like a fast-setting sun.

"Danny, your mind is there, but your parts aren't. Listen to me, why this? Why not—umm, you know, some people make money from their PJs, like answering calls, telemarketing, stuff like that. You would be great at that. and no one would ever even see you. Ol' Charlie could even help." She giggles at the thought and mimes sleeping while mumbling into an imaginary phone.

Danny seethes as his eyes form crinkled slits. "Oh yeah? If it's so good, why don't you do it instead of them?" he says, motioning to a crew of laborers walking by, his vitriol gnashing his teeth.

She replies, completely ignoring the barb. "Danny, they will bring another how many vets from Cleveland in a couple of weeks, right? That's a lot of competition is all I am saying. I would love for you to get the job and all, but—"

"Listen, do you remember those writings on the window, all the symbols and stuff?" he interrupts.

"Well, sure I do."

Danny swivels, surveying the scene for some lurking ear or perhaps the specter who crept away. He hushes his tone and leans in to Trixie. "Those drawings were done by my son. He is in that memory care facility."

Trixie's mouth drops wide open, revealing decades of neglect and violent punishment. "What? So, wait. So you want to *treat* him?" she says, angling closer.

"I want him to be proud, more than anything, I suppose. Of course, I would love to help him, but…" He pauses, absorbing the chapters from only hours prior. "Dementia always ends; it's simply a matter of when and how. Hell, I don't know," he huffs, not having worked out the theory yet. "I know that he is there, he is sick, and whether God is dealing me some shit hand or not, this might be the only chance I get to help. I have almost fifty years of space between us. That kind of time and pressure might not make me a diamond, but somewhere north of a lump of coal, right?"

"I think I get it, Danny. But—even if you don't get the job, you could still make amends, be with him."

"I have to offer more than just this," he says, motioning to his chair and marbled arms, an uncomplicated prospectus of his life. "It's got to be more than this," he fades, tears welling in his eyes.

"Danny," she says, while placing her hand on his knee. "I want you to listen to me. I don't know if you will ever get that job—I really don't. But," she says, her hand patting his lifeless palm, "I believe one hundred percent you will reach him. Do you hear me? You will reach him and you will receive forgiveness and peace. And I don't bullshit. Ever."

She pauses as her head drapes toward the floor, stray hairs clinging to her face. "We all get forgiven eventually—it's only a matter of whether you are alive or dead. You must believe that. You've got your chance now. I've got my list for later."

Danny nudges her chin, lifting her face up toward his. He inspects her eyes and observes a mist welling from somewhere else, far away from the present. Her striking green eyes appear overcast, like a threadbare gypsy tent, blanched from years of solitude and neglect. In an instant, a tear traces her cheek and a facade of granite crumbles as easily as a sandcastle in the tide.

"Are you okay?" offers Danny, puzzled by her response. "Are you crying?"

The words lift above the silence and sting her. Crying, she stews, is the death knell to street dogs like her and the reason why she buried that defect alive so many years ago. *Why does it struggle to live now?* she thinks. With a violent snap of her head, she scrubs any traces of sadness from her face, and yet again begins building walls made of sand.

"Honey, I wanted to be somebody too, you know, like, something relevant. Have some purpose. It's been so long since I have even used my own name. I have become my own—"

"Figment," Danny interjects.

She shakes her head slowly at the thought. "I have spent my whole life hiding from me."

The truth hangs in the air, disarming Danny. He cannot speak.

"I'm so tired, honey. Who knows? Spring is coming, and that always means a new start, clean slate, forgiveness..." She stands abruptly and grinds at the puffed sacs beneath her eyes, now dry and red. "See ya soon, Danny boy," she offers with a slow wave as she strolls toward the exit.

The next morning, Danny is awakened by a newspaper dropped in his lap. "My condolences," shoots a graveled voice, walking off into the shadows. Danny wipes the elusive sleep from his eyes and fingers each headline for some clue, his heart rate mirroring the brisk pace of his fingers. He flips the page and at the bottom, in empty black font, his eyes latch onto the caption: "Body in Mahoning River identified as local prostitute."

Danny drops his hand, the weight crumpling the paper into a disfigured ball. "It's Trisa, goddamn it. Her name was Trisa," he quietly mutters to himself, looking out the third floor window at the bus station. He shakes his head as the paper slides down his leg, closing on top of itself abruptly, like a cheap plywood coffin. "You were always relevant to me," he states aloud as Charlie shifts beneath the blanket on the tiled floor.

Chapter 17

"Crisscross-applesauce. Do you think you could do that for me, Richard?" asks an energetic licensed memory care attendant. She embellishes the movements on her own shoelaces while observing the stoic figure. "If you take the lace over and under, one will never wonder." The singsong cadence chips at his patience as he glares at the high-tops who have become his morning bane.

"Wh-wh-why do I have to do those?" he says, turning away from the nurse. He fumbles with a pair of musty loafers, the soles filed smoother than bowling shoes. "I have *these*." He waves the shoes inches from her face, scattering a musty scent about. Unfazed, the nurse shifts sideways in her chair, off-center from Richard.

"When did you buy those nice shoes? Can you tell me what kind they are?" Her voice soothes the man and navigates around his source of anxiety like a dangerous trip wire.

"Well, these are my loafers."

"Hmm, can you play basketball in those shoes?"

"Well, I—I'm, I don't think so."

"That's right, Richard. That's good. I certainly would not want to play basketball in those loafers either. I am already clumsy enough, but would be afraid the shoes would come flying off my feet without strings. Can you tell me what these strings are called, Richard?"

"Ummm, the things you tie with. Umm, the you know, ropes that hold the shoe together."

"Ah, yes, they *are* little ropes, and they do hold the shoe together. That's great, Richard. If they hold shoes together, then I might be able to play basketball in them, right? Do you think we could tie our shoes together so I can play basketball?"

Richard pans his eyes around the room in search of a hoop, or any context for the game she references. "Ah, yes. Wh-where where is the, the thing—that, the metal circle?" he asks, creeping low as if to avoid banging his head.

"Oh, it's at the gym where I go," she responds, pretending to dribble a ball. The attendant slides her chair right next to Richard. "Okay, can you grab your laces for me?"

Richard looks down and lurches back in his chair, squinting his eyes shut. "Are they dead? I can't look," he says, sliding his feet away from the meandrous black serpents, which mirror his movements and nip at his heels. "They keep m-moving...will they bite?" His feet slam against the bedframe, cutting off his retreat. The black serpents coil a few inches away, awaiting his next move, priming his breathing.

"You know what, Richard, I never thought of it like that. They do look like little black worms. We have these big worms that come out after storms, you know. They help plants grow. Did you know that? They're actually helpful and harmless...I bet you they might even help your little flower near the window."

He stoops cautiously and flicks the hard, plastic end. The rope falls limply, unwound and tame. "I think it's dead," he states flatly, grabbing the strings with a ponderous hand, yanking them high and even with one another.

"Over and under and one will never wonder. Can you do this for me, Richard?"

He furrows his brow and wrestles the shoes off his feet. Setting both shoes on his lap, he again stretches the strings even and high, mirroring the actions of a stranger. She pounces on the opportunity, capturing his attention and willingness to cooperate, even if for a moment.

"That's great, Richard. Let's see if we can tie them like that." She removes her own shoes and places them on her lap, focusing on the tasks at hand. The singsong nursery, though, continues to abrade Richard, like a pencil eraser worn to the metal. "Over and under...over and under...over and un—fuck it—you make them—oh, ummm, make them go together!" he yells, heaving the shoes at the attendant, narrowly missing her head.

"Okay, that's enough for now," she concedes, having tested his limits, and carefully places the shoes on Richard's feet. She ties them and takes a deep, extended breath. "Would you like to play a game of checkers?"

Just a few meters away, the St. Stanislaus lobby is bustling with activity. Staff and patients swirl about each other like leaves in the wind, an orchestrated chaos as intake begins. Cafferty draws his

Oxford sleeves high and allows a quick smile, the kind afforded from an honest day's sweat. He doesn't hesitate, lifting boxes and pushing carts while addressing each of the attendants and relatives with a handshake and a "Mr." or "Miss." "Herb," he calls. Herb walks briskly toward the voice.

"Yes, sir, what can I do?"

"Can I get your help with some of the folks moving in? We have the dollies and come-alongs near the front entrance, and the list behind the front lobby of where each resident will go. Please work with Samantha on the first family."

"Be glad to," he responds dutifully. Herb slips toward Samantha, the obsessive multitasker piloting the front desk. "Samantha, which patient and room is first?" he asks, curiously observing the woman. She sits perfectly upright, head angled down toward the neat stack of files in front of her. Her elongated nose props up sharp-angled black eyeglasses that resemble fairings on an old Chevy Bel Air. The modest lenses have just enough glass for beady eyes to peer through, as if designed for a rifle's scope. Beside her lies a series of highlighters, arranged lightest to darkest, and a series of Post-it notes aligned biggest to smallest. She glances up briefly as if the files might scurry from beneath her watch.

"Mrs. Johnson, room 125," she states with a slight nod, crossing the same off with a precise movement.

"Great." Herb sneaks a quick peek around the room before settling back on the hustling gatekeeper.

"Can you do me a favor, Samantha?"

She nods while double-checking the file of a new resident.

"When new residents check in, please let me know if they have family members or visitors being added to the approved access list. It's real important for me to know what other support structure they might have, even if they aren't here today," he asserts. "It's always good to know their family, get them squared away on our routines and schedules, ya know?"

She nods again as she returns the file into the cabinet.

"Thanks, Samantha. You will do great here."

Herb locates Mrs. Johnson and her family, while serving a gracious smile and encouraging presence. "Good morning, everyone, and welcome to St. Stanislaus."

Across the city, decibels of dissonance measure Forca's progress as men and machinery clash in haste. Slate-gray primer plasters the walls, whisking away tattoos of a wanton past. Cloudless windows stretch end to end, interlacing against the heaven's sapphire backdrop as birds peer from beyond. Even the moss and rats, irrefutable stamps of resignation, have chosen more fitting environments.

Helio towers atop a makeshift scaffolding, observing a band of engineers scurrying beneath. They urgently assemble an immense kiln, one of two proprietary beasts bred for zinc recovery and the gatekeepers to his environmental pledge. "We will be judged by this for generations to come, even more than the steel," he offers to no one in particular, receiving a nervous glance from an engineer.

Helio retreats for a moment, drifting away from the din and chemical smells, reflecting on the effort it took to reach this point in time. He recalls aligning a workforce—a motley crew of engineers and scientists as well as blue-collar, white-collar, and no-collar team members—toward a singular destination. With a chuckle, he recalls the experience resembling a boat adrift at sea, packed full of testy pirates.

"I want each of you to embrace the 'Cradle to Cradle' benefits of our solution, which will positively impact generations to come," he remembers harping. "The first goal of our mission is affordability. Forca would employ the most efficient, lowest set-up cost electric arc furnace the world has ever known." He smirks, thinking of how the blue-collar workers especially groaned at his Chevron charts, bar charts, and anything else he could place on a slide explaining "affordability."

"This looks like fucking Pac-Man," they would chide. Yet one by one, each embraced the flexibility of the design, ramping up and down rapidly, adapting to any political roadblock, budget cycle, or critical event. They would come to comprehend the cycle-time efficiency and the flexibility to scale, and how this would translate to the taxpayer and, ultimately, a sustainable business model for the workers.

He recalls the first time he presented this concept to the public, and the uncertainty in every single eye that was cast upon him. They had been through this before, they groaned, another man's theory on how to build the unsinkable ship. "Why will this be different?" they would challenge.

"The fatal flaws of the blast furnace," he would argue, "are insanely high startup costs and inflexibility. Like bringing your yacht to the bathtub or your rubber ducky to the sea. That old dinosaur was never meant to evolve, and it died when the business climate changed.

"Second, innovation. Forca would demonstrate an unparalleled recovery of ultra-pure zinc, used for galvanizing the very same steel we produced." Helio winces at the thought, his unrelenting personal battle against the Waelz Kiln, the standard technology employed for managing zinc produced by electric arc furnaces. He often lashed out at the technology and process, blaming it for limited competition and high prices, setting determined course to alter both situations.

As he fixes his stare down at the men below, "Leao" looms large, patiently awaiting his master's command for a seminal roar and rebirth of what was once extinct.

As men scatter about its embodiment, Helio recalls the unrelenting push of the scientists. "Continue redesigning and testing that kiln until the zinc reclamation can never be questioned. Less waste is better for the environment and for the business," he would exclaim. "The air must be clean, hence why we will use the acronym AIR.

"Finally, region." Helio smiles at the thought, knowing *this* was what would compel one to believe. He touted the strategic advantages of Youngstown when the city itself was founded—the design of the Pennsylvania and Ohio Canal, the railroads, and the proximity to its neighboring states as it related to the Industrial Revolution's first build of this nation. He underscored that same strategic advantage was even more relevant today with a "regional infrastructure on life support." His fervid speech stirred a pride that had remained dormant for forty years, and endeared him forever to local politicians and community members during a critical US infrastructure rebuild.

"Thousands of bridges, buildings, critical facilities, railroads, etcetera, are within a single shift's drive from this facility. The people of Youngstown will alter the course of the US steel industry again." His lips start moving as he mouths the words that launched the dream:

Forca's research and planning, economic advantages, and method of modern-day steel production have intersected for the perfect answer—lightning in a bottle, if you will—to a decade of unrequited questions. The state-of-the-art electronic arc furnace, our Leao, will be a self-feeding machine, as it will consume one hundred percent recycled scrap metal. The entire tri-state Rust Belt, once entirely dependent on steel production for the very heartbeat it provided, is sitting on one hundred years' worth of available scrap metal. Thousands of bridges, critical infrastructure facilities, roads, buildings, all dust and bones are within reach. It is time to feed our lion.

Helio smiles at the thought as he is brought back to the present, with the thunderous boom of pneumatic drills securing the scaf-

219

folding around the two-story kiln. "Careful with my baby. She needs to outlive all of us," he cautions to the team below.

Just beyond the din and walls of slate-gray, soggy earth and young green shoots wrestle the air. Like a newborn fawn, clumsy and slathered in remnants of change, spring is born and finding its way. Landscapers maneuver chunks of sod and burlap-wrapped maple trees with ease, seemingly unburdened by deadlines. A single fork truck putters between cars and contractors, placing bags of soil atop X marks on the faded old blacktop. With a final thud onto the pavement, the driver shunts the engine and fumbles the knobs on a small black radio. The radio fires an AM sizzle, scorching the midmorning silence. *PFFFFFFFFFSSSTTT-pop.* Suddenly, it locks onto a faraway field of endless green and paths of red clay.

"Hiya folks, goooooood morning and welcome to the Boys of Spring, the 2015 edition of the Pittsburgh Pirates. I'm Lanny Frattare!"

Chapter 18

Rain lashes the bare necks trapped outside the bus parked in front of the VA building. The cramped trip from the newly shuttered Cleveland VA still grips joints and patience like a vice, pushing the vagabond souls into an angry buzz. Insults and hisses fling about like desperate tracers against the night sky, collateral damage an afterthought.

"Get the fuck inside the building or get out of the way!" booms a mountain of a man. He bulldozes the line with a violent shove, and it crumples on itself like an accordion. The rain spatters from his lips with each exertion, but the mass springs backwards with an equal force.

"There's nowhere to go!" fires a man half inside, yet bearing the brunt of an overrun gutter above. "The elevator is stuck between floors. The lobby is full. Where would you like us to go, genius? You go back!" He points to the mountain without hesitation.

The swirl of confusion abrades the new veneer, and Dawson begins absorbing glares. He spins away from the oncoming firestorm as if his thin latex shell will shift the attack to a softer target. His eyes grip his assistant as he snaps his yellow poncho stiff, a sail starched in the gale wind.

"You got a whole shit-show as the matinee here, Jimmy. What's wrong with Otis? A brand spanking new building and that goddamn rickety box of an elevator has us stuck. I told you guys you should have buried that thing first," laments Dawson, shifting blame to his thumbscrew.

A desperate salvo rips through the lobby as an engineer flogs Otis, his door gridlocked halfway open. Through the chaos, Dawson observes figures haphazardly bailing from Otis' clutch, splashing onto the hard tile entry below.

"Jumping Jesus, someone's gonna get killed!" Dawson booms, as he pushes the mass in front of him, descending into the spring downpour. With a violent lurch, Otis bellows as his torso collapses, and releases his arthritic logjam. "Miracles never cease," fires Dawson, now shooing men from inside the covered confines of the bus. With the last vet ambling through the entryway, Dawson slaps the bus door shut and scurries into the building.

On the third floor, a small panel of St. Stanislaus staff is busy combing through potential pilot candidates for their MCF program. The pool of candidates bustles about, some purposeful on the day's agenda, while others join as if deployed to some unknown cause. Danny fidgets with his resume and quietly rationalizes gaping holes in employment to himself.

"Danny," whispers Abby, patting his back. "Honey, you have to be natural, like you are having a conversation. Too much of that rehearsed stuff just runs people in circles. Just breathe and talk." Danny shifts with increasing distress, and scratches at a new abscess protesting beneath his secondhand Oxford. A trace of maroon seeps through.

"It's just that I have to be tight with this, ya know? It's the goddamn gaps I can't hide. I can justify almost anything I've done...but the goddamn space between. If I would have known this opportunity was coming, maybe"—he jabs at the paper—"maybe I would have turned my shit around earlier," he laments. "I know I would have. Fuck." He slams his hand into the resume, creasing the words beneath. A heavy paw rests upon his shoulder, anchoring him in place.

"You cannot worry about any of that now. You need to do what you can in the present. Today is what matters and *que será, será.*"

"Don't pull that Spanglish on me now," he fires, miffed at her seemingly nonchalant approach. Danny buries his face back into his resume as Dawson walks past the long line, offering encouragement to some, screeching to a halt in front of Danny.

"Holy Jesus, is that you, Danny?" he half giggles, motioning to the folded man in the chair. "Are you trying to get into that pilot? What in the hell could possibly have motivated you to move out of your corner? You have a newish shirt, even?" Dawson, half impressed and half skeptical, continues chiseling at the stoic man.

"You do know we can't put you out on the street, right? You'll have a bed here for as long as that rebuilt sump pump of yours keeps a-goin'...tick-tock, tick-tock," he clucks, motioning to some washed-out essence buried within Danny's chest.

"Dawson, when do you leave?"

A smug smile forms as Dawson taps the faux glass cover on his timepiece. "Forty-five days, twenty-four minutes, and...fifteen seconds, my dear man," he responds, tapping the faux glass cover.

"Okay, then. I will do my best to stay out of your way."

Dawson staggers, feigning a sudden shock to his chest. "Jesus, Danny. Uh, I have no idea what has gotten into you, but, whatever it is, you are only half the asshole you were. Now, if you'll excuse me..." Dawson ambles down the hall, stopping briefly to fire a wolf whistle at an unsuspecting and attractive pizza delivery woman. With an uncanny ease, his lips offer a skillful rendition of "Pretty Woman," inciting laughter from the queue.

"Mr. Danny...," a voice chimes from inside the doorway.

"Okay, honey, it's time for you to just be you," whispers the nurse as she pushes his chair, chirping but without resistance. She props him uncharacteristically upright like a plastic mannequin, his ever-present fold in his torso absent. As the carriage settles behind a large card table, his knees, poking skyward like bollards, prevent the tabletop from clearing.

"It's okay, Abby. It's fine. I can set whatever I need onto my lap," he states calmly. With an unexpected stir, a fly settles on the corner of the table, its pronounced eyes fixed on the man. Its brilliant green and red flakes shimmer against the fluorescent light above, like tiny fire flowers, agitating the stage. He senses a twitch beneath his ribcage as he glares at the creature just beyond his reach. He flicks his hand on the tabletop, trying to shoo the creature, but his knees bang the table's edge. *"Jesus! If only the table weren't so low, I would smash you into a puddle.... Do you hear me!?"* he barks in his mind. The vivid pest brushes its feet together deliberately, as if preparing to divulge a dark secret for the room.

"Good luck, honey," Abby whispers as she quietly retreats to the corner of the room.

"So, I understand you are interested in the pilot program over at St. Stanislaus, is that correct?" the woman's voice quizzes.

"Um, yes. Yes, ma'am, I am very interested." Danny fidgets with his wheels, lurching the chair closer to the panel, but the folding table grabs at his knees again. "Um, these gaps here. I want to explain, these—"

"Hang on a second, sir," the voice cautions, dismissing the resume and pulling out his personnel file instead. "It says here you have been at this facility for—" She pauses for a moment, sorting through the various stops within the vet administration programs. "Um, how long have you been here?"

"Well, at this facility, about five years, ma'am."

"And where were you before this?"

"Well, I have had stops at a number of facilities, mostly throughout PA and Ohio. You know, when I got done serving, I—"

"Yes, okay, I see it here," she interrupts, her brisk voice fueled by the Styrofoam cup ascending and descending from her lips.

"How long have you been treated? It says you have a serious—um, terminal liver condition....among other noted 'antisocial-

225

slash-violent' interactions with the staff, notably administration. Is that true?"

"Ma'am, me and Dawson got off on the wrong foot when he first got here. We had some exchanges, nothing too serious, least I didn't think it was. My liver disease—I got it reined in with medication, and my sobriety, for a while now. I have every reason to live, and this is the best I have felt in…well, I don't know how long." He thumps his chest with a precarious vigor, tempting fate.

"I spent the last few weeks busting my hump with these online programs—dementia, Alzheimer's—ma'am, I haven't used a computer in a decade prior to the last few weeks. That's how badly I wanted to be prepared for this very moment. I have got to have some experience over these other humps—sorry—vets in here, no?" His words fall with a thud.

"Danny, we do admire the effort. And I think that effort has more value beyond this role. I think that will serve you well for the time you have left in becoming a healthier and more respectful person to yourself." She closes the file and interlaces her fingers like a chain-link fence between them.

"Dementia patients, and in your son's case, Alzheimer's, are unique in their needs. Their day is entirely dependent upon structure, dependability, a consistently calm approach."

Danny's head begins to shake in protest. His hands squeeze his ears, as if to protect from an imminent crush of sounds waves. "No, no, no!" he pleads. "You don't understand. I worked for this,

226

and I need this. I can be dependable, structured," he says, reinforcing the point with a slap to the tabletop. Immediately, the fly freezes. Neither his secret nor his opinion are needed for what is already known.

"Ma'am. I—"

"Danny. I want to be clear. Fix yourself for yourself," she delivers mechanically, embellishing the point with a firm tap on her desk a world away. "We will not be recommending you for the pilot for the two reasons we have asked about," she says, her words frigid and permanent.

Danny deflates as his wish spoils on the table in front of him. Silence smolders as the man, now hinged at the waist, struggles to turn the resistant chair. He fires a slap at the fly, its colors jittering through the air like a toxic rainbow until they disappear.

"I am so sorry, Danny," Abby whispers, briskly pushing the man toward the exit. But the fuse is lit.

"It was that fucker, Dawson," Danny states flatly, staring off into the void. "He put *that* shit in my folder, that dust-up we had. Christ, that was months ago," he laments, shaking his head while picking at the abscess, now a bright red.

"Honey, it wasn't the—"

"Don't even try and defend him. Once an asshole, always an asshole. Now what?" he whispers, his hands clenching, their normal yellow tinge bleaching from the pressure. "Now what!" he screams, pounding on the chair with ferocity. His hands choke the chair armrest, as if ripping off the foam pad would be an appropriate weapon with which to bludgeon Dawson.

"Give me this goddamn thing!" he screams at the handle, metal squawking in revolt with each bend.

"Danny! Knock it off—you're acting crazy."

As Danny rips at the frame, a familiar voice, bottomless and caustic, rumbles with delight.

"*There's* the Danny I know!' he bellows, laughing at the tornado in front of him. "I knew it wouldn't be too long before you lost your mind again."

"Fuck off!" Danny froths, spitting at Dawson, a repugnant mist defiling the carpet beneath.

"There's no way you seriously thought anyone would take you…. Are you kidding me? Goddamn, son…. There's a mirror in the bathroom. Have you *seen* you?"

Abby tries spinning Danny away from a surefire explosion, but his fingers desperately latch onto the doorframe as if he's hanging from a cliff's edge. Tapping into a vile of hate, Danny wrenches against the door with all his might and topples the chair and himself into a heap beneath his towering foe. The chair smashes against the floor and the handle snaps free, spinning beyond Danny's reach.

"Danny, *no*! Stop it this instant," Abby's voice barks. Dawson's mass drops upon Danny's chest, slamming his back against the tile with a thud. Instantly, specks of red and yellow fling airborne.

"I could fucking kill you right here!" Dawson growls.

She latches onto his beefy arm as it shakes the flaccid rag doll beneath.

"You tried attacking *me*!" Dawson booms, squishing Danny's chest with a primal wrath. "No one would give two fucks if I killed you here. No one. I would be doing everyone a favor—be doing you one too. C'mon, you shit, give me one reason to bash your head in!"

Dawson lurches toward Danny's neck, pinning it like a snake beneath a spade. He snatches the nearby handle and lifts the blunt shaft high above. He drives the weapon into the tile, like a sledge-hammer, narrowly missing the squirming head. Danny whimpers as streams of tears fill the deep cracks like a reservoir.

"I just wanted my son to be proud, that's all. I just needed that chance. I've never wanted something more. *You* took that," he grumbles as Dawson loosens his press.

"I didn't take a damn thing from you, old man—whatever you lost, you took from yourself."

"What son are you talking about, Danny?" asks Abby, still afraid to breathe.

Dawson recoils from Danny as if firing a shoulder cannon. "A what? You have a *son*?" he pleads, his voice climbing. Danny nods and points back at the interview room.

"He has early Alzheimer's and is over at the St. Stanislaus Memory Care Facility."

Nurse Abby, still reeling from the revelation, shakes her head. "Now it all makes sense, your rush to get through this and all." She pauses, filling the space with a deep breath.

"Danny, he doesn't need you as a care attendant, honey. He would be much better served with a father."

Dawson shakes his head and tosses the bent armrest harmlessly to the ground. "Jay-sus wept, I cannot believe what I am hearing here. Not for nothin', Danny, but had I known this, I would have been glad to get you out of here to whatever pipe dream you were chasing. I haven't even spoken to those people," he says as he motions to the interview room.

Dawson rises and runs his fingers through tangled, damp hair. "I'm gonna leave you two here. I'm going to walk down that hall and pretend like none of this ever happened. And you? You are going to do the same."

He saunters down the hall as if the recent scene were water cooler chat, fingering his hair. Abby fixes her attention back onto the dust and bones in front of her.

"Get up, Danny. Let's clean you up and get you fed—hit the reset button on today."

Groaning, Danny climbs into the only home he has known for too long. "I don't want food right now," he mutters. "I need paper, a pen, and some quiet."

Across town, Richard's eyes lock onto the spring lilies, their brilliant white soaking in the midday sun. Sets of three, wrapped in bronze foil, line the St. Stanislaus entryway and flicker against the sun with a blinding flash. But his eyes never waver as a smile hangs from his face.

"Are you ready to go home?" the voice rings with a familiar but fleeting timbre. Something about the question stirs within him, like a chemical reaction, exciting a flurry. First a sputter within his chest, then a thump in the side of his neck. He scans the sprawling facility end to end, but rests back upon the lilies, ignoring the bronze fire around them.

"They look like.... What are the, um.... What's tha—sparkles?" he asks.

Cafferty, perplexed, covers his brow with his hand. "Wow, I never realized how bright those things are under the sun. Doesn't that hurt your eyes?"

"The spark—what are the—they sparkle."

"Maybe glitter? I don't know what you mean."

"Up there!" Richard points skyward.

"You mean stars?"

"Yes," answers Richard, as a sublime ease sinks deep within him. "Stars. I remember the billion stars from long ago. I'm ready to go home."

Chapter 19

"Hey, Fletch, how long does he do this?" asks Cafferty. He motions to Richard, whose face nearly touches the fish tank in the corner. His hands wring against themselves as he ogles the fish pulsing bubbles from within. A whistle slips from Carson Fletcher's mouth as he contemplates the answer. Fletcher, a seasoned attendant and a mountain of a man, steadies his frame as if any question deserves absolute veracity. That same pride and earnestness often generates extended self-conversation, though no one dares to interrupt or question. It is often during these waits, however, that one's eyes tend to drift upward and stare at his massive, bald dome, which—wrinkled and sweaty as it is—has an unfortunate resemblance to a raw turkey.

"Well, he used to wander a bit after lunch—maybe thirty minutes. This is a good thing, of course, as the design encourages such movement—getting his exercise and all. He's always avoided most of the people and activities, but eventually makes it right to this spot each time. No, more like thirty-five minutes. Yes, thirty-five minutes," Fletch corrects. His brow stiffens as he mulls the answer.

"He has been more detached lately. We are trying to get him walking a bit more during the day, as his sleep is tough to come by. But he is refusing the walks with us. Sundowning is brutal, worsening every symptom he already deals with. Imagine that—a basic life function, you are tired, you sleep. But...not here; it's just, well...the longest day."

Cafferty's head bobs as if he has read the book before, the chapters merely obligatory filler. Fletch perks briefly. "For whatever reason, he spends a lot of time there in front of the radio. It seems to calm him. He doesn't want the radio on—just wants to be near it," Fletch confirms, forcibly rubbing his chin as if exfoliating frustration with an imaginary washcloth.

Cafferty recalls the shift within his mom's endless days. The eruptions, fueled by anger, frustration, and even self-loathing, eventually settled into a quiet disassembly within. *He's hollowing from the inside out, like empty space squatting in the very structure that was his self,* he thinks. He settles back onto Richard, the hands now still and a gentle sway keeping time with the bubbles.

Cafferty leans in close and whispers, "I received a call from the VA clinic director today. Richard's father is alive and is actually in hospice care for end-stage liver disease at the clinic."

Fletch's head swivels as he gasps. "Wow. I wonder how long it's been since they last spoke, or if Richard even knows he is living. That's crazy. How did—"

"The father told the director...actually had a note delivered today, as well," Cafferty says, tapping the plain white envelope in his open hand. The words snap at Fletch like a wet towel, as his massive frame recoils just beyond Cafferty's reach. His face steeps with concern as he wipes sweat beads from the parts of his head never seen.

"You do know what I am thinking, don't you?" Fletch quizzes.

233

"Yes, I think I do. I have an idea, so let's pretend I never heard you think that," Cafferty states, his tone serious.

"Technicalities aside, it is his mail. It wouldn't be right for me to withhold it, no matter the circumstance. He deserves whatever's within."

Cafferty approaches the man, cautious with his movement.

"Hello, Richard, do you mind if I watch the fish for a bit too?"

Richard retracts slowly, smiling at the chiseled face leaking words but no more familiar than the rest. His once-distinctive edges, the shape of his jawline, the protruding bones in his shoulder, the ridges in his spine, have melted and congealed like shapeless wax from synthetics and lethargy. He simply stands, smiling as a tacit acceptance of whatever was spoken moments earlier rather than wrestling with the question.

Soon, he drifts past the figures in front of him, far away from curved walls, fish tanks, and color themes, like maps, convincing him he's not lost. Farther away yet from diapers and pills that suppress "the blues," the smoldering embers of depression, simply biding their time for a fatal gust.

And forever away from the Hail Mary nursery rhymes meant to guide his shoelaces secure. He stills his gaze upon the silent radio, the speaker cone prominent, as prominent as a left field loudspeaker, through the tired, straw-colored grille. Like a mirror, the speaker stares back at him. He no longer sees a wrinkled prop in some unfamiliar scene. Rather, he sees an unmistakable young boy smiling ear to ear as he stands atop a windswept, emerald green pasture, ball cap tucked nearly over his eyes.

A man stands in the distance, swinging a mighty wooden bat, which launches a white rocket skyward. The boy's head lifts as fast as the ball, scanning the puffs of feathered cotton strung against the ocean of blue. His feet scatter beneath him, a nervous bundle of energy as he hunts the sky for the pearl of summer. And like magic from the deep blue sea, the ball explodes into sight, its whirling laces emitting a soft red glow. A boom comes from the distant man.

"Not too far in, son. Easy as a can o' corn. That's it, right *there*." The voice cloaks the field with an exactness, almost willing the ball into the leather mitt below. The ball picks up steam, tearing the air with a sizzle, like hot grease popping off the sphere. The leather web spreads wide, casting a shadow over the brightest smile the boy will ever know. The seminal moment of a father's anticipative eyes, smack of leather, and resulting triumph is stamped within his head so firmly, nothing on this earth can take *that*. "POP." The voice whoops and settles back into the exactness, like a science. "Perfect! That's how you play the ball every time, just like that! Just like a can o' corn."

"Richard, can you hear me?" says Cafferty.

Richard winks at the radio, the tired straw grille staring back lifelessly. "Hi, ah—do I know you?" Richard mumbles apologetically, detaching from the radio.

"Sure you do, Richard. It's me, Bobby. Bobby Cafferty. Do you remember what you were just thinking of?"

Richard begins toeing the floor in front of him, like a child's daydream has been brought to light in front of the class. "No, I—the ball…little white bags—"

"Was it baseball, Richard?"

"Yes, baseball." Richard's face sags, lacking the energy that fueled the little boy in the speaker.

"My dad was there. We had the whole grass. He, um—hit the thing real high, ummm, he had…uh, corn, and it's how I learned to c-catch it."

Cafferty fails to make the connection, but presses ahead.

"That's great, Richard. I played a little baseball as well when I was younger too. Well, what would you say to him if you could, you know, like, not in a dream?" asks Cafferty, the attendant honing in on Richard's body language.

"Say what to who?" asks Richard softly, the connection as tangled as the neurons in his brain.

"Richard, your dad lives in Youngstown, just like you."

"Well, I know that," Richard states matter-of-factly. "H-He stays at…argh, the…" Richard taps his temple as if loosening tangled letters. "Ahh, what are they…you know, the goddamn crosses and, ummmm," he pans. "What are the gray things that people sleep un-der…ugm, in the place?"

"Do you mean a church?" grasps Cafferty.

"Not a ch-church. Oh, the place you go to visit ghosts."

"Ah, the cemetery?" offers Cafferty.

"Yes, that's it. He stays over there."

"I understand how that makes sense, Richard. Since you haven't seen him for so long, you think he might have passed, is that right?" Cafferty tiptoes as if lost on a remote path, uncertain if he can find his way back out.

"Well, yes...of course," Richard affirms. "He poofed, never came home."

"You are right, Richard. He did go away a long time ago. But you know, he doesn't live in the cemetery. He actually lives in a home for soldiers. From what I understand, he would like to see you."

Richard's eyes grow wide, as he cocks his head at Fletch. "*Dad?*" he offers, surprised. He observes the mass from head to toe, as if encountering a giraffe in the wild. Without a response, Fletch simply stares at the floor.

Cafferty reels in the drifting man with a gentle tap of the envelope, his handwritten name covering the exterior. "*This* is your dad's letter. He is alive and staying over at the Veterans' Clinic."

Richard's mind flickers like a rusted lighter. Each spark scatters from synapses into a cavernous void and fails to ignite the memory he seeks. His fingers interlace and squeeze behind his head, dispatching a thousand splintered memories across his gray lattice. He lurches at the splinters, each one moving up and down, passing by his reach without a sound.

"Fuck!" he screams in silence. "Slow down. I c-can't see them." As he edges closer, he recognizes that the vignettes are attached to horses on an old carousel. Breath pumps in and out of him as he searches for anyone who might stop the spinning madness.

Soon, he spots an icy figure who grips the lever alongside the carousel. Richard's feet begin to move toward the figure, as if commanded. They no longer shuffle, but march with a purpose, as if carrying a mortally wounded being. *Cli-clack, cli-clack, cli-clack.* His body shrinks as it nears the imposing figure. The presence appears to suck the sunlight to dusk and exhales a breath of doom.

Richard's hands shoot from his body, trying to halt his movement, but the feet continue their march. The figure grows larger yet, until night consumes the dusk. His entire world is the figure and the carousel.

"Please, please. I am b-b-begging you. I only want to remember, that's all," he pleads with the ride operator, cloaked in black. Unmoved, the being teases the throttle. Instantly, a riding crop cracks like thunder and tears into their flesh, sending red streams trickling against their fur. Mottled teeth grimace against the bit as the horses respond with a ferocity, straining against the poles and screws. The wooden slats splinter beneath.

Richard tries to cower, but it is held steady, locked in place and nailed to the ground by an unnatural commitment. Faster yet the horses pump, shedding bolts skyward, tearing through the carousel top and disappearing into the night.

At once, the horses snap free, causing the vignettes to spin recklessly with each movement. The images pirouette faster, as if in a blender, each shard crushed and mixed into indistinguishable grains of sand.

At once, the unseen grip on his body is released, and he slumps to the earth on his knees. "Please make it all stop. I ca-can't do this anymore."

The figure casts down a glare upon Richard. As the hood retreats from his face, an executioner's mask, one from eons past, looms above the kneeling man. Piercing black eyes peer from behind slits, enabling sight of his victim, but absolute anonymity to his deeds. A brownish-red grimace hangs above the chin, ensuring the last vision is one of abandonment and unspeakable terror.

The figure savors the theater of death, as Richard's silent pleas reverberate through his mind. Once the echoes fade, a harsh crackle comes from the figure.

"Let me hear you say it! I can make it all go away. *Away!*" he hisses. A serpent's tongue flicks from behind the grimace, tasting the fear. Richard sobs and slowly reaches for the black robe, grasping at air.

"I want to d-die," he whimpers, fumbling for something tangible, anything to clutch. His eyes scan the night, seeking a compassionate being—a king, a spirit, anything who might afford a quick end. But no one presides over the spectacle, except the figure.

"Why is this happening to me? When does this end?" he screams without a sound. The figure snickers as a gnarled finger extends from beneath the robe toward the merry-go-round. At once, the ride slows, and images from Richard's life begin to materialize in front of him. One by one, he views decades through familiar still frames, a torturous tease of normality. His first kiss and the surge of excitement within him, fireflies and county fairs, graduations, and one image brighter and more vivid than any other: his father's hand upon his shoulder as a young boy ties his shoes.

The figure begins to disintegrate in front of Richard; a small pile of grayish ash grows beneath the robe. A choir of voices moans from beneath the ash, like an opus of agony for the supreme tormentor. In an instant, scores of barren faces flash before Richard's eyes, vestiges of those bound to the same fate.

At once, the robe crumples atop the pile of ash and the figure is gone. "It is not time yet, Richard. But I will burn what remains very soon." His hands claw at the remains, seeking the beast who stood before him moments earlier. "Don't leave me here! You ca-cannot leave me!" screams Richard as the ash slips between his fingers onto the ground below. With one blast of wind, the ash is blown across the landscape, settling into the earth beneath.

"We won't leave you, Richard. You are safe here, at home," a soft voice hums reassuringly. Richard gasps and spins his head around the room, latching onto the bright, plumed tropical fish. "Are you okay, Richard? You're home and safe, Richard," parrots Cafferty.

His skin cold and clammy, Richard stares at Cafferty as his breathing begins to regulate. He dabs at the streaks trailing from his eyes. "N-no, I am not s-safe here. N-none of them are," whispers Richard, resigned to what he has seen.

"Richard. You *are* safe. We will do everything we can to help you. You let me know if you would like this note, Richard. This is from your dad."

"Oh, you f-found my dad's s-s-stuff? Is it a—uh, what is that book—a diary?" asks Richard.

"Sure, I guess it something like that. It's your dad's writing."

His mind twitches like a detached limb, a subconscious reflex toward a stimulus. "My dad?" The reflex twitches again. "Yes, c-can I have it?"

Cafferty hands the note to Richard and wonders, *What did you see, my friend? What did you see?* Richard holds the note, staring at the blue script until the twitches wane and finally subside. He focuses his gaze on the radio.

"Would you like the radio turned on?" offers Fletch.

"Yes—t-t-turn it on." A paw cranks the dial, snapping the piece to life with an AM fizzle. Pops and hisses volley as the stubby red line climbs the dial panel. Soon, a voice breaks through over the fuzz.

"Hello, folks, Steve Blass here."

241

Richard snaps to life, the Bic lighter igniting a powerful combustion from within. "R-Right there.... *That!*" he spits, rocking his body forward toward the emerald field, starched pennant flags swimming in the warming May breeze.

"It's a great day at the ballpark," the voice booms, reaching from within the tan box and pumping life into Richard's soul.

"I'll be damned, he wanted the ballgame all along," says Fletch. "Well...we have a hundred-plus games left this year—no wait." Fletch quietly adds games already played and a smile forms. "We have 150 games left. If you enjoy them that much, we are in great shape!"

Richard clutches the white envelope and closes his eyes, drifting into a safe and familiar world.

In the room down the hall, pint-sized Betty Kimball fumes and struggles to release herself from the clutch of a La-Z-Boy. Her pink floral house dress and white permed hair appear as volatile as a *Southern Living* article. However, red splotches radiate from beneath her white makeup like angry boils. "I know *you* stole my money," she shouts, heaving the TV remote at the bewildered attendant. "I had three hundred dollars in this bill keep right here, three hundred goddamn dollars!" she spits, pounding her knuckles on the coffee table. She wobbles to her feet, but falls with a thud on the carpet.

"They'll cut off your hand when they catch you!"

Herb slips between the pair and slowly squats beside the heap. "Hello, Ms. Betty. My name is Herb. And *you* made my week just the other day."

Betty softens alongside the man, his fabric silky and safe.

"We were putting your money in the safe up front, that three hundred dollars, and you told me about your trip to Italy." He cups his hands around hers, helping her to her feet with ease. "Do you know where I would *love* to go someday, honey?"

Her face waits with anticipation, a childlike smile forming. "No, where?" she begs.

"Italy!" he tickles, setting her gently in the recliner. "I've always wanted to go to Italy." Betty feigns a dizzy spell, covering her heart with both hands as her smile grows. Her red splotches quickly retreat under their white makeup blanket and she presents innocence like a kitten. "I'm happy to handle this from here if you'd like," he offers the stunned attendant.

"Sure, I—uh, have a few others to bathe before lunch, so yeah, I would appreciate the help." The attendant saunters out of the room, perplexed, while Herb settles next to his friend.

"So, Betty. Would you like to do the crossword together? You know we worked through them together yesterday—you were sharp as a tack solving that one," he muses, offering a wink.

Her head wobbles up and down; she is keen on spending more time with her friend. Herb slips about the room, ensuring they are alone.

"But first, Betty, we need to make sure you have taken your medicine for the day. See how good you were yesterday," he sing-songs, motioning to the calendar on the wall. "You even put your initials up there for each dose. You relax, I will get the crossword and the pills." Herb slinks to the counter and nimbly sifts through pieces of mail. He flips past multicolored envelopes and hard block letters. *Past due, final notice,* and *return to sender* leap from the pile, but fail to catch his attention. Buried within, he retrieves credit card offerings and one envelope stamped "Important Notice—End Year Statement." With a tap on the counter, he snaps the medicine trays shut and strides back toward his crossword partner.

"Here, Betty, I need you to make sure we stay on schedule with these," he says, sliding a few oval pills in front of Betty.

"Ooh, I like these ones…. They are, umm, like cold stuff—what's the name of that—"

"Yes, cold as ice, Betty."

She snaps up the three pills and deposits them into her mouth, crunching down on the tablets.

"Good, honey. I am glad you like them. So, I have your mail here too. Not too much to take care of, just a couple signatures and your checkbook."

Later that afternoon, Richard grabs the shower curtain, dips his toe onto the bathroom floor, and retracts the curtain with force. "What do you want me to do?" he asks, squeezing the large safety bar as if hanging off a ten-story scaffolding.

244

"It's okay, Richard. Watch me." Fletch walks to the discolored tile and thumps the square with a foot resembling an oar. "See, it's just the way it was made. Kinda silly, I think. It should be the same color as the others. But it is safe."

Richard leans away from the secure confines of his scaffolding and places his foot on the square. "Ooooh, whooaaaa. It's not moving. It's still."

"Yes, buddy. I will not do anything that would put you in danger, right? Now, the clothes are right here. Can you show me how you put these on? Just follow the clothes in the order they are placed." The clothes are arranged in a stacked sequence: underwear, pants, shirt, and finally socks, with each piece further away than the first. "Okay, let's start."

Richard struggles, but eventually completes the tasks with some guidance, with the exception of the buttons. "I hate these things," he mutters, fingering the ivory-colored plastic.

"I sometimes have to redo them myself," Fletch admits, securing the final button.

"Wait! Where is the…the white thing. M-my—"

"Your letter? It's right here, Richard. Do you think you might open it soon?"

Richard turns the envelope and scans the piece, now dingy from repetitive groping. "Where is the—how do you get inside it?"

"Here, would you like me to do it? Do you know who this is from?" he asks, reading the return address.

"Yes, my—uh, my dad is in there."

Fletch inserts a finger between the seal and, with a ponderous jab, releases forty-five years of deafening silence. He plucks a trifold white paper and unfolds it, instantly revealing an ornate black script. "Wow—what is this? This looks like it should be on a wedding invitation or something," he marvels. "No one writes in cursive anymore. Everyone is too busy texting or emailing. The writing is amazing."

Richard draws a breath, and, as if grasping the hand that produced the words, traces the pen's trail. Emotions pour through an ever-present fog, like a lighthouse piercing thick black clouds. He *feels* the Spencerian script, the only nutritive hobby he recalls observing his father practice. Intricate shading graces the script, while polished ovals and brushed feathers evoke a delicate artist's hand. Richard's fingers slip effortlessly along the ink, careful not to smudge the words beneath. He rests his finger on the "D," and for a moment, he is clear, present, and filled with crisp images. His mind, an empty cupboard traced in cobwebs, is stocked with precious memories that fed a boy through lean years of separation. "Th-this is how he wrote cards, birthdays, Christmas, so-sometimes we would si-sign baseball s-s-s-scoring sheets like this." Richard traces the remaining portion of the word, and with a soft voice, says, "Dad."

Chapter 20

Cafferty's truck rolls past the bus depot as he studies transplants spilling onto the roadway. For the first time in three decades, buses teeter, lugging their haul, punishing the axels and lashing the breaks until they gasp with duress. Anticipative feet descend the worn rubber steps and settle as strangers in a strange land. Despite untold penance dished from the road, eyes flit across the landscape, seeking the magical beast Forbes dubbed "The Brick Lion" or "Leao."

Cafferty marvels at the blind faith in a city people once begged to abandon. *Can they all be right*, he wonders, shaking his head in mild disbelief. A primal impulse flickers within him and a chill pricks beneath his collar, trickling to his fingertips. *Can we all be right*, the little voice begs.

As Cafferty's truck settles near the mill entrance, Helio eases toward the truck, wearing a buoyant smile. "My friend, we still have many miles to go, but…. Have you seen—"

"Yes, Helio," Cafferty cuts in, while retrieving a shadowbox from within his cab. Alongside a recent *Forbes* cover are two Youngstown clippings of yesteryear signaling the demise of domestic steel production.

"I thought the *Forbes* cover had a much better photo of the mill than the shots I took. Besides, I think their name carries a bit more credence." He winks, offering the frame. The midspring sunlight laps the shiny magazine cover, reflecting sparks with each turn of the hand. The olden news clippings lie dormant as the sunlight sinks into the thin corkboard behind each.

"America's most livable city in three years? This is quite a reach, don't you think?" asks Helio.

"Probably so, but everyone wants the underdog to win, right? And everyone has a story to sell, Helio." He pauses momentarily, observing the photos within. "Job production, more disposable income, a low cost of living…. Who knows, maybe they are onto something. We are sort of fucked on the cultural front, but…"

Helio chortles at the thought. "Perhaps we can make an opera house or art museum someday," he pans.

Helio's smile fades as a cautious edge emerges. "I think we overestimated the candidate pool—you know that, um…substance problem? It's bigger than I ever would have known," he laments as his voice trails off.

"You know, we started our first test run over the weekend. It's as if she awoke from hibernation, a younger and stronger animal. We have the bridge contracts starting soon in Venango and Mercer counties."

Cafferty pauses on the news, a whirlwind of events having been sown and reaped in part by his hard work. "That's encouraging, Helio," he offers, shaking his friend's hand.

"By the way, there is something I wanted to show you as well, Bobby. Come with me." The two walk through the front gates bypassing the transplanted maples, now equipped with bright green leaves. As they near the main entry, Cafferty spots an imposing sculpture, a marbled serpentine ball, basking in the light.

"What's *that*?" Cafferty asks, stumped.

"Well, I hope you don't mind. I asked Mr. Dawson to save some of the rebar over at the VA demo. That right there was the original steel which came from this very mill. The one where your father worked. We took our initial test run and twisted the pieces around each other. I can't speak for the artistic quality, but my engineers tell me this looks like some DNA strand. God knows what twisted species came from it. We wanted to engrave the plaque with a title, but haven't figured out what to name it yet."

Cafferty's eyebrows arch as his friend's tender cues strike a perfect chord. "Perhaps you can give it a name, you know, with all the cultural experience you have gleaned from Youngstown." He winks, poking his friend.

Cafferty offers a modest grin as he digests the exhibit. "How about for now, let's let it marinate a bit. If it's on a plaque, I need some time so I don't embarrass myself."

"Perfect, my friend. Take your time, and when the right name comes, you will know."

"Thank you, Helio."

Back at the MCF, Herb situates himself in the lobby alcove. He rides a trimmed thumbnail along the ridge of a tin container. With a final jab, a frigid whisper rises into the air.

He studies the journey, a hectic crossroads of family and residents, classifying each passenger's ultimate destination with deft precision. Soon, his eyes fasten onto the families as they serve like contrast stains, illuminating the specimen he studies. Quickly, he dispatches the first family, two children modestly attired, escorting an elderly woman in a wheelchair. He flicks an icy sliver into his mouth and draws a breath, savoring the numbness creeping about his tongue.

Almost immediately, his pupils dilate and constrict with a yearning, locking onto a sturdily built, tattooed man aiding a long-suffering figure. The buffed, two-tone Oxfords and tweed blazer hint of a proud man, but the wearied face and childlike gestures expose the vain ruse. Herb relishes the man's obvious fog before resetting his eyes on the escort. He is confronted by a calcified glare, nearly shaking him transparent. His skin flinches from the tacit threat and he swiftly retreats from this hunt.

Finally, his eyes locate a sharply dressed man, barking into one phone and scrolling through life on another. The juggling act falters as the silver-haired woman he leads shuffles back outside into a sea of confusion. A rush surges through Herb's veins, like a shark stalking a stray pup. He flips two more white crystals into his mouth and slips through the lobby, intercepting the woman in the parking lot.

"Hi, honey, can I help you?" he offers.

"Uh—where's my brother? He's—ah, he is supposed to be here for our dinner. We all have to wait for him—he's momma's faaaavorite. He *never* shows up on time," she rattles, her words biting from years of resentment. "That—uh, sonofabitch is gonna make the food cold and I'm tired of all the cold food. Can you find him before our food—"

"Sure, honey, you know we can't be late for dinner. You are right, no one should have to eat cold dinner. I promise you a hot meal this evening, okay? What's that favorite meal of yours again, honey?"

The resentment dashes from her face as she places her hand on Herb's shoulder, following him back into the facility.

"Sell, that's what we do. We still make an easy three hundred on the shares and move on—do you understand?" the man barks, still unaware of time and place.

"There's my brother right *there*—you little shit, you were going to make us late. Momma was hollering for you—"

"Geez, Mom," the tense man fires, cramming the phone into the nook of his armpit.

"If I am on the phone, I am working and you have to—"

"Oh, Frankie, get off that phone—dinner's getting cold—I want…. Oh my God, Frankie, when did we get this fish tank? We can't afford a fish tank, can we?" Rose continues, slipping toward the feathering colors, leaving the man shaded red.

He snaps his attention back to another life, and, for one moment, focuses on the primary task at hand. "Make. The. Sale." His finger jabs at the screen and washes his hands over his damp, reddened face. Herb, sensing the despair, pats the man's shoulder.

251

"Let me help you," his voice soothes.

"For God's sake," the words tumble from underneath the man's clenched hands. "My mom thinks I am her brother. Her brother died before I was even born." The man, exasperated, laughs at the thought. "Can you believe that? How the hell can't she see the difference? I know they forget stuff—like when to take medicine, the car keys, you know, typical bullshit. Hell, I forget where my car is parked half the time and I have owned that building for ten years. But how the hell does one confuse a ten-year-old dead kid with this?" he says, pointing to his bald dome. Herb clears his throat.

"You know—Frankie, is it?"

"No, it's actually Warren," he scoffs. "Frankie is the ghost."

"Okay, Warren. And Mom's name is?"

"Rose," the voice fires back.

"I want you to hear me say this: I understand. I understand the frustration, the hurt, the guilt, the anger—and yes, it is natural to get angry. Mad as hell."

Warren stops for a second, relief slowly washing down his face, his shoulders hunching forward.

"When I was a kid, I used to play down by this creek, this beautiful, perfectly clear, slow-moving creek. You could see for miles, every stone, every log underneath this beautiful, quiet world. A few friends and I would occasionally roll up our jeans and wade in that creek, looking for crawdads." Warren draws a breath and, for a moment, forgets juggling and allows life to simply move. "We spent entire summers doing this—some of my friends would catch fifty to a hundred crawdads in a given day, and they would make fun of me for catching maybe five. But unless the crawdad walked into my hand, I had no interest in catching them. I was so mesmerized by the clarity of the water, the life happening beneath the surface, the moss wafting back against the gentlest current, the schools of minnows that would brush up against my shins, that I never thought to take something from that world…. It was perfect." The words tickle the man, transporting him away from phones and ghosts.

"One day, five of us jumped into the water, making a racket as nine-year-olds do. Once we got done pushing each other, splashing about, and whatnot, we began looking for our mud bugs. I toed a few flat stones beneath the surface and watched the dust rise and settle back to the bottom, when I got this sense something was watching me. Didn't know if it was a big ol' mudbug just waiting for my toe or some water moccasin slipping closer to my calf. But you know when that hair stands on the back of your neck, and you just sense you are the prey," he states flatly.

"I just knew *something* was observing me in *their* environment. I never wanted to run so badly in my life, but something held me to that moment, that spot. About twenty feet from me, I saw the most beautiful pinkish-blue streaks you had ever seen. It looked like a Frank Webb watercolor painting. I saw pictures like that before in books, but never *here, and never this beautiful*." His fingers trace a delicate streak through the air as the man follows the dream. "A gorgeous rainbow trout, just being…a gorgeous rainbow trout, seemingly indifferent to the jackasses around him. He was pitched just slightly skyward as if he was showing off the beautiful reflections to the heavens. He was the largest fish I had ever seen in real life. I was close enough that I could see the fins brushing gently against the water, like he was dabbing the final strokes of color onto a canvas beneath the surface."

Warren offers a nostalgic shake of the head and smiles. "God, do I miss trout fishing, just beautiful." As Herb nods his head in agreement, the majestic scene evaporates as quickly as the smile does from his face.

"So, I motioned to my friends to be real quiet, you know, not to make a peep, but to come toward me, because there was something they would not believe. One by one, they step as quietly as awkward boys do, mostly avoiding the moss and stones to get to where I was standing. It seemed like it took forever, but the fish was oddly patient, like he wanted to be the memory we would never forget, or at least the highlight of our summer. So, we finally stood on the same sunken log and watched this beautiful creature in its finest glory. Just breathing, watching us, painting the water with those delicate gills when all of a sudden, he made the slightest turn toward us and just froze—he stared at us with a beggar's eye, you know…desperate as hell, but with this awful guilt written all over his face. And we all screamed, falling off the log."

Perplexed, Warren's face scrunches. "Well, what the hell was it? It's a fish, for Christ's sake, what was so—

"Hanging off the side of that beautiful fish was the most grotesquely bloated leech that ever existed. It had drained every ounce of pinks and blues from that fish, so much so, it was like an anchor to his body."

The man cringes at the thought, his mouth framed wide open.

"The entire side was collapsed. It looked like someone had thrown a cup of rock salt onto a sheet of ice, all pitted around bones. You could actually see the insides on this thing, turned this whitish-gray, like someone spilled bleach all over the damned creature! We ran for shore, climbing over each other, like that leech was going to do the nearest kid just like he had done the fish. When we reached the shore, that fish used whatever life was left, or maybe the current pushed him there, to float about ten feet from where we were. He stared at us as if saying, 'You ran toward what you thought was me, and now? You run away from me. I am asking you to help me.' And yet, we couldn't move. We could not stop watching that thing die, its mouth pulsing so slowly."

A gasp evacuates the man. "Well, what happened?"

"I remembered we sat there and felt sick and helpless, but most of all, sad. Not because something would be so cruel as to take life so it may live. No. Even at our greenest, we knew that was nature. But sad because something in this world could be so cruel as to take what people *remembered* of his pinks and blues." He pauses, tipping his head as if the black eyes are still desperately waiting.

"But after watching this thing stared at us for what seemed like hours, so desperate yet helpless, the sadness departed. I looked around at my friends and to a person, saw the anger building in their faces. We got furious at the fish! We blamed it for everything. We screamed at it in every way imaginable."

Warren sinks on his heels, a wash of confusion running down his face.

"'Swim faster, go brush up against the rocks, call the other fish friends to help…do *something*, you stupid fish, or you will die! How could *you* let this happen to *you*?' we yelled. We were furious. That fish just floated, just staring at us with these big, black empty eyes.

"It had no concept of how disgusting it looked, couldn't remove the leech itself, and on top of dying in such a horrible manner, it now had five kids demanding for him to do something, anything differently to save itself. Of course, it didn't do anything but grow weaker in front of us. So, we began throwing rocks at the fish, trying to dislodge the leech or kill the fish—all the same, we thought. It would be over either way. We hit everything but that leech or the fish, and that parasite fed until it could not strip another ounce of life from that creature. It slipped away at one point amid the screams and splashes."

Warren stares at the ground before his eyes reach gingerly for Rose.

"The next morning came and we spent hours replaying how gross the fish looked, how clueless it must have been, and ultimately, how unloved it was, that none of his friends would help. We saw one hour of that fish's life, and that's how we remembered it and judged it. Do you understand what I am saying, Warren? Your mom has had *decades* of beautiful pinks and blues," his voice chimes, effortlessly slipping through the lobby's din. "We will celebrate those above all else."

Warren slowly shakes his head as lines carved from years of frustration soften for the moment. He observes Rose, tapping the fish tank's thick glass, and staring into two lifeless black eyes. "What do you think she sees in that darkness?" asks Warren.

Herb flips the top of his tin and offers the container to the man. He shakes a dose into the hand, with flecks of spearmint dust sprinkled about. He neatly flicks a rock into his mouth. "Sometimes," Herb theorizes, "I think they see a vault of memories within those black eyes, like they are roaming a library filled with a million books, and buried within each of those books is a memory. They are absolutely certain a specific book is in the library—for instance, they know they had a mom and dad. They had to come from someone. But instead of those books being categorized in some logical sequence, they are thrown into a pile, stories high. Unfortunately, life doesn't

wait for them to locate the specific book and simply keeps moving."
Herb shrugs for a second and clears his throat.

"I fully believe that because I don't think this disease can take love from someone—the love of a child, a spouse, any love that was built before the disease came. I just believe those memories are simply buried in that pile of books, and we need to do all we can to help find them."

Warren contemplates the analogy, while his eyes find their way back to Rose. "Or maybe that's just a convenient way to make sense of some boogeyman no one can see," Warren pans. Both men watch Rose smile at the fish and wave for them to follow her.

"Let's get Rose and help her checked in to her new home. I promise, I will take care of Rose for you here. I know your life must go on as well."

Chapter 21

"Okay, how do I look?" begs Danny. His hands fidget as he tugs at the sleeves. They stretch past his knuckles as he tamps the billowy material accentuating his frailty.

"I should've chosen a blue." He winces as the Oxford shirt appears to blend against the drab yellow skin. "Can you see anything through these sleeves, like my spots?"

Abby scans the figure, but avoids meeting his eyes.

"Honey, you look fine. It's what is inside you that matters anyway, and no shirt or tie can dress that up."

"What does that mean?" snaps Danny. "I've got one chance to make an initial impression and you're back there cracking jokes?"

"Danny, what I meant was you look better on the inside than at any time I've known you. I believe they call that a compliment," she fires, her sarcasm thick.

"All right, all right," Danny moans.

The memory care attendant ogles the pair uncomfortably, as if sitting between an old married couple having a spat. "So, if I could, I'd like to level-set expectations here, Mr. Danny," she says almost apologetically. "Neuropsychiatric symptoms—or NPS—are symptoms commonly seen in dementia patients. Things such as aggression, depression, agitation, apathy, delusions, and hallucinations are all challenges the patient, family, and caregiver face every day. The OTs at St. Stanislaus cover a broad range of ADLs...or activities of daily living—the IADLs."

"Hang on, ma'am. I am trying to understand what you are telling me here and how I might be able to help my son."

"I understand, Mr. Danny—"

"Christ, just call me Danny. I know I'm old—let's just move past the pink elephant in the room."

"Okay, Danny—let me be frank. Our main goals within the program are prevention, symptom relief, and reduction of caregiver stress. The core concept of this approach is to understand what has preceded the symptoms we spoke of. Think of it like a movie—we describe in detail what was said, done, etcetera, that led up to a specific response. If we can identify those issues that triggered the responses, both positive and those we seek to modify, then we can alter our approach to achieve a different outcome. Typically, this would be done for the caregiver, but..."

"Yes, I understand. I am not the caregiver, but—"

"But you might still be able to play a positive role in a portion of the ADLs we support. For instance, leisure and social participation would be good areas in which to offer help. Also, positive memory recall—there may be some long-term memories still intact which could provide some common ground. Do you have any of those you might be able to share at some point?"

Danny squirms as the memories prick from within. "I think I do, yes. But there are other memories as well that, umm..."

"Yes, those could be some areas we should perhaps avoid. Unless brought up by Richard himself, it's best to divert att—" A rap on the door interrupts her message.

"Hello, may I come in?" Cafferty states, as he proceeds without a response from anyone. "Hello, Danny—I wanted to drop by and wish you all luck on your initial meeting."

Danny lurches forward as if desiring to stand, but winces against the pain. "I'm sorry…I can't."

"It's okay, Danny."

He extends a trembling hand to Cafferty, who tempers the invisible demon with a firm grip.

"I have spent a lot of time with Richard over the last year, getting to know him, learning about what he has accomplished." The words descend upon him heavily like a cellar musk, pressing into his secondhand costume. "You are his father, and I believe this is an opportunity for both of you to make a connection before—" Cafferty halts, his eyes wandering toward the damp patches surfacing in the Oxford. Danny looks up, catching Cafferty's gaze.

"My mom was on the same journey as your son. There were many challenging days, the kinds where I never knew if that connection would ever be made again. My mom and I had a moment before she passed where I am convinced she heard me. That's what I hope for you and Richard." The words, genuine yet foreign, soothe the man in the chair.

"Mr. Cafferty, if you would have said that to me when I was thirty, forty, hell, even sixty, I would have told you I wasn't ready for this," he states with a brutal candor. "I am at the end of the line…dying. There is nothing left to chase or to run from. Couldn't even if I tried." His fingers thud against the faux leather armrest.

"But the moment I saw him was when I realized why I kept breathing. There's nothing I would want more than for him to know I love him and to say I'm sorry. I appreciate this opportunity."

"I believe that, Danny," Cafferty affirms. "Oh, one thing. He did recall a moment with you and baseball. There was something there which made him happy. He's also less anxious when he listens to the ballgame on that old radio, as if he understands what is going on."

Danny stirs in the chair as memories flicker in his mind.

"How I would give anything for those days, endless summers, the smell of cut grass and wet clay. That was our thing. I would turn the game on and that little boy would slide on the green grass until we both caught hell. He would imitate every play on our little patch until—"

"Yes, you know, then," says Cafferty. "You do what you can to make a connection for him, Danny. I will leave you now, but if I can help, please let me know."

"Thank you, Mr. Cafferty."

Soon, the door closes with a stiff thud, leaving the trio alone again. "Okay, Danny, just like a movie. We keep reworking scenes until we find an outcome most positive for Richard. Be patient and selfless. That's the best advice I can offer. Are you ready to meet him now?"

With a deep exhale and twist in the chair, the man presses his shoulders back, unafraid. "Yes, I am ready."

Four doors away, the MCA taps the door just above the name-plate and calls out for the man within. "Richard, it's Dawna—is it okay if I come in?" A moment passes without a response, just the soft hum of the A/C breathing throughout the hall. "Richard—can I—" A loud crash startles the trio, each covering their head as if the ceiling is about to give way. Dawna freezes for a moment, contemplating the noise.

"That sounded like glass," she states, depressing the door handle. There, behind the befallen TV, sits a man on the floor. Danny peers past the MCA and observes a shoe flailing at the heap of glass and wood, a shoelace flicking about with each strike. "Danny, it's okay, let me help you up," Dawna states, kneeling by his side.

"I—I—couldn't make them stop," he snaps, kicking the TV glass again. "I keep asking them to, but they don't listen."

Danny and Abby sit motionless, staring through the entryway as the two struggle to their feet. Danny is gob-smacked, devastated, looking at the fractured man who looks a universe away from the boy he once knew. Words leak from his mouth, without his lips moving. "Hello, Richard? Son, this is your father." Almost immediately, Danny's hand retracts over his mouth, as if the words shocked even himself.

Silence smothers the room, even hushing the breath of the A/C. Stillness spreads like the calm before a tornado, not a blade of grass moving, simply awaiting the funnel's direction. Richard ogles the wheelchair like a cast-aside jalopy, an eyesore to society, as his feet begin to chisel at the carpet. *Ch-ch-ch-ch....* The soles brush the carpet with a plodding pace, their cadence led by a deep-seated timepiece.

"Son, are you okay? It's your dad." The feet begin to inch closer, but promptly stop against his recliner, as if the barrier would prevent a sudden lash from an asp. But his eyes reach from behind the recliner, inching closer yet, touching every part of the man in the chair.

"Are you a—a—*ghost*?" pries Richard with an unexpected inflection. The words shake up Danny, as he contemplates what god would be so cruel as to deconstruct a man.

"No, son. I am not a ghost." Danny taps his arms, his legs, and pinches his cheek for proof. "Would you like to check for yourself?" he asks as Abby and the attendant view the scene from afar.

"Ghosts are white, like sn-snow," he pans. "Why are you a yel-yellow ghost?"

"Well, I made some very bad choices over my lifetime.... This yellow is part of my sickness and why I have a nurse, this chair," Danny states without budging. "Do you see ghosts, son?"

"I see g-g, arrr, what the ffffffuck. You *are* a ghost! Liar!"
Richard slams against the recliner, sending it crashing against the
floor. Danny remains motionless and unafraid as his resolve swells
within.

"Okay, Richard. You are right, I *am* a ghost. But I am a gentle
ghost and would very much like to be your friend." At once, the eerie
stillness that had assembled like a tornado moments earlier fizzles
into a gentle breeze.

"Ah, Richard?" Dawna begs. "Would you like to go outside
for some fresh air with your friend?"

As if the ghost vanished, Richard's feet resume their plodding
chops, shuffling past the visitors as his chin droops against his chest.
As he reaches the door, he stares hard at the silver handle with a
grueling determination, wishing it to move. His hands wring together,
as they squish an imaginary lather between them. But the lever stares
back with an icy indifference, intent on keeping him captive. Danny
winces as he twists, the wheelchair creaking and squirming in sympathy.

"Excuse me, Richard," Danny's voice rings. "May I get the
door for you?" Abby pushes his carriage slowly, as if approaching a
crosswalk. She is careful not to hit the confused man. Danny depresses the lever and immediately the room releases Richard.

"Th-thank you," the voice mumbles as he initiates a slow
shuffle into the hallway.

"This is very good for him," Dawna states, leaning in to Danny and the nurse. "If we can get him to do this each day, well, that's excellent progress." With each step, a wash of colors greets the group, marking progress through an infinite labyrinth. Assorted faces, like masks at a masquerade, dot their journey and frame a single emotion in time. Chatter between the three ebbs and flows as Richard pushes unchartered distances since arriving.

"It's almost as if he is walking toward something he wants to find," whispers Danny. As Richard approaches the door, his hands wring again.

"May I help you, Richard?" the voice eases as the door draws them inside. As the three dissect the scene recently played, Richard rests his hand on the stranger's shoulder. Danny flinches as if stung by a bee, uncertain whether venom was discharged. "What is it, son? What can I help with?" Danny spins, facing his son, ignoring the pain within his body. Richard rocks back and forth like a pot chattering above the red-hot source.

"What is it, son, you can say—"

"Wh-wh-where did you go?" Richard spits, the contents spilling onto the man beneath. "Where d-d-did you go?" he fires again, his hand gripping the collarbone like a door latch. Danny steals a glimpse toward Abby, as if seeking privacy to the only secret left within his past.

"I will, ah, leave you folks be," she says, slipping into the hallway.

"Where. Did. You. Go." The question echoes again, this time without a sway or stutter. Danny reaches for air, as he finally stops running.

"I just left. I didn't go anywhere but to this wheelchair," he admits. "All I knew back then—" Danny's eyes mist as he slams his arm pad. "Goddamn, I never knew how hard this was going to be. All I knew back then was I didn't want your sister, your mom, or you. I didn't want that...that restraint. I couldn't breathe," he says, voice cracking and losing any momentum.

"The night before I was going to leave, it was—"

"I remember," Richard says, his words piercing the still room. "I remember. It was s-s-s-s-so c-cold, my window had ice on the inside. It was after New Year's. My door was open and I could see mom's, umm—the glass let me see her face."

"Her reflection? Could you see her reflection?"

"I saw her on the glass. She had water—tha—tha—" The words escape him and ignite a charge within his hand, smashing the side of his tangled mind.

"Jesus Christ, son, don't hurt your—"

"Don't f-f-fucking touch me." The words blister from a shaking man. Danny's hands retract to his body and slide between his legs and confines, hidden. "Tears, she had tears and scary looks on her face. Th-the whole room smelled like m-mouthspray, it always d-d-d-did when you drank tha-that stuff. I saw you in the glass too, your mad face. I went closer, like I was, oh, wa-wa-watching on you. But

267

you couldn't see me. Sis-sis-sister…never woke up." Richard stares through the floor, his teeth gnashed with a ferocity and hands balled. His memory is primed, almost cued from something within. The attendant and Danny can only hush, affording him undisturbed clarity to let the words flow. His hands now wringing, Richard sways precariously, like the last leaf on a naked fall tree.

"You t-told Mom, I was the mi-mi…fuck."

"Mistake," Danny states, his lips cinched shut.

"Yo-you said if you c-could have taken me out of her, you would have d-d-done that." Danny sits statue-like, the words course through his limbs as his eyes fill and breach the puffed bags beneath.

"I wan-wanted to run then, b-but you always said yo-you would hurt all of us. When you drank that stuff, you were a m-m—" Danny's voice breaks. "A monster.

"It made you a monster. I don't know when the yelling stopped. I woke up because my toes h-hurt, were blue." Danny's face sinks into his hands as he shivers with each breath. "I went back to my b-bed and drew the b-b-baseball signs on the icy window. Th-the next day, you were a g-g-ghost." Danny raises his head as he paws at snot and tears. His mouth stumbles as if words are fleeing a burning building, trampling over his lips. With each breath, he hacks against a death creeping within, its cold fingers filling the voids.

"I am so sorry for what I did to you all, Richard. I will take those sins to my grave. But, I want—" Before Danny can finish, large pink bubbles inflate and burst against the exterior window. Richard's eyes grow wide and a smile beams across his face.

"The bubble m-m-maker is here!" A man wearing goggles appears as if on cue and squeegees the windows clear, waving at the group inside. Richard shrieks with joy, as ghosts and monsters scurry away. "I love b-bubbles!" Richard shuffles to the window, craning his neck to see his friend.

"Is this normal?" Danny begs, still stunned.

"They are rare," Dawna whispers, grateful for the distraction. "He has fleeting moments of recall, like if you dropped a puzzle on a floor...you might recognize a piece goes to something much bigger, but...that clarity was, ah, a first with him."

As the bubble maker vanishes, Richard turns back toward the room, startled by the two strangers watching him. "H-hi, do I know you?" Richard chimes apologetically, his finger pointing at the man gripped by the chair. "Wait, are you a *ghost*?" he chimes, his tone suggesting a random encounter with a familiar face of decades past.

Danny clears his throat, as the resignation anchors within. "I am a ghost."

An innocent smile cracks Richard's face as he cocks his head. "I *knew* you were," the voice affirms with glee. "But are you friend-ly?"

Chapter 22

"Did you hear about Betty?" whispers Samantha, removing her black finned glasses and, with that, her habitual laser-like focus. She leans closely to Herb as he fingers through a pile of resident applications.

"Uh, what about her?" he replies, never looking up. His fingers hasten their pace, as he senses a distraction coming.

"Well, it was just the craziest thing. You know how she never speaks to anyone? Just sits there clammed up, watching church services all day long? She rarely even comes out anymore; just to get her hair done. Doesn't have any visitors. Sad, really."

Herb shrugs his shoulders and his lips move as his fingers trace words beneath them. Samantha leans in, her stare nudging the side of his head. "Ahem," she grunts, causing Herb to snap the folder shut.

"Well, she does crosswords with *me*," Herb states, with ample smugness.

"Well, I *know* that, Herb. You know I work here too," she fires, miffed at his response. Herb sets the file down and turns to face Sam.

"I am sorry, Samantha. That was rude of me. Please, go on."

"Okay, so, one of the new maintenance guys was fixing a nameplate outside her room last night. He hears her mumbling, or grumbling…just making these noises, which, as you know, some of this stuff here can kinda freak you out if you aren't used to it. He didn't know at first if she was struggling for air, having a nightmare, or whatever. So, he leans a little closer and hears her talking about ordering cookies." Herb shrugs his shoulders as if waiting for a punchline. "You know, like ordering cookies from a Girl Scout or something. But according to him, it's a conversation she was having. Perfectly clear, appropriate responses to whatever questions she heard in her head.

"Well, the maintenance guy—he was relieved that she was okay, not hurt or anything like that—he had a little giggle about it and went back about his business. This morning, he was doing shift-change and thought to mention this to one of our attendants. He told her the whole story—Betty ordering cookies, having conversations with herself, whatever. No biggie. So later this morning, the same attendant dropped by to meet with Betty, who as normal was quiet as a mouse, not moving a finger, church program on TV. She was not answering any questions."

Herb, always curious to visitors, sharpens his focus. "Well, yes. Not uncommon for delusions, conversations, for a hundred different reasons. Maybe medication was off, er, maybe it's the progression of the disease, dehydrated, who knows."

Samantha shakes her head. "No, no. I understand that part. Here was the catch. She was floored when she noticed her nightstand. It had this beautiful old artist's sketchbook sitting there, left open. The page had this beautiful farmhouse scene, you know, cows, horses, fences, trees, tractors, all this intricate detail. It's *not* Mrs. Peterson, Herb." Her voice pricks like a tiny burr in his side.

"What do you mean, not her?" he pries.

"The woman has not spoken, cannot move those rigid fingers of hers to open a door, let alone the dexterity to draw this." Herb, shaken, looks confused. "I check on her a couple of times a shift, you know, just to make sure she is doing fine. There was never a sketchbook in that room. I am one hundred percent certain she has no one else dropping by to see her." He gazes across the lobby, staring into the fish tank at the bubbles forming and then vanishing without a trace at the surface. A silent audience stares back at him.

"She sure as hell isn't drawing in it." An uncomfortable heaviness descends upon him, like a cold wet blanket. For the first time he can recall, a visitor might have slipped around his guard.

"No, I am certain she had no one. Did any attendants or doctors visit her?"

"No, that's the thing. No one has signed into this facility or that room for Betty. It just, well, appeared."

His head wobbles back and forth as scenarios appear within him and chip at his resolve. "Well, I am off to see her after breakfast. So…" His voice dissipates.

Down the hall, Richard ogles the hi-top tennis shoes beneath him. His eyes scan the length of the coiled laces, and upon reaching the plastic aglet, his body recoils with a shiver. As he snaps at the laces, they shrink in defense before falling helplessly to the ground.

"Richard, are you excited to have a visitor today?" sings Rita, an enthusiastic transfer attendant from Pittsburgh. "I think we might try to get these tied today for our walk. What do you think—would *you* like to try?" Richard folds in half, resting his chin atop his knees, staring at the lifeless strings below. He touches the string with one finger and traces an infinity sign, the head chasing an imaginary tail over and over.

"Richard, can you take your other hand and hold the two strings like this?" she says, pulling her own shoelaces high and tight. Richard plucks the two strings and draws them straight, his eyes running the length of the twine. "That's perfect. Just like that. Okay, now we take the one string and fold it over and under the other, just like this." Her delicate hands ease through the movements, like fingertips tracing in white sand. His fingers tense and clang, like misshapen cogs. They start and stop erratically, misfiring and eventually stalling.

"Why—why do I wear these? I have th-those!" he fires, pointing at the closet. The strings loosen from his fingers and plop into a serpentine coil atop his foot. "That's okay, Richard. You got the shoes on your feet today and got the strings up high. You are making progress."

"P-progress to what?" he begs. "It's l-l-like a lake that h-has one of the things…the things that stop water."

"Like a dam?"

"Yes, a d-dam. The dam broke and water is coming out. I h-have a bu—" Before Richard can complete his thought, a loud knock startles the pair.

"Hello, Ri—" A vicious hack interrupts the crackled voice. "It's your da—" The voice, robbed of air, simply ceases. A nervous smile forms on Rita's face, if only because family should make one smile. Richard wrings his hands and mouths the words *a bucket*. "It's like I have a small bucket..."

"Hi, Richard. Hmmm, heck, look what I was able to bring to you," the grizzled voice spouts from inside the doorway. Richard twists toward the voice, locking his eyes on the worn brown grille of a radio. As the moments pass, three elongated bars inside the grill press and strain against the cloth, nearly ripping the fabric. His heart flutters at the sight and an awkward smile forms on his face.

"That looks like an umpire's mask," he mumbles to himself. "I thought maybe you and I could listen to the ballgame today." A whistle, like a simmering tea kettle, can be heard with each labored breath. "You know, the Cardinals are in town. I once told you one of my favorite players of all time was—"

"Stan Musial," Richard blurts out, his face still fixed upon the umpire's mask barking out strikes from within. Danny retracts and slaps his armchair.

"Yes—Stan—"

"You s-said he was one of your favorites because he was f-f-from Donora, PA. A h-hometown boy."

"That's right, Richard," nods Danny, "a hometown boy." Quiet peals the room when Danny finally nudges Abby. "Can you hand me the program? Do you remember when I taught you how to keep score of the games?" Abby hands Danny the weathered baseball program, its corners long stashed away within a rat's nest of a farmhouse attic.

"I figure if we listen to the game, we might as well score it. Just like the old times, right?" he rasps with a force befitting a lumberjack. Richard gradually hardens, like a clay sculpture fired in a kiln. His mind is stainless for the moment, absent any reason to disagree. But something anchors him put; he cannot move, not first. With more commitment than he has ever known and disregard of fear, Danny reaches his arm to his son, what for decades was an impassible gorge, splitting two pieces of the same earth. The bridge that long ago was abandoned and left to rot into the gorge beneath, never again to join the lands. But instead, his hand is met halfway. For a moment, there is no space between, rather a conduit of love and memories spanning the void. Richard squeezes the program's edge, like a child grasping his father's hand, and gives a gentle tug. The pages slide across one another, decades of gravity and humidity having beaten the musty rag lifeless.

With each brush, heaven wafts from beneath his fingertips, a thirty-year distillation of crackerjacks, wet grass, sweat, and, of course, beer. Not just any beer, but warm Genesee Cream Ale, the kind of rank barley pop one desperately until all other medicine is gone.

The trickle of pages comes to a halt as an unknown grime has glued the centerfold open, revealing the most beautiful boyhood creature on the planet. Faded numbers, letters, and lines laid bare, utterly stripped of veil and frills. They lie there, scabs and dazzling beauty alike, without commentary or bias. They lie there as the purest form of universal communication and truth one can find, a snapshot in time. His heart staggers within his frame. Ks litter one side of the page, broadcasting a gem by the home team pitcher. Danny thumps the arm's chair. "Christ almighty, Bibby had a heater that day! I remember taking you to that ballgame. Do you remember? It was bat day and..." The voice wanes, as Richard traces the Ks as if they hold the sum of the parts listed on that afternoon decades ago. Flashbacks streak through his mind like the fireworks exploding after the home team wins.

His mind is no longer barren, but suddenly exact in respect. The voice within shouts: "Yes, Dad, I *do* remember bat day. The first five thousand people in attendance received that miniature wooden black bat, the kind they don't give out anymore. We didn't get one—we got two! I could've gone home right that moment and never had a better day in my life. But it would get better before...I always dreamt of catching a home run ball, and what better chance at that than batting practice! We made our way to the outfield, left field to be exact.

But when we got there, you got real angry because they wouldn't start selling beer there until an hour before the game. But I had my bat. You could have told me the game was canceled and it wouldn't have mattered. You made a dream come true, and it was *our* time.

"We walked back to the home plate, where we found a beer man—I remember he wasn't ready to work yet, but somehow you convinced him to sell each of us two beers. I remember the foam on my face and giggling because I had a mustache—but I hated the taste. We got the scoops of ice cream in the little batter's helmets and started walking back to left field.

"I was petrified during that entire walk, afraid I would spill what you looked forward to most. You would stare at me and warn, 'Don't you *dare* drop that. It cost more than I paid for the tickets!' I squeezed the bat and helmets underneath my armpits so hard they made my hands numb, but I wanted to be sure I didn't disappoint you. When we finally made it to left field, batting practice started and baseballs were flying so fast and so often. I remember the sounds that day almost more than anything. The hum of those seams, my God, like wet hornets flying all around my head. I didn't like batting practice anymore. I was *scared.* I remember thinking, what would happen if that ball hit me coming that fast? What if the ball hit *you?* But as you drank, you changed. You weren't my dad. You were anger. As the balls would buzz by us, you would howl with laughter and scream at the batter. 'You call yourselves big leaguers? A bunch of bums, that's what you are. Bums! I can do *that.*' You would close your eyes, stick your chin out as far as possible, and spread your arms real wide, taunting them to hit you.

"'God strike me dead,' you would scream to them, promising not to move no matter what. You got angrier as they missed. And then, I remember. It happened. This giant of a man stood in the batter's box and smacked his cleats so hard, I thought he might break the bat. He stretched both of those gold wristbands up to his elbows, his forearms as big as my thighs! When he looked out in our direction, he tipped that telephone pole of a bat directly at you and he smiled. And he smiled until he didn't, as if he knew. He then turned toward that pitcher and channeled every bit of his skill and power against that ball, hammering the covers off them like he wanted to reach out and smash your face quiet forever.

"The batter must have been four hundred feet away but I saw it in his eyes after each pitch. He wanted to knock the bully out of a bitter man. Finally, he launched one pitch that screamed toward the very spot you stood, as if there was a rope hung from his bat to your nose. It was your chance to prove something, whatever it was you were trying to prove. I heard the ball sizzle and saw your eyes grow wide, as wide as fear can make them. Instead of fulfilling your promise, you cowered in fear. You tried lunging behind me, but instead knocked me over and sent every bit of what was important to each flying. I lost everything—beer, bat, and helmets. That ball ripped into the seats behind us and I began to cry. The beer that splashed all over me also washed down the outfield wall beneath where we stood, pooling on the warning track below.

"Your screams were so powerful that day, echoing off the empty left field seats. It was genuine anger and disappointment, not the kind you can hide. It was lingering and bright, like the July sun. 'Nice, real fucking *nice*. Well, guess what? You're sure as shit not getting *my* bat!' Somehow you managed to save one of your beers from spilling. I have no idea how, but I remembered thinking that was *your* bat. We stayed in left field as I watched fathers catch home runs and hand them over to their sons. You told me to chase the ones they missed. But I was always late, someone got to them first.

"With one final gulp of that miserable piss, you told me my time was up. We headed back to our seats, where the beer men were all too happy to serve. And as if all was normal, you taught me how to keep score.

"By the time the ninth inning came, the game was all but over. The Pirates were destroying them and you had fallen asleep in your chair, leaning against the man next to you. Do *you* remember what happened to me? No, you don't, and never will.

"The usher took me by the hand and walked me down right behind the dugout! I had the whole row to myself, and it was absolute magic. I could smell the tobacco and peanuts wafting up from these mythical creatures below. I could hear the umpire's grunts every pitch and see the stitching on the batter's sleeves on deck. I watched that inning until the final out, as the ground crew began shutting down the field.

"The stadium was beginning to empty, and only then did the usher tell me he wished he could let me stay longer. I was about to walk back to where you were sleeping when it happened. This massive forearm, as big as a tree trunk and veins popping out like one of those relief maps, appeared from under the dugout. No body, no head, just this massive arm that knew I was there. It had two golden wristbands rolled all the way up to his elbow.

"That hand slowly rolled the ball right toward me! I watched the red seams and the blue 'Official MLB Baseball' stamp spin around and around until it plopped into my hand. He gave a thumbs-up to me and his arm disappeared under the dugout like the Loch Ness Monster, some creature you had to see to believe.

"That moment was supposed to be our time. I didn't want to wake you, but the ushers were telling me it was time to close the stadium. I never told you this, but right before I woke you, I took your souvenir bat and kept it long after you disappeared."

"Richard," Danny chimes in, breaking an uncomfortably long silence. "Do you remember the bat day?"

"Yes, Dad," Richard mumbles. "Y-y-you ta-taught me how to k-keep score."

"That's right." Danny smiles, looking at Rita. "Do you think we might be able to kickstart this old box and get the game today?"

"Of course, as long as it fits around his other schedules, I don't see a problem with it." Danny nudges the nurse for a push and slowly stretches his arm toward the outlet, grimacing and groaning. A buried sackcloth, like a penance for a lifetime of immorality, chafes inside his gut. His body and spirit, estranged from birth, are reconciling for a final migration. But with each passing moment of reconciliation, wrongs seep to the surface of his skin, varnishing it with blues and purples. He is the living dead.

Danny drops the cord and is knifed in the side trying to reach the old, frayed cable. "Fu—um, fudge," he yells, forcing a smile through pain and a mist welling in his eyes. Immediately, Richard kneels and grasps the cord, like he once fetched tools as his father lay underneath an unwilling Volkswagen bug. Richard stands, unsure of what his father would like, but wanting to help. "Wh-wh-what do I do with this?" he asks, staring at the little brown wooden box.

"You see those little slots right there? Would you please plug that in those slots?"

Richard presses the little silver tips into the slots, and a crackle spatters from the speaker.

A few doors down, Herb slips effortlessly through a vacant hall, and steadies himself against a silent room 223. As he rests his ear against the door, his calculated mind reassures him that no one comes to see Betty. With seconds yielding to minutes, Herb's heartbeat courses from within the door itself, almost too loudly for comfort. He recoils as if slapped and gently raps the door. "Hi, Betty? It's

Herb. May I come in?" he mutters softly. Muffled laughs emanate from the room and then others.

"Shhhhhhhh," he hears as the giggles dance off into nothingness.

Herb raps on the door again, this time with urgency. "Hi, Betty—are you okay in there? I am going to open the door now." Herb twists the lever and firmly pushes the door open, certain to catch the source. As he approaches, he encounters a resistance like an ocean tide. For a moment, he is cheated of breath, and stands frozen while an eerie mistral surges toward the door. In a final sprint, the door is vacuumed shut like an ancient tomb, terminating sound and motion. Betty rests perfectly still in her recliner, her arms crossed over her body as if she is prepared for her final resting place. Her lips are pursed and parched, and a listless stare is fixed on the sliding glass door, offering a view of the St. Stanislaus memory garden a few feet from her back porch.

Herb toes the ground, testing the familiar yet wavering realm, the transitional void between life and death. "Betty?" he whispers again to the figure, the words gulped by the heavy air before they reach the vacant chrysalis. As Herb leans closely and touches an icy, stiff shoulder, he is met by a wisp of a sickly sweet, cascading over him like week-old sour, peace lilies.

The odor multiplies, seeping into his clothing and glazing the back of his throat. His body cringes as he struggles against a building pressure within his stomach. He forces the swell back with a hard swallow. "Jesus, what the hell is that?! Honey, did you forget about bananas in here somewhere?" he whines as he covers his mouth. As he scans the room, it appears undisturbed, the bedsheets untouched and crisp. A flicker within him warns of nightfall and shift change, prompting him to move quickly. He combs the kitchen drawers and cabinets, bypassing dulled silverware, mugs, and sunglasses. He pauses briefly, examining a few stray pieces of cheap china. He recalls finding a Royal Copenhagen butter plate, tucked away in a refrigerator, in Detroit. That find sends a smile across his face even now. "A lot more time then," he whispers to himself.

He continues a swift but precise search, an adrenaline high fueling him as he eventually reaches the bedside table. He recalls Betty warning him that she watched that table above all else as she knew, she was certain, the VA janitor, "the one with all the paint on his arms," was stealing her money. Herb is cautious with this search, looking for only a few scraps, knowing he has already netted his bigger payday from Betty. As he opens the table, an ornate, distressed jewelry box equipped with a foggy, palm-sized mirror sits unclaimed and alone.

"Hmmm, this must be ancient," he mutters as he twists the container, looking for some indicator of the maker and age. He sets the box atop the bedside table and marvels at the depth and clarity of the grains, the dulled silver corners, and mother of pearl surrounding the tiny drawer handles. The work is impeccable and reminiscent of bygone days when craftsman knew the customer by face. "Jesus." He

283

doesn't recall this piece being on any inventory list for check-in. But the constant skepticism of the janitor needles his mind, an otherwise rocksteady foundation in thievery.

Did he know about the box or was this whole thing in her head? he thinks to himself. The mirror, flickering like a lighthouse, begs for his attention and causes him to stare. The seduction to act teeters on a tightrope, and for a moment, his heart steadies the mind.

Perhaps Betty smiled into the same glass sixty years ago while preparing for her wedding vows. She most likely wept in front of that mirror, during her life's darkest hours, manufacturing a face that compels one to get through the day. Surely that mirror has a thousand memories of Betty and the ghosts before her. Should *this act* be a part of Betty's chapter, a helpless spectator to an opportunistic vulture, picking through scraps? The mirror is staring at a thief of the most wicked feather and doesn't lie. Shrugging off the constraints of conscience, Herb fondles the wood and traces his finger around the mother of pearl while contemplating his own golden rule again.

"Pigs get fat, hogs get slaughtered, pigs get fat, hogs get slaughtered," he whispers, loosing the reins on a runaway greed train. "Fuck it." He draws a deep breath and quickly opens one of the small drawers, eying neatly grouped bills, separated by denominations. Thumbing through the hundreds, he peels a few off and does the same with each denomination, a high coursing through his veins.

He spins quickly as if trying to catch a living statue, slipping out of character, but instead finds a fossil. "You got nobody to give it to anyway," spits Herb, as he stuffs the full stack into his bulging pockets. He focuses his attention on the second drawer and draws the little knob toward his body. There in front of him lies a small, rectangular, wrapped box, the kind perfectly suited for a Christmas stocking, yet two seasons early. Its crisp and shiny edges suggest a recent wrapping. "Getting a head start, are you? Maybe that's why you've been laughing lately," he surmises. "But what could it be? Actually, who you gonna give it to?" he whispers, perplexed at the finding.

He plucks the small box, rotating the item like a child trying to solve youth's cardinal riddle. As he twists the container, he hears pieces moving, like chalk sticks inside a wooden container, startling him. The box slips from his fingers and bounces into the jewelry drawer, revealing a nametag on the bottom. There in black block lettering, "For Herb Bandusky *Only*" pierces his soul like the mirror did moments prior.

"Ah, Christ!" he shrieks, lurching away from the box. His head snaps, catching a glimpse of the placid figure behind him. "What could this be?" he gasps. With a deep breath and a stomach churning with trepidation, he snatches the little box and tears at the paper. He immediately recognizes the wintery scent of pine needles stinging his nose and the slogan "Curiously Strong Mints." His breath chops and heart raps within his temple, as if this frigid mountain air is too scarce for a moment longer. His hands shred the last ribbon of dime-store wrapping paper, revealing a small, pink sticky note. The blood-red cursive omen shoots through his limbs, numbing them white and lifting the hair on his neck:

"*Hogs get slaughtered.*" The box ejects from his hand as he tries to scream, but the air thins briskly and abrades his lungs to an uncontrollable hack. "Ahgh!" His head spins with disequilibrium, revolting from the verdict as he vomits twenty years of calculated preying and guilt onto the tan rug beneath him. "What the fuck? Oh God, Oh God. No, no. I didn't..." The words rattle from the man as he staggers to his feet, as if being dragged to the gallows by something all-powerful yet unseen. The motion whirls him toward the door, but not before crossing paths with someone no longer cold. The chair no longer faces the garden but confronts him. Her eyes, once fixed on the memory garden to the west, now rest squarely on his, like doll eyes tracking the slight sway of a sickened man. Her body appears responsive and malleable, her cheeks with a natural blush to them. There is a growing presence, an aura about the room, that is alive and breathing.

"Agggghhhhhhhh." Life is drawn from his lungs as he gulps at the thinnest air. His skin begins to gray and blister from the cold as a heavy cough cracks his ribs within. The room is ripped with violet blasts of frigid currents like those born at the top of the world, eventually prying the door apart. Like a bullet, Herb is fired past the chair with great force, and thrown into the hall. Without hesitation, he sprints past the front desk, ignoring the stares of patients and administration alike, into the late spring afternoon.

Cafferty arrives early the next morning, gripping a hot tea and flicking lozenges into his mouth. "What's this—a bit late for the cold, no?" Samantha pans. "You should stay at home and rest. Things are well enough along at this point to take some time." She nudges a dismissive Cafferty.

"I wanted to speak with the team and get a read on the first quarter here. We still have some kinks to work out with intake, some facility issues, etcetera, but all in all, I have to say the staff has been pretty impressive." Cafferty hacks into his handkerchief, drawing a stare from the front desk. "How were the rounds this morning?" he pushes.

"All rooms checked out fine, no major issues. Oh, we had a little mess in room 223 early this morning. Betty got a little sick last night and we had some cleanup today. She made a bit of a racket, but made it to her bed fine, though. Oh, and something must be going around here. Herb sprinted out of here end of his shift, looked sick as a dog when he left here."

Cafferty shakes his head and rubs a stiff growth of whiskers outlining a chiseled jaw. "He did send a rather cryptic note late last night, like he needed a few days.... Didn't mention about being sick, though."

Chapter 23

Helio stands atop the variegated catwalk, content, despite the oversized ear protection drooping over his face. The mayor, wearing a white sweat-stained Oxford, looks as misplaced as delicate china in a coal mine. However, neither he nor Cafferty would miss this event, each for very different reasons.

As the wall of sound rises and falls with a herculean synchronicity, the Fortis DNA emerges. The red-hot, malleable rods wobble with movement, still fragile like newborns. The skeleton begins to calcify in front of their eyes, as Helio awaits vital signs from his foreman beneath. With a quick peer above, a white hardhat figure below signals the success of the batch.

"This is exactly what we waited so long for, gentlemen. I know the first run we shipped was for testing in the Pennsylvania bids. But this, right beneath us…this is steel for *here*. The next three generations will benefit from this. That piece right there will be going to start the refurbish on the Shaler Bridge, if you can believe it. This will begin to connect parts of the city that have been fragmented for years. How many neighborhoods were segregated due to these bridges being deemed too dangerous or closed?" he laments, considering the long-term impact.

"People will be able to walk to parts of the city they basically only stared at previously. Now the rail bridges and pedestrian bridges will connect again." The mayor bubbles with excitement as he offers a generous slap to Helio's back, startling the Brazilian. "Ah, sorry, Helio. If you would have told me this ten months ago, even five months ago, I still wouldn't have believed watching this." His thumb lifts up, sending a stamp of approval to Helio.

Cafferty glances at the workers beneath, ignoring his colleagues for a moment. His head whirls as he contemplates the enormity of the day. The occasion is bittersweet and déjà vu, he recalls, as he remembers the metamorphosis of the VA building too. Soon, all the bridges in Youngstown will bear a Fortis Steel symbol, an explicit transition marking the end of everything he once knew. The prideful yet abandoned Youngstown steel, the very sight of it crumbling all around him, has been chopped down and fed to the beast beneath him, like an industrial-age crematory. He ponders further. Soon, no bones will remain from his father's generation. The sights and sounds of the struggle, the bitter winters, families poisoned by addiction, decades of the "whistle," the waning screams of the foremen, and finally the echo of a bullet.... Each wait in line for a final burn, shattered forever.

And maybe that's just the point, he thinks to himself. *Perhaps the whole game is a planetary puzzle still being cut, one of such size, we cannot even comprehend the insignificant piece of which our lives occupy. A series of events that simply go on eternally, rendering each separate puzzle piece that much more negligible.* He gently toes the steel grating beneath his feet, oblivious to Helio motioning to him.

289

Or perhaps this puzzle is indeed finite, one in which once the pieces are connected, every single aspect makes perfect sense in context and by themselves. The clues, like the picture on the outside of the puzzle box, come in various fashions, he thinks. *The death of his mother, the funeral and the girl, his decision to pursue better care for those suffering...all of it paints the picture to your puzzle.* He smiles and turns back to his colleague, reaching around the mayor. Hello looks at him. "I believe this should be the name of your piece out front, the rebar from that past to the new. Let's just call it 'The Puzzle.'"

"It sounds magical," Helio offers.

Back in the VA clinic, Danny labors within his chair, a futile pursuit for a tolerable fifteen minutes. With each shift, a new barb twists within his side as if he is being corralled, minimizing his freedom of movement inch by inch. Just beyond his gasps, his fate plays out like a crude sketch, minute details unnecessary.

"We are reaching the end of the road at this point, Abby," Dr. McGuire hushes, his voice flat. His former private practice, which he once described as "financially modest but filthy rich" in personal satisfaction, began to wither earlier in the decade. "Lobbyists, Legislation, and Lawyers. The diseases with the highest mortality rate to a family practice," he would snipe. The eventual death of his practice etched deep crow's feet touching either temple and sagged his cheeks south of the chin. But it was his heart most noticeably ravaged by the "Killer Ls," leaving him listless and stony.

McGuire observes Danny's face trickling with sweat and simply shrugs. "Not much more to do; maybe up the painkillers. He has very little time, maybe weeks."

"Doc, you don't need to whisper any longer," grunts Danny. "I been here five years. I have been sitting in this chair hearing you tell that same woman, 'He doesn't have much time left,'" Danny mocks with a pretentious air. "Easily for a year and a half or more. She might have believed you back then, but even she's got to think you're full of shit. Don't get me wrong, I got more wires running through me than Otis over there, but...this whole charades game of yours, 'maybe weeks, maybe months, maybe years,' it's such a copout for not having a clue."

McGuire stares at the ground, then approaches Danny. "Okay, Danny. You want me to be candid?"

"No, Doc, bullshit me," he fires. McGuire steadies himself, kneeling at eye level in front of Danny.

"When I spoke of your decline, what, almost a year ago now?"

"Actually about fourteen months, Doc," says Danny, manufacturing a painful but forced smile.

"Okay, fourteen months ago. I gave you a range of time based on the token services you receive here. This right here"—he motions with his finger—"is the shit-house door of medical services, Danny." Danny's chin sticks out, like an eighth grade child gloating in front of his friends. The doctor cocks his head and squints his eyes.

291

"Hang on, hear me out. I made a short-term prediction based on the minimal services here *and*, more importantly, the fact you had no one, Danny. No emotional anchor, no support system. Just a five and dime soul waiting for God to admit even he makes mistakes." The very words fall like a lead blanket, oppressively heavy, pressing a fragile frame against a cold, steel table. "But that's my struggle, Danny. Even he doesn't want to take you, and somehow, you are still you. People like you, and this place," he says as he motions around him, "have ruined my faith. Is this my penance of some sort, taking abuse from you and the others while I tried one last time to help patients again? Or am I simply as naive and dumb as the day I was born, some puppet for death's amusement? Do you hear what I am saying?"

Danny's smile is snipped from his face like some malignant growth. "I have wanted to tell you how I really felt for years now, but professionally I just bit my tongue. Fear of being fired, I suppose, but then I realized, who would they get to take the role? No one would take this for long. But now? I don't give a damn. I was one hundred percent certain you would die so quickly from being alone, they would have deposited your unclaimed remains in the old TICO cemetery." A gasp rips the air as Abby delivers an elbow to the doctor's ribs. Danny shifts uncomfortably, catching his catheter on the elbow pad, grimacing. He clears his throat and manages to steady himself between pangs.

"I don't have a clue about your faith, and my little ol' role in that, Doc, but my guess is you just insulted me."

292

"Read a little history about your state, Danny. You would have had a number and a brick for a gravesite. Did you ever hear of a spouse dying days after their life partner has gone? They literally die from *being alone*. You should have been dead last century, Danny." The candor lashes Danny like a squall, its effect pondered with each passing breath. Danny slumps, listless and deflated from the truth.

"Listen. I only tell you this because you have an opportunity, a dwindling one, but one nonetheless. I hear you have been making some good with your son over there. I don't fault him for you. He's got himself in a pretty good groove—the best he can hope for—of you fitting a piece of his daily routine after so many years." McGuire rises slowly, towering over the sunken man in the chair. "This," he says as he fingers Danny's rusted chassis, "doesn't just affect you, and for once, you should consider how your actions and words impact others." The doctor begins a slow stride away from Danny but is stopped with a gravelly snare.

"Hey, Doc, I do appreciate you firing the warning flare." Danny loosens a viscous wad from within his lungs, depositing it into a Kleenex. "Do you remember the Lockerbie bomber?"

McGuire, stumped by the connection, shrugs his shoulders. "Well, I don't remember his name, but yes, I am familiar with the bombing."

"Shit, I can't remember his name either, and couldn't pro-nounce it if I did. He was Libyan. But I do recall something about that

293

event which always struck me as not only odd, but also the cruelest irony ever.

"The bomber killed 270 people. Eleven of those were *on the ground. Scottish* ground, that is. He of course was convicted and locked up for life. End of story, or so thought the family members of the 270 victims."

McGuire squares his stance toward Danny, not certain where the bitter man treads. "Well, he came down with cancer in a Scottish prison— terminal, as you guys call it. Hell's bells, kind of poetic justice, don't ya think? A real shit-sandwich meal." Danny chuckles to himself, slapping his arm pad and releasing more noxious drool, this time, onto the floor. The doctor and Abby are frozen, staring at the man in the chair.

"Sorry, Doc. I mean this is what the world would describe as 'karma.' You know, committing some horrific act, rotting away in a foreign prison, and then being consumed by cancer. A perfect ending that couldn't be ruined by anyone or anything. Or so the world thought. As it turns out, the *only* thing that could fuck up *this* karma was a doctor. Not by actually treating, but by speaking.

"See, Scotland has this 'compassionate grounds' law. If doctors decide some shit-heel's death is imminent, the prisoner can be released. Now if ever, and I mean ever, there was a circumstance which could have used divine intervention, like a fucking lightning bolt, this was the case. But no lighting ever came," he hisses.

"Instead, Libya hired doctors, mercenaries in my book, to assess his fate. They consulted with the Scottish prison doctor and somehow drummed up a prognosis of three months to live. Take a guess what general timeframe is acceptable for 'compassionate grounds,'" he sneers. The pair simply stare at Danny as he seethes. "Three months. Two words, uttered by doctors, killed 270 families and tossed their bodies into a sea of lawyers.

"Well, lawyers couldn't help but feed, and they argued some humanitarian angle for this case. Can you imagine that, being able to breathe free air again after what he did? He was freed." Silence grips the room.

"He got a hero's welcome back in Libya, adding further salt to the wounds of the families. And do you know how long he lived?" huffs Danny. "He lived almost three years longer! Three. Fucking. Years!" He slams the arm pad for emphasis.

"My point, Doc, is the doctors didn't care how their actions would impact anyone. Nothing stopped them from doing the right thing—they *should have* said that devil had another fifteen years—but they didn't."

The heaviness presses down upon the room, and the silence is only broken by a diseased Otis groaning in the background. "I understand more than I ever have in my life that my actions back then and my actions now impact others. But thank God, or whoever, I never for once believed in what it was you had predicted for me," he states as his eyes well up. "I have one more chance to do right by my son."

Danny's rough facade disintegrates forever like a paper house in the rain.

"I'm sorry, Doctor McGuire. What I want to say is that we all make mistakes and don't realize the impact they have on others. I am sorry for mine," Danny finishes.

McGuire's eyes cast upon the man, as if staring at a tombstone, contemplating the message carved in stone. He draws a deep breath and rubs his eyes. His hands rest upon the vet's shoulders. "I hope you do prove me wrong, Danny."

In room 227, Richard stares at the attendant ripping cellophane from a green cardboard box. His heart flutters, sending an errant smile across his lips. "Is it Christmas?" Richard quizzes as if awaiting a gift within. The bouncy white letters, and a smiling aged couple gracing the box, only stoke his excitement.

"I—I love Christmas…the pre-presents…I remember getting a BB gun from my d-dad," he gushes with a rare moment of clarity. Staccato gasps gush forth from the attendant as he struggles against the stubborn grip of the adhesive.

"Well, these are for you, so I do suppose it is a bit like Christmas, right? This box—" The attendant gasps again while ogling a custodian scrubbing excrement from the floor. "The box is like new underwear," he states in a rosy manner. "They will help with any accidents…" The voice fades into a hum as Richard eyes brown smears across the floor. He follows the smudges from the bathroom to beneath the bedside where he sits.

He observes his shoes and hands, streaked with mud, like when he once played down by the riverside. "Mud pies," he thinks to himself, remembering summer camps long forgotten. "We go out after rain and"—he cups his hand as if dragging a backhoe—"scoop the mud from the pu-puuu—the—"

"The puddles?" the voice chimes in.

"I am not sure if I can finish this right now." The custodian gags into the nook of his arm and releases the mop handle. "I need a break for a bit."

"We need to get this cleaned up before lunch, Jerry."

"Just give me a minute, will ya," fires the custodian in between desperate huffs. The pair meet midway to the hall, their words hushed and actions discordant. Richard, sensing something off, begins shuffling against the carpet grain, wringing his hands raw.

"Y-you told me to go in th-th-that room if I felt something. I-I-I don't know what to do with it, wh-where does it go?" he whines to no one, exasperated. Primitive functions now confound, collateral damage of the tireless tormentor. He sways as if he was assembled in the dark, his hands cupping his head and trembling. The voice begins to screech between his temples.

"Look! There at your feet! The snake flicks his tongue, tasting your fear!" His eyes peer from within his hands, spotting the serpents coiled about his ankles. He cannot breathe or move an inch as the tongue appears and disappears.

297

"The serpent will slither about you, always close enough to strike. And one day, while you plead for sleep, it will happen. Fangs will bury within your calf and spit a foulness into you from which you will never recover. With every heartbeat, you will nourish death, yet you will fight to breathe," the voice delivers. "The reptile will slither up your leg, but you will be unable to move. You will only be able to watch. Finally, it will coil around your chest and neck as you lie in some hospital bed. You will hear its muscles tighten and feel the give in your ribs and the thump within your neck. You will..."

Richard's hands compress his head as if trying to crush the beast within. A mop sloshes beneath his feet, crashing into him like a rogue wave. His body lurches forward as if bracing for impact. His head touches his knees as he leverages every ounce of power against his temples.

"Please, fu-fucking stop," he howls toward the floor. With one powerful thrust, the room envelopes in black. Richard's heart taps, but cannot be heard through a vast nothingness, a vacuum of eerie silence. Moments pass around him, but time stands deathly still. A glow warms beneath his feet as a single bulb illuminates his body. His eyes survey the area, drawn to meshed hardwood floors. His shoes trace the seams, as if following a maze to some answer. The room appears unsullied and motionless, almost sterilized, as if preserving something of value. His eyes steady against an overwhelming white in front of him, and he notes people holding cameras and wine glasses. Their lips ripple as if speaking, but not a sound is heard.

298

Their fingers point at him, and their faces wince and heads shake. They ogle his build, his jowls, his hunch, dissecting him like an insect while scrawling on index cards. With each step he takes, eyes prod further and strip him bare against their conformation.

"Where am I?" asks Richard. His voice is compressed as the sound stops just beyond his lips. He reaches the edge of the hardwood floor and bangs into the perfectly clear barrier. His hands explore the glass as shadows reciprocate with movements along the walls behind him. Moments pass, and the caravan moves beyond his view.

He is alone again, now facing a wall adorned with thousands of shadowboxes containing images. Immediately, he recognizes it as his life's discourse arranged sequentially. His eyes gravitate toward the right side, nearest the ground, where black ashes have accumulated. Above the ashes, a charred outline mars the wall.

"Am I dead?" he offers. There is a break in the still air, and a breath draws from somewhere unseen. A voice descends upon him.

"Were you alive in that school two years ago, when they took the only thing that mattered to you? When you killed your own mother? When you couldn't even remember to tie your shoes?" Richard stares blankly ahead as a voice within him screams. "But you *do* remember me. I saw you at the carousel. I told you I would be back, yes?" Richard stares at the shadows on the floor, uncommonly lucid.

"Yes, I do."

"You are in your own head, a museum of the past," the voice spits back. "Every single thing you have ever done, every memory you have ever created and every dream you have ever had, is kept within these boxes," the voice informs. Richard grasps at the flat glass surface, trying to touch something impossibly out of reach.

"But those are mine," Richard whispers, barely audible to even himself. A long silence festers before the voice responds.

"They were yours, Richard, but now? They are mine. Do you see the candle on the floor?" Richard's eyes drift down, spotting the luminary beneath a shadowbox.

"With each passing hour, a candle is lit beneath your wall." Richard's eyes pump, like a creaky well run dry. "I am so tired." His limp hands slide down the glass, surrendering his forehead against the cold window.

"I know you are, Richard," growls the figure. "But I am not." The robed figure appears, gashing the light and bleeding the room black. His finger extends and a wave of heat ripples the air. An icy blue flame travels in its wake, stopping just shy of the wick beneath the box.

Inside the shadowbox, he sees a man carrying a sleeping boy through a county fair. Fireworks flicker and dance off the boy's forehead as he clutches a stuffed panda. Richard observes the man, content and unrushed, parting the sleeping child's hair. The boy's arms drape along the man's neck as a picket-fence smile speaks of unbounded happiness. Richard's eyes recognize the tattoo's crisp colors on the left forearm and he is filled with joy.

The wick spits and a burst of light fills the room before settling into a teardrop. The soft orange flame laps the wood, painting the box sienna and then black. Richard's eyes lock onto a little girl standing near the carousel. She observes the man smiling as he holds the sleeping boy. However, she appears unsettled as the pair meander toward the park exit. As they are swallowed by the night, she is left alone within the smoke-filled box. She turns to face Richard and smiles before the memories fall to ashes below.

"Honey, please stop, you are going to hurt yourself," the nurse says. Richard is partially naked, his bare legs puffed with fluid.

"What are those f-for?" he mutters, pointing at the large white briefs.

"Honey, these will help keep you dry if something happens, if you can't get to the bathroom in time. It's to help you—"

"F-fucking help me?? S-stop the man from burning my boxers! T-this is how you can h-h-help me," screams Richard, pushing the attendant away from him.

Chapter 24

"I am not sure what happened—he just left and never came back," the voice explains a second time to a perplexed Cafferty. "It's been two weeks. I don't see him coming back now. His paycheck was returned too, no forwarding address."

Cafferty scratches his chin while contemplating what could have caused the eager young man to simply vanish. "Well, that one's on me. I suppose now is better than later," he glosses against the little voice inside. "Let's hit the reset button here and move forward." The administrator plucks a large, black Sharpie from the drawer and crosses out the name "Herb" from the schedule, shifting his employee folder to "Storage."

In front of room 237, Danny watches sweat surface and spread across his shirt like a rising sea. He observes the advance until no island remains, only an acrid cloak of sulfur. "It's hot in here," he whispers. Abby dabs cream at white splotches on his cracked skin. A little voice within speaks as Danny's frame quivers in little bursts.

"You are sweating in mid-May...*in Ohio*," the voice pans. "No one does this, certainly not inside with air conditioning. Look at your arm." Danny knows what the voice cues. A fresh purple bruise stains the entirety of his bicep. "Fifty years ago, you'd be showing this off to your teammates. Standing your ground against that fastball, taking one for the team," the little voice recounts. "But."

A gentle rap chases the little voice away as Abby slowly opens the door. "Hi, Richard? How are you feeling today, honey?" As the pair enter, Danny winces as he peers from behind her mass, seeking his son. "It's absolutely beautiful outside today. It would be good to get you out of here and breathe fresh air."

"Where's my boy?" he asks, his voice laced with urgency.

"We are just finishing a bath right now, so he will be out in a moment," the attendant calls from behind the bathroom door.

The response pegs Danny as he recalls bathing the same boy so many years ago. "Can he not do that himself any longer?"

Abby slowly shakes her head. "It can be quite overwhelming."

Danny reflects momentarily, the gravity of the statement tolling like a passing bell counting moments. "I can't either," he states. "That's something we have in common, right?"

His eyes wander from Abby, gazing out the window. He observes motionless residents standing in the vibrant garden. He thinks they resemble translucent gnomes, warming beneath the sun. He notices life and time passing *around* them, just as a creek would flow around a fallen branch within its path.

Beyond the fence, a bright green extends as far as the horizon permits. The single interruption is a stretch of blacktop running from one ocean to the other. He fixes his stare on large trucks that appear, their rubber clutching the asphalt with a muffled howl. They carve slowly across the vast landscape, their howls gradually reducing to purrs and eventual silence as they disappear past the gnomes.

The bathroom door cracks slowly, and the distinct shuffle announces Richard's arrival. "Good morning, son. How are things today?" Danny's voice crackles. Richard glances at the new black box in Danny's hand and slumps into the chair.

"Would you like to go outside today? The weather is beautiful," Abby chimes. "I thought it might be fun to listen to the game underneath one of the trees in the garden." Richard scans the strangers and eventually settles back on Danny. He sits silently, his hair matted, as his eyes take in the new blemishes on his father's arms. The colors punctuate like an Afremov oil canvas, begging the eyes to dig deeper. But it is a lifeless break in the canvas that catches his attention.

He observes the dull, blurred image that once showed brightly against unblemished skin. "Where's the ta-tat—the paint?" asks Richard.

"It's…well. I guess it is part of my past now, son. Looks like it's almost gone." As if cued, the bluish-green hue of a fly catches the sunlight. Its colors paint a brilliant contrast against the pale white blinds before settling on Danny's arm.

Danny sits stoic and resolute, observing the pest. The fly grinds its twiggy legs and jitters about, unleashing a series of chaotic movements. Danny stills his body as if not to startle the creature, no longer desiring to fight, but only to accept. *It's inevitable, like the danse macabre*, he thinks to himself.

The room is hushed and motionless until Richard leans and swipes the creature from his father. "Th-they are b-bad," he quietly offers, as the fly buzzes to the far end of the room. "I do-do-don't want you to g-get s-sick."

Danny smiles. "Thank you, son. Would you like help putting on your shoes?" he asks.

Richard stares at the loafers, dangling from the attendant's fingers, as they approach Danny. "No, ma'am, not those. Can we take a crack at these?" he offers, nudging Abby to retrieve a box beneath his carriage. Abby flicks a glance to the attendant. *I'm sorry,* she mouths silently. Danny plucks a bright white pair of new shoes from within, eliciting a look of concern from the attendant.

"Well, those probably aren't the best choice. They're kind of tricky to—"

"I understand," Danny interrupts calmly, "but I would like to help him with them."

Richard's eyes begin to widen with excitement. "Who are those f-for?" he asks.

"They are for you, son. Would you like to wear those today?" Danny motions toward Abby, as he guides him in front of the hunched man, carefully navigating the motionless bare feet.

Danny lifts one foot-peg away from the chair, then a second, affording space. "Here, buddy. Do you remember when you played baseball? You were a catcher?" Richard sits motionless, watching the man scrunch the socks for some unknown task.

"He would have such a hassle with those stirrups in Little League," he speaks to the room. "Eventually, after all the tears, we would get them on and every now and then, one would be on backwards, high opening in front and low in the back. But not once did it matter a damn bit on his game." He waves a finger, motioning up and down Richard's body for full impact. Clearing his throat, he continues.

"I always told that boy he could do anything he wanted with that sport. He was effortless, fearless out there against the older boys too. I was his coach, you know, spent every day with him in that dugout until he was twelve years old," he says, his voice crackling as he dusts a memory caked in mildew and mirages.

"What happened after twelve?" a voice pops from behind Richard. Danny ignores the voice, trapped in the moment. He maneuvers the first sock onto the foot. Richard's eyes close as he tries locating a memory, like a needle in a haystack. He squints, prying into the little glass shadowbox, trying to recall. His mind sputters like wet flint, crumbling with each strike. He stares harder at the boxes, and immediately the memory flickers within and begins playing out.

I remember the fear always being present, even before you reached the field. I remember my heart racing, never quite certain which man would show up to coach, or, worse yet, which one would show up to father. I remember loving baseball because it was important to you, more important than it should have been for a nine-year-old. The feelings coalesce into something tangible, a script

306

etched in stone for permanent reference. *The game meant Winston cigarettes and Black Velvet whiskey, or "aftershave," as the other kids told me. I never wanted to be a catcher; I was strapped in oversized gear one day and told, "You're a catcher." That was the "quarterback of the team," you would tell me. The guy in charge. But I realized very quickly, it was the closest position to the dugout and the one which forced me to look straight at you for every single pitch call. I could hear every comment you spoke against the kid in the batter's box, their pitchers, the umpires. Like the kid—any kid—needed to hear that stuff. Even when a ball was hit, I could feel you bristle when a mistake was made. That was the worst time, after a mistake—I had to look your way and make eye contact before you would give me the pitch. One day, we were playing a night game and the field lights grew dim. It was like we were on this grand stage and everything else—the audience, the ground, the other players—were cloaked in darkness, so the only two actors were you and me. There was no more pitcher, just the ball exploding out of the darkness and bursting into my glove. But after each pitch, you sank further into the recesses of the dugout, where I began losing sight of your arms, legs, everything. It was as if you were retreating into a cave and I was the only one left in space. I leaned closer to the dugout, and stared hard into the darkness, awaiting the next call. Nothing came, just a funeral box hush. Moments passed like years as my heart pressed inside my temples and chest, and for that single moment in the blackest, starless night and absolute aloneness, I felt...fine. I removed my mask and gently laid it down on home plate, taking one last look in your direction. But smoke billowed from the dugout, and your voice boomed... "LOOK. AT. ME!" I remember your face appearing as if it were suspended from the sky, engulfed by smoke and a smoldering ember tip glowing like the devil's eye. I stopped cold, couldn't help but stare at that thing, watching it breathe and exhale, pulsing a life, or some beast, into you. Your face would glow a bright, deep orange as you would inhale, casting shadows across the deep cracks within your face. You looked old and broken. It was as if the veil of darkness and fear were your tether to love and, once removed, nothing but broken glass. But when you would exhale and the cracks slipped behind the cover of smoke, you lurked like every nightmare I never outran.... You played catcher; I couldn't stand it.* Richard looks down at the man beneath him, gently pulling socks onto a pair of spiderwebbed feet. He can hear the man labor with every breath, but his fingers are gentle. The memory begins burning hotter.

You know what position was my favorite? Right field. You could never understand that, would get upset if I asked for it. Right field was perfect, so far away and peaceful. I couldn't see anyone's eyes or hear their voices. You would ignore me when I made it to the dugout, when it was our turn to bat. I knew you weren't happy, but sometimes the quiet made it easier. Two innings would go by and I wouldn't see a ball in right field. But then, a hollow tink *sound would lift a ball like a bottle rocket high into the sky. The feathered cotton in the sky served as the perfect summertime backdrop against those red seams. I loved the sizzle of those seams announcing its arrival, me just waiting for it to smack the leather shut. POP. "Can of corn," you would tell me after I tucked the glove underneath my armpit. That split second of catching that ball and hearing you tell me it was "like a can of corn" erased all the smoke and darkness, just for a moment. It was a moment in time that was pure, unblemished, and proud. That feeling and the look in your eyes is what I held onto for fifty years.*

"There, how do those feel?" Danny asks Richard, his sneakers on but laces untied beneath him. "Would you like to try and tie them yourself?" The nurse and attendant observe Richard, their eyes nervous. Richard grasps the strings and pulls them high and tight.

"That's it, Richard. Just like a can of corn. Do you remember how we used to do this?" Silence descends upon the room as the A/C vent whispers a breathy lullaby. "This is the very first thing I taught you how to do—well, maybe the second. You could catch a ball before tying your shoes." He cackles as his lungs fight thick cement, hardening by the minute.

"I had a little corny jingle I gave you—I am shit for writing rhymes, but it worked. 'Runner, runner, on first base, pull the strings to your face. Wrap around and under through, runner, runner on base two.'" Richard pulls the strings hard as his fingers blush red against the pressure. He begins to tremble against the taut strings, his bones covered by a wet papier mâché. Danny senses the struggle, and only now can understand and accept failure.

"That's okay. It's quite okay, son. We will work on that whenever you'd like and someday, we'll get. We'll learn how to do it together again." Danny folds against the revolt inside him and gently plucks the strings from clenched fingers, securing them snugly. "Let's get some sun and fresh air—does that sound okay?" Richard's eyes never leave the shoes, but his head slowly nods in agreement.

As the door cracks, the sunlight and early May warmth rain down on the caravan, rendering the harshest of winters extinct. Colors and scents dance freely and timelessly like an Elysian field, stimulating blood through a labyrinth of constricted veins. As the caravan passes patients, distant smiles and an occasional wave greet the group.

"This is some kind of beautiful," Danny remarks. Across the garden, a stately red maple sits, flaunting its brilliant spring flowers. "How about we go set up over there?" The nurse and attendant nod dutifully as they too soak in the landscape.

Danny clutches the handheld radio and twists the knob to a harsh AM crackle. In a matter of moments, he lands on the sweet spot, the same frequency of yesteryear that taught them both everything, from sun to rainouts, shoelaces to tethers, love to hate, and father to son.

"Perfect," he peps up, as the crack of bats, like a nostalgic balm, soothes his struggle. Men banter over the airwaves, a volley of letters and numbers that wash over Richard like a firehose. "RBIs, HRs, AVG, IP, BBs, 2.37, .337." The letters and numbers that once came so naturally to a man educating the future now render him as mute as the day he first heard the alphabet.

"Do you know who we are playing today, son? Those Redbirds, the goddamn Cardinals. If we can just get past them this year, you never know what might happen," he convinces himself. Richard slumps against the large tree, watching nameless faces pass time. The rapid-fire bustle of the radio and roar of the crowd whoosh together like the sea in a conch. His eyes begin to drift beyond the fence, an open sea of green, a single highway traversing the Earth. His eyes trace along the path, eventually consumed by the massive horizon and heavens above it. The point ends, somewhere down that road.

Where does it end? he thinks to himself. What begins beyond it, or does it stop? He stares hard at the confluence of Earth and sky, awaiting some movement, any clue that there is something more. As the moments pass, a little girl's hand extends from above him.

"Come with me," her voice guides as a set of dark eyes tug at his spent instincts. The ocean whoosh idles behind him, letters and numbers flowing from a box and drifting aimlessly. Richard's body lifts with a surprising ease as he latches onto the little girl's hand, and a sudden flush of warmth fills his limbs.

She leads him beyond the fence, walking in silence, barefoot as the knee-high grass tickles their legs like feathers. He can *feel* the change within him, like a rebirth, as his presence and self-awareness take shape. Her little frame twists toward the man, tossing a shock of darkish curls across her shoulder and a smile across her face.

"I would like to give you something," she says, pulling his hand. At once, he stands in front of a wall, as immense as anything he once imagined and as clean as an afterlife promised for millennia. There along the wall stand three boxes. His body, once so tired and so resigned within this very room, fills with an excitement. He glances around the room and recognizes the glass enclosure he was in some time ago. But now, he is free from the enclosure, and nothing but a child's first steps to reach them. His feet jostle the ash as he moves, sending a fine mist of snow falling behind him.

"Where is the figure?" he asks, as if driven by curiosity.

The little girl smiles, gripping his hand again. "I promise you, he will be gone forever soon, and then you will never fear again. Until that time comes, I want you to have these three boxes.

"No one can ever take these from you, from those who came before you, do you understand?" Richard peers into the boxes, crystal-clear artifacts perfectly intact. "Once you have seen and touched, you will need to help those who ask."

The words puzzle the man as he gazes at the girl. "I don't under—"

"You will know when it is the right time, and the memories inside will guide your direction."

The words comfort him, like a familiar hand upon his shoulder. His head bobs in affirmation as he redirects his attention to the boxes, slowly approaching the first one. With a quick tug against the brass handle, a rush of air and matter washes over him like a hurricane. He gasps against the current, but steadies as the fragments join as if magnetically drawn to a perfect, singular counterpoint. Ashes from the floor swirl all around him, matter from decades prior inter-mingling together. Each sequence of memories is hardwired into him like a pianola, its large, metallic role as brand new as the day it was made. He gasps deeply, as if taking a child's first breath, while emo-tions flood with each measure of script, exploding sparks across vast, empty space within his mind.

At once, the rush of wind ceases and the door vacuums shut, naked and empty. Richard presses urgently through the other two boxes, wind and matter coalescing with ashes of the past. With the final rush of matter, the last door sucks emptiness from within, and ashes softly float like snowflakes back to the floor.

"It is time to go back now," her soft voice calls, as she extends her hand gripping his. At once, he senses the tall grass flicking against his legs as endless acres of green and yellow pass by. He observes a figure gliding effortlessly toward him through the tall grass, buoyant and nimble as if gliding on rails. Uncertainty bubbles within and he seeks the little girl's hand once again, only to grasp the warm May breeze.

"Hello, Richard," the woman offers, pressing her delicate flesh into his palm.

"Hello. Do I know you?"

"Not by name, but by our journey," she comforts him, placing her hand on his shoulder. We have both traveled together—you, me, so many to come—and your path is nearing its end. But it's not just us, those that have been chosen for that odyssey. There are loved ones who will never understand what that journey looks like, what it feels like, and what we are left with at the end. Our purpose and identity have evaporated, and we are left to rely on photographs and faith to help them make sense of the senseless."

The notes strike Richard with perfect consonance, and his head gently nods, as if guided by marionette strings from above. The woman cups his lax hands between hers as a message slips through the air without being spoken. A blanket of compassion wraps around his core, embracing the man and imparting assurance and design to something fitter than now.

"I now understand and promise, I will not forget," he whispers. A smile forms across her face as she pirouettes into the horizon and beyond, leaving Richard alone.

As his eyes locate the large, bright red maple in the distance, he is struck by a man in a wheelchair flapping his arms as if trying to fly, almost toppling in the process. His hands come crashing down upon the arm pads as hoots and whistles shatter the silence. He surges with vitality, almost leaping from the chair despite the meaty hand of the nurse.

"You've got to calm down, Danny! Your heart cannot take this. Please, just relax, honey."

"Holy sweet mother of Jesus, did you hear that?! Did you hear *that*," he fires to everyone, his voice luring Cafferty's peek from inside the office bay window. The glance is not driven by concern, but rather by curiosity and gratification, as if witnessing the bloom on a dormant seed. "I'll be damned," he whispers as he leans against his chair, observing the scene unfold.

"Richard—they just turned a four-five-four triple play," Danny gargles, as he hacks a bloody discharge into the air. "I cannot believe we heard it together. We did it!"

"Danny, you're gonna blow a leak here if you don't calm down," the voice presses again from behind him.

Richard observes his father, his shirt mottled with fatal stains, overjoyed and lucid, life bursting through his veins for the first time. He cannot help but smile as his hand reaches across the divide once more, gripping a part of him. "Dad, I am h-happy we got to d-do this t-together. I bet y-you it w-was a can of c-corn," he muses, wringing a tear from his eyes.

With the post-game AM crackle and the cool evening air setting in, the group is the last beyond the four walls. "Guys, it's time to come in," the voice breaks from the back door. And with the red maple bearing witness, the caravan begins their slow journey back inside.

Later that evening, Cafferty eases back in his chair, kneading the fatigue from his eyes. The cool night breeze squeezes through the screen with a gentle whistle, stirring a vintage but ever-present memory within him. "That whistle," he whispers to the shiny black mesh, "will always make me think of you." Lurching forward, he ambles toward an old walnut office desk across the conference room, smiling at the gift from Bain years ago. He soon drags his finger across the desktop and examines the chalky drywall remains. A perfect streak of luminous wood surfaces, as if a snowplow has liberated a remote mountain pass.

"How many times did we shovel that driveway together?" he whispers to the trace of wood, the wind ebbing as if drawing breath to answer. But the answer doesn't come, only a gentle whistle barely audible over the leaves resisting beyond the walls.

"Not as often as I would have liked," breathes Cafferty. His eyes gravitate toward a striking, black wooden box from within the desk, drawing a sheepish grin across his face. He recalls Helio flogging his dismissal of Scotch, even once suggesting a defect in his palate.

How can a man of your professional standing not have learned to appreciate the finest spirit on Earth? he would chide. *There must be something wrong with your mouth, or you were given that Irish shite rather than the real stuff. Someday, I will give you something that even your Irish blood can't deny,* he threatened, following through with the retirement gift Cafferty now ogles.

"Highland Park, aged forty years," he states in a crude Scottish timbre, chiding the politesse of such lofty potables. As he releases the cask, a polished silver amulet graces the bottle. A leatherbound booklet further pokes Cafferty, brandishing virtues and refinement more suited for royalty than a man still calling the Rust Belt home. Cafferty peeks over his shoulder for a cup or any vessel, while scanning for Helio, who would be appalled by such flippancy. He eyes a sleeve of plastic water cups and chuckles aloud.

"Absolutely perfect." Plucking one from the sleeve, he rests it atop the powdered walnut surface and tears into the wrapped bottle. Without hesitation, he tugs the cork, releasing a breath of something familiar, yet shrouded. "Pine. I smell nothing but cheap pine, Helio." He smiles, tipping the bottle. A rich, oily mahogany slithers from the mouth into the ribbed vessel below. He grips the cup, and with the surrounding wind whistling again, Cafferty offers a nod into the blackness outside.

"Cheers." He pulls the drink and closes his eyes tightly while a warm numbness simmers from within. With a quick gulp, he fires the liquid down, bracing himself for the streaky burn of a shooting star. But the resultant warmth is comforting and measured, like a late-night campfire ember pulsing and glowing with a subtle rhythm. His skepticism falters and sharp features soften as the liquid slips effortlessly through his body, radiating from limb to limb and settling gently across his face. Vignettes scroll across his eyelids, a montage of life summoned by a friend's gift and a chilly evening whisper. He affords each image a breath of satisfaction or pause of reverence, but each one resolving and resting comfortably with acceptance. Except one. It is that single image, over a lifetime, that haunts of inconclusiveness.

What was that? he begs. *What were you trying to tell me, Mom?* His voice is swallowed by the cheap plastic. As he raises the potion to his lips again, he feels a presence behind him and a voice breaks the stream of silence. "Bobby, s-she wanted you to know, she has never been more alive than when her s-soul was set free, right there in room 233. Bobby, she has never stopped dancing since."

Chapter 25

As the sun peaks during its midday ascent, an urgent rap rips through the blackened room. "Hi, Richard, honey. It's Nurse Abby from over at the clinic. I'm here with the attendant—can we come in?" A heavy thud shoots from beyond the wall, a sound increasingly routine. The door releases with force, flinging hall light into the darkened cave. A pasty white body is folded in half on the floor, disoriented and shaking.

"Honey, your daddy was taken over to St. Stanislaus early this morning—that's the hospital in town." She props the naked body against the bedside frame, while covering his lower half with the spread. Abby sits next to him, as the attendant bustles with urgency, gathering clothes and disappearing into the bathroom. An immediate surge of life whooshes through the walls behind them. The tub churns with a violent force, like ocean waters lashing against a weathered pine hull.

"Do you remember we spoke about your dad not being well and needing doctors all the time?" she tests, as Richard grows anxious of the crashing waters.

"C-can you s-stop that?" he blurts, as the attendant quickly shunts the water and prepares to make do.

"Honey, let's get you over to see your dad." The message marinates for a moment among the stillness of the room. Water drips from the faucet into a calming body of water, plopping a labored cadence as if wringing every ounce of life from the pipes beyond. "Honey, we really need to get you moving, okay?" her voice prods with a slight break. Richard's body remains fixed as his eyes slip shut.

He *feels* the final drop wrung from some buried valve within the structure, trickling through a network of vessels. With the hush in full throttle, a last drop disappears beneath the water's surface, giving birth to a series of gentle ripples. "They never disappear, they j-j-just change," he offers, his face breaking a smile. The words slip past the woman. "Okay, I am ready to see him," he states calmly, oblivious to his bare skin.

"First, let's get you bathed and dressed, then we will go."

"Okay. B-but I want my sh-shoes today," he says, pointing to the front door. "We will get you your shoes, honey. We just have to go now."

As the trio evacuates the second floor St. Stanislaus elevator, figures covered in white and blue appear and disappear with a mechanical precision resembling army ants. One figure slows, observing his graveyard tan and heavy shuffle, offering a sympathetic smile.

"Hello, we're here to visit room 233," Abby whispers to the ward attendant. As she examines the paperwork, Richard's eyes wander the hallway. The walls pulse with life, as dozens of faces, garnished with legacies of grandeur, gaze upon him. Their visages seem to radiate a youthful glow, as if the perpetual recounting of their lives fuels their immortality. *It's like a classroom*, he thinks to himself, smiling. His eyes offer a silent exchange with each, sending a comfort through his core.

He observes the vivid, polished floors, without a winter's scar, as his eyes travel from the most remote window back again to the ICU entry point. There, as if tending to her flock of souls, is the imposing figure of Mary gracing the landing above the doorframe. Richard observes the diminutive but principal woman, looking only upon him. Her brilliant aqua eyes and tobacco hair dazzle against the lights, casting a rebirth larger than all of spring.

"Richard, honey. It's right this way." Soon, his arm is led toward room 233, shoelaces clicking and dragging a beat behind the shuffle. "Honey, let me—"

"No," he states flatly. "N-no more tying."

"I'm sorry, honey. You're right, it's not important," she returns dutifully.

As they approach the doorway, he tugs briefly against Abby, reflecting on the figure between the tan frame. "St. Jude, the Patron Saint of Lost Causes" greets the visitors, a single flame perched atop his dark mane.

"Honey, I want to make sure you understand they gave your dad some medicine so he doesn't feel any pain, okay?"

Richard is transfixed by the flame, no longer an icy blue finger of havoc, but instead a sun as he stands at the edge of darkness. Words continue in the background, trivial compared to the voice of *this* flame. *Tubes...chest rising...beeps...strange noises...no*

321

pain...forgive, the words tumble like crumbs onto the floor beneath. "Letter."

"W-what letter?" he states as he turns away from the flame.

"Your dad had written a letter some time ago, right after the first time he saw you again. Honey, your daddy knew this day would come soon, and wanted to make sure you had something from him after..." She pauses momentarily, uncertain of how to say it.

"Death," he says, flatly.

"Yes, honey, after he passes."

She retrieves an envelope from her purse and places it in Richard's hands. "Son." The letters no longer bear the trademark of a gifted hand, one that could make any message charming. They are primitive and labored, their edges reminiscent of a trembling hand. Yet they are the most authentic and beautiful he has ever seen. "Thank you," he breathes, clutching the envelope.

As they enter the room, they are confronted by a cadence of beeps and a network of wires, running like tributaries from an original source. Liquid courses to and from the core, completing a circuit and providing life. Richard observes the liquids' paths, disappearing into arms and hands, until eventually settling on a single black cable running into the wall.

"Honey, he can definitely hear you. I will wait over here in the chair as long as you like."

Richard peeks from the wires and into the man's face, gaunt and ashy, but untroubled. "He looks l-like he is sleeping." Richard tears at the white envelope as the machine staves an encroaching fate. The single paper bears broken letters and smeared ink, as if errant water fell from above. Richard hands the letter to the attendant, without taking his eyes off the man.

"Would you like me to read it to you?" she offers, while quietly shifting to the corner of the room. His head nods.

Softly, she begins:

"Purpose, Forgiveness and Remembrance…

"Son, I wanted to teach you everything about life. That was my *purpose*, my reason for being, when I became a father. But as I write, my only lesson offered is what *not* to become, what not to do. That's a helluva way to arrive at what you have become. I would have loved to have lasted long enough to begin again. To give you one thing, no matter how small or seemingly insignificant of a task, that you learned from me. I simply met a stranger, who I always loved, too late. In the end, my only purpose in life was to learn what love *is*. How it hurts and heals, loses and finds, dies and lives. Despite everything I have done or failed to do, here love stands before me, and my life ends with purpose. Thank you.

"Forgiveness. I once told you 'the true measure of a man is how much he forgives.' I stole that quote from somewhere and in hindsight, certainly wasn't written for people like me. But, I said that to you and every other relationship I treated like a dime-store rummage sale, articles no one could justify keeping, wouldn't be caught dead wearing. It became addictive, that transfer of responsibility and blame to someone else, as if their failure to forgive *was the wrong*. And yet here I am again, but this time, I am the rummage sale. Son, you owe me nothing, but one day, I hope you realize how very sorry I am. Please forgive me."

The voice pauses momentarily is if affording the words room to breathe. But the beeps persist, counting the rise and fall of ribs against the white cloth. He shuffles to the side of the bed as his shoe-laces click against the floor, flopping into the nearby chair. Leaning forward, he rests one elbow on his knee for support and stretches across the divide, touching his father's shoulder.

"Should I continue, Richard?"

"Yes, please."

The voice chimes within Richard, a perfect consonance within a sea of disharmony, sending waves of warmth throughout his body. Richard *feels* for the first time as his body rebels against his nemesis, the veiled coward, intent on destroying his life from the inside out. He is *alive* again, his senses piercing the thick fog like a cannonball. His heart pounds from within his chest and his eyes flicker, pushing small streams down his face.

His hand slides down his father's arm, pausing on the faded splotch. The ink, once screaming of rebellion, now whispers as inno-cently as a birthmark. He settles his hand on his father's, clasping it as both pulses flicker against the other, filling the space between heartbeats. Despite a lifetime apart, they are forever interconnected.

Richard nods his head for the voice to continue, a tear flicking from his cheek onto the bed.

"Finally," the voice begins, "we all want to be remembered. My single greatest regret is not knowing if you remember a single memory of us that makes you happy. Until my last breath, I will hope to learn of one from your lips. I love you, son. Dad." The voice trails off, immersing the room in silence and beeps. Abby rises quietly and slips to the door, cracking it.

"I will be right outside. You take all the time you need, honey," the voice whispers as the door clicks shut. Death hangs in the air like a black cloud, but is oddly patient. The machines continue to rise and fall, as the cloud drifts to neighboring rooms where the skies have opened.

"He can hear you, honey. Anything you want to say…he can hear you," a soft, youthful voice percolates from the corner of the room. The voice rings familiar and summons his attention. There he sees the little girl again, smiling. At once, he is filled with peace.

"Your words will reach him before the ashes fall." He gathers a breath as he focuses on the man's eyes, drawn shut. He clasps the hand again, as the words flow from his lips, uninterrupted and precise.

"Dad, I want you to know I forgive you. Life is about choices, and we are a product of those we make. It never occurred to me to judge you for those you regret. You always were and always will be a part of me. Whatever good choices I have made, I believe within my

325

heart you helped make those with me. So for that, I forgive you."
Richard squeezes the hand, rubbing his thumb along the ridges of a
sunken landscape. He feels the once-steady pulse slowing and stray-
ing from the perfect consonance from moments prior.

Richard steadies himself, glancing to the corner of the room
again. The little girl nods for him to continue. "You wanted to know
if I had a memory of us. I do, Dad. It was late Christmas Eve and I
was six years old at that point; sister still wasn't even born yet. That
was the very first time you called me to the garage, telling me we
could put the sand in the luminary bags together. You bundled me up
in this big, white snowmobile suit. I looked like a giant marshmallow
and was sweating like I was in the confessional.

"You carried me down the stair and plopped me on the floor.
You placed all these white bags around me and handed me a measur-
ing cup, telling me to put two cups into each. Do *you* remember? You
told me to be real quiet or Mom would be upset we used her measur-
ing cups. We muffled laughs as I filled every single bag. You patiently watched, showing me how to level the sand off with a spackling
knife, telling me what a good job I had done. Once I finished, we
opened up the garage door to the crisp night. I had never seen such a
beautiful white blanket covering the ground. The snow was this
high!" he fires, placing his hand as high as the man beneath the sheet.

"The snow was falling so slowly, fluttering down like we
were in a snow globe. It was so quiet, like the world had earmuffs
on," he whispers, leaning close to his father. "You grabbed the little

326

red sled, the one with electrical tape piecing the rope handle together, and told me to hang on. You stacked the white bags all around me, and dragged me to the top of the hill, panting the entire time. I guess that was the one good thing about your smoking," he chuckles. "You sounded like our Lionel train chugging along. *Cha-cha-cha-cha*," he huffs as his hands churn along an imaginary cold steel rail. The memory is flowing and alive, like quicksilver.

"We placed every bag down on the driveway. Your sweat began to frost up all over your eyebrows and beard, looking like you had been searching for the North Pole or something. But my God, you looked so happy. I have never forgotten that smile. You know what you did next? You looked up at the picture window, just to make sure Mom wasn't watching. You took that long match—those that looked almost like a baseball bat, with the massive red end of the barrel. You then struck that match—pffffffffff! It lit the whole ground up all around us, a billion little diamonds reflecting off that perfect white sheet. I couldn't tell the sky from the ground—the shimmering of stars was everywhere." He flicks his fingers slowly, watching the tips flutter like snowflakes toward the ground. A smile cracks his face as he watches the snow settle into a perfect white canvas, everything new again.

"A big flame started chewing on the end of that wood, and you handed it to me. I couldn't believe it—you let me light every one of those candles." Richard reaches for his father's wrist and hand again, squeezing it. For a moment, he feels nothing but rigid bones pushing back. He rubs the hand with his thumb again, warming the spot as he feels for any sign. A faint thump taps back from beneath the skin, nudging him to continue.

"When every one of those candles were lit, we sat at the top of the hill, admiring the most beautiful scene of my life. Our road, untouched by a tire, lit on both sides like a runway in the woods. When our lips turned blue, you counted down from ten and pushed me to the bottom of the hill! I screamed and laughed until porch lights flicked on throughout the neighborhood, Mom telling us to get in out of the cold." Richard chuckles to himself, an impish grin hanging from his face. "We went inside, peeled the clothes, and sat in front of that fireplace. The crackles and the glow, the smell of the wood, and the tree in the background.... Every Hallmark card would have blushed." His smile wanes for a moment as he looks up to the ceiling. "There isn't a damn thing on this Earth that can take *that* from me." He wipes a stray tear from his face and refocuses on the man in front of him.

"I woke up late that night and tiptoed all the way to the backroom, until my feet hurt. I wanted to see what Santa had brought, and sure didn't want to wake up you or Mom. Right before sneaking in, I saw the beautiful red glow—the embers were still casting their light—onto a figure beneath the tree. Here I am thinking I just caught the fat man in the red suit performing magic!" He chuckles loudly, slapping his father's arm with great force. "Jesus, sorry, Dad. But you can imagine what I must have felt, right?" he says, gently rubbing the point of impact.

"So, I knelt as quietly as I could and leaned in just enough, hoping I could catch a glimpse of his face. But it wasn't Santa—it was you!" he says, giggling at the thought. "You were so quiet and so meticulous, stacking the boxes under the tree, around the train tracks, making tunnels with the boxes. Who knows how long I sat there? When I guessed you were done, I quietly snuck back to the room and never slept that night. I watched every luminary shine off that perfect blanket of white until the very last one burned out at daybreak. And I smiled the entire time."

He nudges his dad's arm and watches it fall back, limp and heavy. With one strained swallow, he halts a lump, bubbling from his chest and climbing to his throat. "The next morning, I couldn't help but tell you what I had seen. I didn't know how you would react, if you would be mad, or whatever. But you didn't care. You were happy; we were happy. We played trains around that tree until the New Year's ball dropped. *That* is the memory I will carry of you until the day those endless ballfields of green turn to hay."

Richard arises slowly and surveys the room. He is alone with two chairs and a single white line, unflinching and explicit. His heart thumps peacefully as he observes the man one last time. "I love you, Dad." His voice rings strong.

His feet move steadily toward the door, unencumbered and agile, as shoelaces clack a familiar cadence. As the latch releases him to the outside world, a gentle tap lands on the small of his back, as if nudged by a persistent child. He smiles as his hand pats the front of his brow.

"I almost forgot, Dad." His body lowers to one knee as he plucks the shoelaces from the tile. "Runner, runner on first base, pull the strings to your face." The words guide his fingers as effortlessly as his father whispered decades earlier. "Wrap around and under through, runner, runner on base two." He can sense a hand upon his shoulder pressing firmly, as his father once observed the little hands moving as taught. A little voice whispers in his ear as his fingers continue their dance, looping the bows together.

"Just like that, son.... Now send the runner for home." His fingers cinch the knot, and at once, the touch of his father's hand is gone. "Just like that, Dad.... A can of corn."